OBSESSION

NEW YORK CITY SYNDICATE
BOOK 2

SETTLE MYER

Contents

Author's Note

Deadly Obsession is a dark, cozy romance meaning the romance is sweet... but the story includes dark themes. It's the second, and final, book in the New York City Syndicate duology, and a standalone, however, it will spoil Deadly Deceit.

This book includes:

Torture (explicit), Murder, Violence, Abduction, Human/sex trafficking, Domestic Abuse (Emotional and physical), Death of a parental figure (murder-off page), Death of an abusive parent figure (on page), Cursing, Alcohol consumption, Drug use, Sexual Assault (groping), Discussions of: depression, grief, child abuse, rape, sexual assault, and attempted suicide.

Explicit sexual activity: Choking, Edging, Breath play, Ass play, Period play, Breeding kink, Exhibitionism, power exchange/power play.

If you have a specific trigger, please reach out to the author.

Please also be aware: this story is set in New York City/Connecticut area and includes both real and made up locations/businesses.

I will also add that this book has been edited, but I am human. My editor is human. We might have missed things. I also intentionally left at least 1 grammatically wrong piece of dialogue in this book because I felt the character would not say 'whom'

Help is available
Suicide & Crisis Lifeline — Call or Text: 988
https://988lifeline.org/
https://afsp.org/
https://nami.org/Home
National Domestic Violence Hotline: 800-799-7233 or
Text START to 88788
https://www.thehotline.org/
Please consider donating to St. Jude:
https://www.stjude.org/

Dedication

This book is for the baddies who've always wanted to tell a man to get on his knees.

Playlist

You'll notice this playlist isn't a typical one for a mafia book.

These songs are all mentioned in the book!

My playlists aren't meant to be listened to while you're reading along; however, you can! Enjoy!

PLAYLIST

JOHNNY B. GOODE - CHUCK BERRY

GREAT BALLS OF FIRE - JERRY LEE LEWIS

LA BAMBA - RITCHIE VALENS

CAN'T HELP FALLING IN LOVE - ELVIS PRESLEY

UNCHAINED MELODY - THE RIGHTEOUS BROTHERS

CAN'T TAKE MY EYES OFF YOU - FRANKIE VALLI

IN YOUR EYES - PETER GABRIEL

GROW OLD WITH YOU - ADAM SANDLER

BAD ROMANCE- LADY GAGA

NEW YORK STATE OF MIND - BILLY JOEL

SCAN TO LISTEN

Chapter 1

Sage

I'm getting railed by the man who owns the hottest nightclub in Brooklyn.

He has me folded over his office desk, slamming into me from behind. The front of his legs slap against the back of mine, forcing my eyes to roll back into my head. His strong hands grip the fabric of my rolled-up dress like a saddle's horn, allowing him to fuck me deeper. I scream with every vicious thrust as the tip of his cock repeatedly grazes my g-spot.

"Yes, Boss," I whimper. "Like that."

I don't know his name, he never gave it to me, and I never asked for it. The first time I called him Boss, paired with a salute, he clenched his jaw and flared his nostrils. I don't know why that made him so mad. He's literally a boss. He owns the nightclub.

I so badly want to give him orders. I want him on his knees in front of me, licking my pumps.

They're Louboutins—a splurge upon getting my first payout from the app I signed up for where all I do is order men around.

I spent too many years being controlled by my ex. When I left him, I promised myself I'd be the one making the demands. Especially in my sex life. It began with the app and then I started going to sex clubs where I learned to dominate my partners.

But tonight, when I was brought into the office of the owner of Underground Park Slope, I knew he wasn't the type to wear a collar and let me call him puppy.

I mean, I've never done that before, and this man would look delectable on all fours, but he's also intimidating and powerful and there's something about him that feels... *dangerous,* so I decided to let him take the lead.

Another orgasm builds, and he grunts the moment my pussy walls pulse around him.

"Fuck, Reine," he wheezes, but doesn't let up.

Reine?

Did he forget my name too? No, because he addressed me by Sage when I was brought to him. He knew my name before I even gave it to him.

His hand crashes down on my bare ass, the sound cracking through the near silence of the room. Silent except for my moans, his grunts, and the muffled beats of music from the club downstairs.

He spanks me again, harder this time, and I buck underneath him. When the third lashing lands, I'm sent over the edge.

Orgasm number two!

The moan I let out is mixed with a sob. Tears roll down my face and stars dance across my vision as pleasure from the orgasm ripples through my body.

Am I going to pass out?

That's how well this man has fucked me.

He removes his cock and walks around the desk where my head hangs over the edge, as I try to catch my breath. He swipes his fingers over the condom, then grips my hair with his other hand to lift my head.

"Open," he demands.

He barely gives me time to comply before he shoves his fingers past my lips—the fingers coated with my pleasure that he literally just swiped off that condom.

"Clean them off."

I shouldn't find this hot, but I groan as I flail my tongue over the digits.

"Do you like the way you taste?"

"Mhm."

Once he's satisfied that I've had enough, he removes his fingers to peel the condom off and pushes his cock into my mouth. I suck the shaft down to his balls before flattening my tongue and withdrawing back to the tip.

He lets out a sharp breath.

He hasn't come yet, so I slide his length down my throat again. He moans and sinks himself deeper, causing me to gag. My eyes water, the tears spilling down my cheeks, adding to the streaks of mascara.

I'm ready to Hoover this man and let his cum pour down my throat, but he releases my hair and steps away, taking his hard cock with him.

I might have whined a little.

He walks to a black leather couch on the other side of the room and sits down.

"Come here, Reine."

Reine.

He said it again.

Now that my brain's not jumbled from getting fucked, I'm pretty sure the word is French. I took French classes in high school, but I don't remember shit because I'm about to turn thirty-three, and high school was a long freaking time ago.

I dismount the desk, adjusting my dress to cover my bare ass and wonder where my panties went as I cross the floor of the office—which might be bigger than my studio apartment.

I stand in front of him.

I can't imagine how unhinged I look. He'd been tugging on my hair. It's surely a blonde bird's nest on top my head. My lipstick is certainly smeared to match my streaked mascara. Red splotches decorate my body either from his mouth sucking my skin, or his hands leaving beautiful marks.

But whatever this man sees, his eyes light up with desire. "Undress."

Fuck he's bossy.

Boss.

I can't stand it.

Then why did your cunt just flutter at the order?

He combs his hand through his sweaty midnight hair. It's short on the side and longer on top, and aside from the strand that fell across his forehead just now, most of it stays slicked back.

He really is a gorgeous man.

He's wearing a suit, or he *was* wearing a suit. The jacket is tossed on a chair at his desk. His black dress shirt is partially unbuttoned and open, revealing a tattooed chest and soft stomach. His cock stands straight up through his unzipped pants.

He's a big guy with a belly that jiggles, and he towers over my five-foot-eight frame.

"You first," I say with a smirk.

He raises a brow as if no one has ever challenged him before.

Maybe no one has.

I also find myself having a hard time saying no to him.

Despite being intimidating, I don't break eye contact with him because I'm determined to get what I want.

And that's for him to be naked too.

We didn't have time to fully undress before his mouth and hands were all over me.

It all started with me on the dance floor, moving my hips to a song I can't remember, but I was feeling myself, so my hands sensually scrubbed over my body. My eyes closed as I swayed to the beat. Then a creep came up behind me, wrapped his arm around my waist, and cupped my pussy through my dress.

I didn't hesitate to swivel around and punch the asshole square in the nose.

Turns out, the owner of Underground Park Slope doesn't tolerate violence in his club, and security escorted the handsy man out a side door that I assumed was an exit. I was then brought up to Boss's office.

"Tell me what you'd like me to do to him, Sage," he said.

I was confused at first.

"He touched you without your consent. I can turn him over to the police or I can make sure he'll never touch another woman again."

I chose option two because, in my experience, police won't be able to do anything unless there's evidence, and even if he's arrested, the jails are too crowded, and he'd likely be released only to go on and find another woman to violate.

Boss seemed pleased with my answer and made a phone call. I overheard him saying something about 'tying him up' and 'I'll be there soon to take care of him.' I pretended not to know exactly what that meant, and I should have felt bad for dooming the groper to that fate.

But I don't.

When he hung up, he approached me, putting himself between me and the door, never letting his eyes stray from mine.

"How do you know my name?"

"I know the name of every person who walks through my doors."

"Are you kicking me out?"

"Why would I do that?"

"Because I punched that guy?"

He shook his head, some of his dark hair falling across his forehead.

"Okay. If you're not kicking me out, then I think I'll go back downstairs. I could really use—"

I tried to walk past him, but he grabbed my arm.

"What do you need? Tell me."

I needed a good fuck, but I wasn't about to tell him that, especially with him being all demanding. Mostly because it pissed me off how much I wanted to obey his orders.

"Tell me. Whatever you want, it's yours."

Instead of telling him, I showed him. I grabbed him by the lapels of his suit jacket to bring him down to my mouth—since he was so goddamn tall—and devoured him.

Then I let him fold me over his desk and fuck me into a near catatonic state.

Boss narrows his blue eyes and stands, realizing I'm not backing down.

So he *can* take orders.

Good.

"Go on then," I say when he doesn't make a move.

The corner of his mouth twitches.

"Come over here and undress me," he says.

Touché.

We're both fighting for control. I would fight harder if he hadn't just given me two of the most mind-blowing orgasms I've ever had.

I walk to him. I'm taller than the average woman, but that's nothing compared to this man's height. He's at least six foot six if I had to guess.

I unbutton his black dress shirt the rest of the way and place my palms flat on his meaty chest. It's covered in an elaborate tattoo design: a skull in the middle wrapped in barbed wires with black roses mixed in. There's a gun on his right pec and a knife on his left.

He closes his eyes as I skim my hands up to remove the shirt. When it falls to the floor, more tattoos riddling his shoulders and arms are revealed to me. My fingertips ghost over the design on the left: a snake hidden within greenery, slithering down his arm and its fanged mouth open and aligned with his thumb and index finger.

Boss sighs, but he doesn't move. He also doesn't stop me.

On his right arm is a design of butterflies perched on black roses and green vines down to his wrist where there's a name and words written in script.

In Loving Memory.

Imogen.

She's someone he lost. A grandmother? Mother? Sister? Wife?

It doesn't matter. This person meant enough for him to immortalize their name in ink. I bring the inside of his wrist to my mouth and kiss the name.

His body freezes when my lips gently press over the permanent memorial.

Then something flips inside him, and he jerks his arm away.

He drops his pants to the ground and tears open another condom packet, rolling it onto his still hard cock. I yelp when he grabs hold of my dress and literally rips it off my body.

What the actual fuck?

With his hands on my hips, he drags me to the couch and once he sits, I mount him.

Fine.

He wants it rough and dirty?

That's what he'll get.

I sink down his length and groan at the feel of him inside me. As if he wasn't inside me just minutes ago.

I hate how controlling he's being, but at the same time, my body wants to be dominated. I'm confused and turned on.

Which is why I slap him.

His head jerks to the side, his eyes are wide, clearly not expecting the sting of my palm. I don't give him time to react to the slap and start moving my hips. He moans, his head falling back against the couch—all is forgiven.

With his thick neck exposed to me, I wrap both of my hands around it. They barely reach halfway around his throat. I'd never be able to successfully incapacitate him.

Maybe that's why he lets me choke him.

"Come for me, Boss."

He growls and takes hold of my hips, holding me in place while he thrusts up into me.

"Elias," he grunts, fucking me hard enough that I'm confident I won't be able to walk properly for the next few days.

"What?"

"My. Name. Is. Elias." The words are enunciated with each thrust. "Say it. I want to hear my name on your lips when I make you fall apart."

My grip on his throat fails as lust builds within me. I let go, allowing Elias to lean down to catch the peak of my breast with his mouth. He grazes my hard nipple with his teeth before lashing his tongue over it.

He lifts his right hand off my hip and brings it to my mouth.

"Open."

I do, and he shoves two fingers inside.

"Coat them good, Sage."

Once they're soaked, he moves them to my asshole. A fingertip traces down my crack until it presses against my puckered hole.

"Yes," I whisper, bucking into the touch.

He releases my nipple. "How tight is this little hole? Have you ever taken anyone here before?"

"All the time."

"Don't lie to me, Sage."

Sage. I kind of miss Reine already.

I growl, frustrated and in need of release.

"Just put your finger inside my asshole already, Elias."

And he does.

Orgasm number three.

After railing me in his office for over an hour, Elias is summoned away for club business. Or maybe he left to take care of the man who touched me. Elias insinuated that he was going to kill the dude. Does that mean I'm an accessory to murder? Yeah... I'm trying not to think about that.

He ordered me to get dressed and wait for him.

I can't wait, though.

I can't stay.

I'm not ready to get into another relationship, and Elias is giving me relationship energy.

Not to mention that I've never had a man fuck me so passionately... so... thoroughly. Staying here and spending the rest of the night with him would spoil me. I'd never want to leave. I'd ruin it by falling too fast, too hard. The last time I let myself fall for a man, I married him, and he turned out to be a horrible person who did a lot of shitty things.

I shouldn't have fucked Elias.

I definitely shouldn't have let him give me five orgasms.

Elias.

No last name.

Since the man ripped my dress to shreds, I grab his suit jacket from the chair in front of his desk and thank whatever sex god is looking over me because it fits me more like a dress.

A very short dress, but at least my ass is covered.

I find my panties on the ground and slip those on, then use the shredded dress as a belt.

My clutch is in another chair in front of Elias's desk. I grab it, open it, and pull out a ballpoint pen. I find a piece of paper on his desk, write out a note, kiss the paper, then leave the pen on top.

My heart is racing when I crack the door open and peer outside.

It's not like I'm a prisoner. I can leave. But the demand in his voice when he told me to stay put tells me he's going to be pissed when he finds out I'm gone.

I hate to do this to him. It's my fault for letting him kiss me. Letting him fuck me. Letting him give me hope that there are good men out there.

Is he a good man if he vowed to 'take care of' the asshole who groped me?

Eh. Tomato, tomato.

The upstairs office area of Underground Park Slope is like a maze, but I manage to find an exit without running into anyone. I slip out the back door. While waiting for a taxi to stop, I shift on my feet and glance over my shoulder a few times. After a painful five minutes, a cab stops, and I blow out a long breath of relief when I get in and it takes off.

Then I cry because I'm an idiot for running away.

Like I always do.

Like a fucking coward.

Chapter 2

Elias

A pained sob rips from the man's bloodied mouth. Piss and vomit sting my nose, and my knuckles are split open with how many times I've punched this fucker in the face—enough to break his nose and cause both of his eyes to swell.

Yet he's still alive.

"You think you can go around touching women without their consent?"

His words are gurgled, and he coughs, attempting to clear the blood from his throat.

"How many, Adam Shaffer of the Upper East Side?"

I don't need to clarify. I've asked the question three times now, but he's vehemently denied being a predator.

He's lying.

I can always tell.

The way they panic and come up with any excuse as to why they're not a rapist.

I'm a good person!

I'm educated!

I'm successful!

I donate to charity!

I go to church! tops the list.

I pick up the pliers, then grab his hand. He tries to tug his arm away when he feels the teeth grip his thumbnail.

"I will rip these out until you start talking. And don't lie, Adam. I know everything about you. Where you work, your credit score, how many times you've been arrested. Who your family is. They're quite well known in New York City. Wouldn't it be a shame for the world to find out that the socialites' son is a sexual predator?"

My team has been busy the past hour gathering this information while I fucked Sage in my office.

I'm anxious to get back to her.

But first, I need to kill the asshole who cupped her cunt on my dance floor.

I clench the pliers and jerk my hand up at an angle. It takes a few tries before the nail dislodges from the bed. I tug and it rips out. He squeals like a pig and flails his body around in the chair I have him tied to.

"One down, nine to go. And there's always your toes. Or maybe I'll just cut off your cock."

"No. Please," he says, his voice scratchy from yelling.

I wait, expecting him to talk.

He says nothing.

Nail number two goes, and Adam nearly passes out. I backhand him, and he coughs himself to full attention.

I line the pliers up with his middle finger.

"Okay!" Adam yells, though it's more of a wheeze. "Six."

"Six? SIX?"

I snatch my knife from my torture tray and sink it into his cock.

Adam's piercing screams echo throughout the room, but I'm not worried about anyone hearing us. We're in the basement of my club, and the room has been sound-proofed.

I pull the knife out of his groin. Blood spurts out, staining Adam's lap and spilling to the ground. I yank his head back by his hair and dig the tip of the knife into his throat.

"Six what, Adam? What did you do to them?"

He's barely hanging on to consciousness, so I dig the knife deeper, hoping the pain sends a jolt of alertness.

"Rape... I... roofie them, then rape them."

I've heard enough and slice the blade across his throat. A shower of blood pours down his front, and I step back to make sure none gets on my shoes and clothes.

I'm fuming as I head to the bathroom to wash my hands and check for blood splatter.

Covering up the details of his death won't be easy. I have contacts with the NYPD and the city's medical examiner who can report it as an overdose or something equally believable. Then I'll hand over audio of Adam confessing his crimes. I already have my tech guy, Phil, looking for physical evidence, in addition to the video of him assaulting Sage. I haven't watched it yet, but I already told my security team to pull it. That way, if Adam's parents try to investigate his death, I'll threaten to leak his crimes to the world. I doubt they'll chance a tarnished reputation.

I change into a fresh shirt and head back upstairs to Sage. Hopefully I can talk her into coming home with me where I can properly bed her. I'd love nothing more than to wake up next to her and fuck her again before making her breakfast.

I've never been so utterly attracted to a woman that I literally kill a man for her. Not even my ex—who broke up with me last month—made me so... passionate. Lori was a beautiful woman. But too innocent for my world. I hid this part of my life from her for two years before she uncovered my lies. It's my own fault for not locking my office door at home. She walked in on a less than legal conversation. I asked her the cost of her silence and after paying off her student loans and setting her up with a PR job for one of the local sports teams—she loves hockey—she agreed not to say a word.

It was an easy decision for her because our relationship had been over for months.

Because I pushed her away.

I slow my steps as I approach my office and notice the door ajar.

My phone is already to my ear, calling for backup, before I tuck it away and grab a gun from the holster at my side. My heart beats erratically with worry that something's happened to Sage. This place is highly guarded, and someone would have to be invisible to get past my security team, but it's not *impossible*.

I should have left two men up here at the door, but I didn't want Sage thinking she was a prisoner who couldn't leave.

I peek around the doorframe and listen but no one's in there. Still, I enter cautiously. There's nowhere to hide in my office so after a quick scan of the room, I put my gun away.

She's not here.

Gone.

Except for the note on my desk.

Had to leave. Thanks for all the orgasms.
- Sage

What the fuck?

I take out my phone and call my head of security, Jax. Maybe she's still in the building. If not, I'll have my security team track her down.

Everyone who enters my club hands over identification that I log into a system. I keep a database because rich pricks have been known to frequent my clubs, and it's always good to have dirt on the powerful schmucks for blackmailing purposes.

If Sage is gone, I'll be able to track her down.

She caught my eye the moment she walked in earlier tonight. Her green dress clung to her thick body. Her wide, perfect ass and soft stomach begged for my hands to worship them. Her blonde hair was up in a high ponytail, waiting to be tugged and wrapped around my wrist.

She was by herself.

Confidence radiated from her as she moved her hips to the music. The crowd gravitated toward her.

Including that man.

I saw red when Adam approached her from behind and cupped her pussy.

In that moment, I knew I was going to kill him. Sage choosing not to get police involved solidified my decision.

I never expected to fuck her. At least, not right away, especially after she'd just been groped. She obviously had different plans, lunging for me and initiating a kiss.

She melted into me. Then for a few minutes, she took control, pushing me back to my desk.

It was strange.

I'm always in control in both my personal and professional life. But there she was, trying to lead.

It didn't last long. The moment I slid into her wet cunt, she submitted.

Until she ordered me to undress.

And slapped me.

Then choked me.

My cock jerks remembering the sting of her palm on my cheek. Her small hands squeezing around my throat.

How she begged me to fuck her ass with my finger.

She's going to ruin me.

She's going to ruin sex for me.

I'll never be able to fuck anyone else.

That's why I'm determined to find her.

Obsessed with finding her.

Chapter 3

Sage

It's barely been a week since my one-night stand with Elias, and I can't stop thinking about him.

I've tried masturbating him out of my system, but that only made me hornier.

It's a constant need.

An itch I can't scratch.

Which is why I invited my bestie, Noah, to come out with me tonight.

I need to get dicked. I need to forget about the man with the magical cock who gave me five glorious orgasms.

Even logging in to the Madam app has been lackluster. I don't make a ton on it, maybe a couple hundred a month depending on how mean I am. Consensual humiliation.

Most of the time, it's sexual.

For example, I was paid $200 after ordering a man to stand in a corner with his pants down for ten minutes... in his office at work.

I ordered another man to jack off in the bathroom at work without getting caught. $100.

Some men just want to be yelled at because that gets them off, so I call them through the app and curse them out—totally anonymous.

Easy $50.

But the messages in the Madam app are piling up because nothing is appealing to me.

Noah and I arrived at Club 99 SoHo thirty minutes ago, and she's already found a hottie to take home.

Now I'm on the prowl.

I finish my drink and flag down the bartender, Harry. He nods, letting me know he saw me. Noah and I come to this club enough that Harry has our drinks memorized.

While I'm waiting on my vodka soda with a splash of cranberry, I scan the dance floor.

Ugh.

There are some beautiful people here tonight, yet I have no desire to walk up to any of them and start flirting.

My resting bitch face must be in full force because a man appears before me with a smirk.

"You look mean."

"I am."

"I don't believe it. You're too pretty to be mean."

"I could throw my drink in your face and slap you. Would that convince you?"

"I'd let you slap me around any time, baby."

I narrow my eyes at the dude.

He's cute, I suppose.

Tall—six feet if I had to guess—with wavy dark red hair and freckles across his nose. He's a big guy, but not nearly as big as Elias. This man who is scanning his eyes down my body, his thumb skating across his lower lip, is packed with muscles... which means he's likely a gym bro.

Gym bros love big girls.

"Can I buy you a drink before you slap me around?" gym bro asks.

Harry arrives at the perfect time, setting booze on the bar in front of me.

"Put it on my tab," gym bro says and gives Harry the name Ryan Bradford.

Harry looks at me for confirmation, and I give him a nod.

Ryan holds up his beer, and I accept his cheers before taking a deep sip of my drink. I'm tense as fuck, and I need to loosen up.

"So... what's your name?" Ryan asks.

"What makes you think you deserve my name? Because you bought me a drink?"

He raises a brow, intrigued by my brash response.

"Then tell me what I can do to earn it."

Hell yeah, he wants to play.

He's giving me submissive vibes. Compliant men somehow always find me.

This is exactly what I need.

"Kiss my feet."

It's a little strong off the top, but I'm not messing around tonight. If I'm going to fuck someone else to forget about Elias, I need them to do anything I want.

Ryan pauses and glances around.

No one is paying attention to us so he sinks to the ground on his hands and knees.

He moves in to kiss my Louboutins, but I take hold of his hair, stopping him.

"You think I'd let that dirty mouth on my designer pumps?"

He groans, his pupils expanding. "Please, let me take you home. I need..."

I tug on his hair harder and force him upright on his knees. He's a tall man so his head aligns with my chest. I lean in and whisper across his lips, "What? Tell me."

I pull back when he tries to kiss me.

What the fuck?

I never refuse a kiss from a hot guy.

"I need you."

Boring fucking answer.

"Get up," I nearly growl because my body tells me we want this, but my brain is trying to steer us off course.

Because of Elias.

"Pay your tab, and we can go."

He smiles, and it lights up his face. He really is a gorgeous man. I just wish I'd stop comparing him to someone else.

"And tip your bartender—generously."

It takes about ten minutes for Ryan to cash out, then we're making our way through the crowd to coat check.

He calls a ride share and after getting our coats, we're heading to the Upper West Side to his apartment.

My heart races, and I know it has nothing to do with Ryan.

I'm nervous... no, anxious. NO. This is guilt. It's me feeling as if I'm about to do something wrong, which makes no sense.

Elias was just a one-night stand!

Ryan talks my ear off for the rest of the ride, and I expertly tune him out while giving him generic answers: 'oh?' 'wow' 'that's cool.'

His apartment is a small studio, but big enough for a queen bed, couch, coffee table, a few bookcases, a dresser, and a tiny table with two chairs in the tiny kitchen area.

As soon as he shuts the door and locks it, he's on me.

He tries to kiss me on the lips, but I avert my head, and his mouth lands on my jaw before trailing down my neck. He walks us to his bed, and I pull away.

"What? What's wrong?"

I twist us around and push him, causing him to fall onto the bed.

"Get in the middle, back to the headboard."

He sucks in a sharp breath but does as I order.

"No touching me, or yourself, until I say so, got it?"

He nods, then immediately tries to reach for me.

"Ry-guy, what did I just say? Can you not take orders?"

"I can! I promise!"

"Hmm. I don't trust you. I'll just have to tie you up."

I go to his dresser to start opening drawers in search of his ties and luckily find them in the top one. Picking two, I return to the bed on his left side.

He doesn't resist when I take his arm and secure his wrist to the bed frame's corner. As I walk around the end of the bed to bind his right hand, I notice his cock straining in his pants.

"Do you need help with that?" I ask, nodding to his crotch.

"Yes, please..."

His eyes widen, just now realizing he still doesn't know my name.

"You can call me Madam Manilow."

"Holy shit," he nearly whispers. "Are you really a dominatrix? I knew you were the moment I saw you tonight. That's why I came over to talk to you."

I stifle an eye roll. I brought this upon myself. The whole reason I wore this body-hugging midi dress with the sweetheart neckline and built-in corset was to attract a submissive man. This outfit seems to call to them.

It must be the red.

Like an angry bull, except they're horny gym bros needing to be told they're bad little brats.

I turn to Ryan's dresser for another tie, then crawl onto the bed between his legs.

"Shut. Up."

I stuff it in his mouth, gagging him. He whimpers, and it's music to my ears.

I turn my attention to his tented pants. Slowly, I unzip him and tug his boxers down.

His cock springs free.

It's a nice dick, average I'd say.

But it's not Elias's cock.

Goddamn it.

The man will not leave my head.

Which means, I can't fuck Ryan tonight. Hell, I won't even let him kiss me.

I get off the bed and grab a chair from the kitchen area, then return to the end of the bed. Sitting down, I spread my legs and hike up my dress.

"You're going to watch while I touch myself, and if you're a good boy, I might let you come too."

His cock jerks, leaking precum.

I close my eyes and find my clit, pressing down and massaging in circles, slow at first, then picking up speed as

I remember my night with Elias. How he fucked me like I was the last person he'd ever sleep with. Like I was a god, and his thrusts were prayers.

Like a starving man, and my cunt was a feast.

"Yes, Elias," I moan.

"Elias?" Ryan mumbles.

Damn it. The tie is falling out of his mouth. I should have secured it better. I ignore him and move my fingers to slide them inside me.

My walls spasm around the digits, and I snake my other hand up my body. Tugging at the neckline of the dress, I free a breast and pinch the nipple.

"Fuck, Boss, yes!" I scream.

"Boss? Who the fuck—"

I don't hear the rest of what Ryan says because I explode with an orgasm. My body shakes, and I squirt all over Ryan's floor.

Once my shaking ends, I remove my fingers and stand, readjusting my dress to cover my ass.

"Can I taste you?" Ryan asks.

I shake my head.

"Sorry, Ry-guy. Turns out, my pussy belongs to someone else. I need to go."

I find my purse on the table where I dropped it.

"What the hell? Aren't you going to untie me?" He squirms, tugging on the binds.

That's only going to make them harder to unknot.

I smirk. "You have a few options. One: call a friend to set you free. Something tells me a little humiliation turns you on, doesn't it?"

He doesn't answer, but his cock jumps at my words, telling me everything I need to know.

"Wait, what's the other option, and can you at least get my phone out of my pocket so I can prompt the voice assistant?"

I pause, considering. I should feel bad for getting myself off in front of him and refusing him his release.

But I don't.

I hold up a finger and dig in my purse for my phone. I call a friend I met at the sex club I've been to a few times. She's a thick goddess like me.

"Hey, Raya? It's... Madam Manilow. I have a situation needing taken care of. Can I text you the address?"

Ryan's eyes widen.

"Yeah, he's cute. He likes to be ordered around too. You're going to love him."

I hang up and turn to Ryan.

"I'm not really a dominatrix, but my friend Raya is. She'll be here in fifteen minutes."

I wink and walk out the door, leaving it unlocked.

I'm going to need a bestie night with Noah to talk about this. She needs to convince me not to return to Underground Park Slope.

To return to *him*.

I've got to be strong, though, because the last thing I need is another man in my life.

Even if that man gave me the best sex of my life.

Chapter 4

Elias

I stare at the piece of paper for what must be the millionth time.

Had to leave. Thanks for all the orgasms.

- Sage

Five orgasms, and she ghosts me?

It's been three weeks.

Thanksgiving has come and gone, and the worst time of year is approaching. The holidays remind me how lonely I am. How much I miss my mother. How I miss my brother even though I'm the one who constantly pushes him away.

I twirl the pen Sage left between my fingers. It's all I have of her. The note and a goddamn pen.

No phone number. No address.

I have her name that was logged when the bouncer scanned her ID at the door.

Sage Manilow.

My contact at the NYPD ran the information but came up empty-handed.

Sage Manilow doesn't exist.

The address on the ID is to a laundromat in Harlem.

Searching Sage Manilow on the Internet pulls up pages upon pages of Barry Manilow results. Even my tech guy found nothing on the woman when delving into the depths of the dark web.

I scoured my security camera footage from that night, trying to find a good shot of her face for Phil to use in his searches. I found plenty of her on the dance floor, including the moment that man sexually assaulted her, but none of it was usable. Her face was either too blurry from dancing or too dark and pixelated in the club's dim lighting.

Even when she was brought upstairs, she kept her head low and out of view of the cameras.

I have a camera in my office, too, but I turned it off before she walked inside, knowing we were about to have a less than legal conversation.

I also don't film women in private settings without their consent.

I questioned if she was real. If my men hadn't seen her, hadn't escorted her to my office after that fucker touched her, I would have thought I was going mad.

A knock on the door pulls me to the present.

"What?" I bark out.

My underboss, Martin, pops his head inside. He's my uncle on my mother's side and looks nothing like me. He's short, maybe five six with light brown hair and brown eyes. He likely weighs half of me.

I'm a big guy. Six foot six and over three hundred pounds if I had to guess. I have no idea because I don't give a shit about my weight. I take after my late father who was just as big with black hair and blue eyes. Anytime I look in the mirror, I see his ghost and it fills me with rage.

I will never be my father, the abusive prick.

Martin holds up an envelope. "This was just delivered."

He enters my office and hands it over.

The envelope is opened already, which isn't unusual since I have someone who checks all mail and packages delivered to any of my businesses.

I own a few nightclubs in Queens and Brooklyn. Underground Park Slope was my first business, and it's now a front for my criminal empire—one that was left to me when my father died.

He began preparing me for the role since my teens, and I took over at age twenty-two, which means I have a long list of enemies who've tried to kill me more than once by sending poisons through letters and packages.

I extract a thick piece of paper from the envelope. It has beautifully written script on the front in gold with a Christmas-themed border of holly and mistletoe in silver.

It's an invitation to Gio Lenetti's Annual Christmas Party this weekend, held at the Wyndock Hotel in Midtown, Manhattan.

Gio Lenetti is the Don of the Empire Mafia. My rival. Why would he be inviting me to his party?

I'd understand if the invite was addressed to one of my aliases that I use for my businesses, but it's not. It's addressed to Elias Carter.

People know my name. They know I lead the Queensboro Mob but not many know my face. I tend to stay in the shadows during business deals. I'll act as security and let one of my soldiers who has a similar build and appearance as me act in my place. Or even my uncle, Martin, leads meetings sometimes.

It's worked well for me so far.

The invite alludes to a neutral night of festivities which could be the perfect opportunity to make connections, maybe try to lure some of Lenetti's power players over to the QBM.

I don't trust Gio, but he's not an idiot. He wouldn't be dumb enough to start a mafia war at a luxury hotel in Midtown, Manhattan.

What will happen if I show up and give them my name?

I guess I'll find out.

Fucking Christmas.

Fucking Lenetti.

Why did I think it'd be a good idea to show up to his Christmas party?

I tried talking myself out of coming a million times because I hate both Christmas *and* Lenetti, but I'm too curious as to why I was invited.

Two Empire soldiers nod as I enter the hotel's entrance.

They don't stop me or four of my men who walk in behind me.

Either these Empire dickheads are new and don't recognize me or were told not to do shit.

As we walk through the lobby, I point out spots where my soldiers can station, ready to move in if needed. I leave them behind and turn into a hallway outside of the ballroom where the party is taking place.

Two large men stand beside a woman with a clipboard, checking invitations while she verifies names. She doesn't react when I give her my name, however, the two security guards make sure to give me a thorough pat down. They also inspect my invitation closer than anyone else in line ahead of me. With a curt, but somewhat suspicious nod of approval, they let me through.

Interesting. I at least expected some pushback at the security checkpoint.

Maybe all of Gio's guards hate him as much as I do and don't give a fuck about letting his rival in. Or maybe this really *is* a 'neutral night of festivities' as the invitation stated.

Or this is a trap, and they don't expect me to leave this place alive. I don't doubt Lenetti's already been alerted of my arrival.

The party is well underway when I enter the grand ballroom.

The decor is tacky as hell. Reds, greens, and golds everywhere as if Santa and his elves got drunk and threw up all over the walls. The tree is nearly as tall as the room. Bows are wrapped around columns, and gold streamers hang from the ceiling. A string quartet plays an instrumental version of a popular Christmas song, and the cheerful music almost makes me turn around and leave.

I don't celebrate Christmas. Not since my mother was killed the night before, twenty years ago.

I was the one who found her. I was only sixteen.

That's the main reason why I decided to show up.

Tonight is a chance to listen. To overhear drunk conversations for any information that might accidentally slip from loose lips.

My brother and I are convinced Gio is the one who ordered the hit on our mother all those years ago. We've been trying to gather enough proof to bring him, and the Empire, down. If we're going to start a mafia war against the most powerful man in New York City, we have to be sure.

Someone here at this party must know something—especially the powerful fucks at Lenetti's side. I've got dirt on plenty of them. If I can't get them to squeal on Lenetti, then I can at least blackmail them into aligning with the QBM.

I stop at the open bar and grab a whiskey before weaving through the crowd. People stand around chatting while drinking and eating, fake laughing at horrible jokes, and slapping on charm that's just as fake as their smiles and bodies.

I hate it all.

The corrupt gravitating to the powerful.

Gio Lenetti is the king of corrupt and powerful. He has blood on his hands.

Not that I don't, but the blood I spill is from the veins of living monsters. Pedophiles, scam artists, human traffickers.

The list could go on.

It's what I've been doing since taking over the QBM. I've been working to clean up the streets and bust dealers who target kids and teenagers. My father really fucked things up twenty years ago. He's the reason New York

City has a drug epidemic. Percy Carter dealt dirty and dangerous drugs.

There will always be drugs in this city. I just make sure to regulate them the best that I can.

I snatch an hors d'oeuvre from a passing server but pause before putting it in my mouth. The woman has walked on, but she's not far because of the crowded space. I tap her on the shoulder, and she turns, lifting her head because of my height.

Her cheeks blush, and she sucks in a breath.

I get that a lot. I'm a giant. People always ask if I'm a wrestler. If I hadn't been born into a life of crime, I would have loved to be a wrestler. My brother, Lance, and I would watch it on television as kids. Then we'd clear a space in the living room to create a makeshift ring and body slam each other.

I always won.

"Does this have nuts in it?"

"Oh, um, no. I don't think so. It's smoked trout croquettes. Mashed potatoes, smoked trout, mozzarella, parmesan, and chives. Would you like me to double check?"

I shake my head. I have my EpiPen, and cross contamination won't incapacitate me like eating a whole fucking nut.

I pop the food into my mouth and groan. Fuck, that's good.

While I chew, I scan the crowd. No one seems to be paying attention to me, which is fine. I like to be invisible. Though, I do appear to be one of the taller and bigger men in the room.

Wait one damn second.

My eyes land on a head of hair belonging to a man who looks like a slimmer version of me.

My brother.

"Lance?"

He startles and whips around, snatching the wrist of the woman standing next to him. He shoves her behind him.

"Del, why are you trying to hide me?" she scoffs and peels out of his grip.

Del? That's cute. His name is Delancy, but I call him Lance. He hates being called Lance, and now this woman has shortened his name to Del. Like the fucking computer.

I stifle a laugh.

"Hi. I'm Noah," the woman says, holding out her hand.

This is my first time meeting Noah, but I know all about her. She's Lance's neighbor and a contract killer who goes by the name Colpa Sicario—one of the best in the industry. My brother had no idea he'd been living next door to his rival when she moved in a few months ago.

They somehow ended up on the same assignment, to kill Cillian O'Connor, the son of the Don for the Lords of Staten Island. I've been trying to take down that sad excuse for a crime organization for years. Cillian was the worst of them, a rapist, low-life scum.

His father, Finn, is a piece of shit too. Finn is involved in human trafficking, and I have no doubt he's helping this new fucker, Moonlight, who we believe is behind recent shipments.

If the Lords are working with this Moonlight douchebag, then they both need to be taken down. But dismembering a whole mob isn't easy. I can't go in with guns blazing. It's too big of a mess to clean up that would involve utilizing my contacts with the FBI. I'd rather keep them out of this if I can.

The Lords are already under the agency's eye because of the crimes Cillian committed. He was messy and one more crime away from getting the Lords slapped with RICO charges.

But he's gone now. Dead.

And Noah was the one to take him out.

But now she's found herself in trouble. The day after she killed Cillian, her apartment building—the same one where Lance had a safe house—blew up. That was just over two weeks ago. We spent a week trying to find the person responsible with no luck.

But now they're both here? At Gio Lenetti's Christmas party? Lance didn't tell me he had been invited, so this was either planned or a coincidence, and I hate coincidences.

Time to piss him off.

I scan Noah's body and rub my thumb over my bottom lip. She's beautiful.

Not as beautiful as Reine.

"Elias. This idiot's brother," I say, then take Noah's offered greeting.

I lift her hand to my mouth and kiss her knuckles.

"A gentleman," Noah purrs.

"He's not a fucking gentleman," my brother growls.

I laugh, full belly. "I have to say... I've never seen my brother so... protective of another person before."

The woman takes my brother's fisted hand and weaves her fingers with his. His anger immediately fades.

A pang rips through my heart and stabs my insides from my heart down to my stomach.

I want that. I want a woman who can calm me down with just her touch.

What if I had her and let her go?

"What are you doing here?" Lance asks, his voice low. "If anyone were to find out the leader of the QBM is at an Empire party..."

I glance at Noah, expecting her to react to my brother calling me a fucking mob boss, but she's Colpa Sicario. She likely knows all the heavy hitters in this godforsaken city.

"I was invited," I say and take a drink of my whiskey.

"By my father?" Noah asks, and I whip my head back to her.

"You're Gio Lenetti's daughter? I thought Noemi Lenetti—"

"Died? No. It was a lie." She snorts. "It's weird hearing my birth name again after all these years."

What the hell is going on? Noah is a contract killer *and* a mafia princess? Even worse, she's the daughter of the man who Lance and I believe ordered our mother's death?

I turn my attention to Lance. How long has he known she's our rival? Is she making a play? Using my brother to get to me to take down the QBM?

"We're working together," Lance says.

"And fucking," Noah adds.

My face heats with anger. How could he do this? It's... betrayal. He's literally sleeping with the enemy.

My brother wraps his arm around her waist, bringing her closer to him, clearly seeing my rage. Which pisses me off even more. Did he really think I would do something to her? We're in public for fuck's sake and on Empire territory.

"I wanted to meet yesterday to tell you everything," Lance continues. "But you never answer my text messages. I even called and left a voicemail. So, don't act surprised. I tried, like I always do. We'll meet tomorrow to talk."

My anger dissolves and is replaced with guilt. I'm trying to be a better brother. I want to start involving Lance in my life more. I've been pushing him away since Christmas Eve, twenty years ago. Because the men who were hired to kill our mother forced my little brother to slit her throat instead. He was only twelve. *Twelve.*

I wasn't there for him. I wasn't there to save our mother and protect Lance.

I was a failure, and I haven't been able to forgive myself. It makes me angry and instead of telling him how I truly feel, I lash out at him. A part of me worries that if I keep him close, I'll lose him just like we lost our mother.

That being said, I'm still pissed about him hooking up with Lenetti's daughter.

"It better be a good fucking explanation, little brother," I say through gritted teeth.

"It will be," Noah says, trying to ease the tension between us. "Oh!"

Someone behind me catches Noah's eye, and she squirms out of Lance's hold. She waves, and I turn to see who she's bringing over to us. After learning Noah is an Empire heir, I can't trust her. I have to watch my back.

"Sage," Noah says, and my heart stops beating.

My breath is captured by the blonde goddess walking toward us. I slink behind my brother, not that my big body will be hidden by Lance.

Noah hugs the woman who's been haunting my dreams for the past three weeks.

"You look amazing."

She fucking does.

Her red strapless dress sparkles, and the fabric falls to the floor aside from the split where her leg peeks out. Her long hair falls over her shoulders in curls. She's wearing white gloves that come to her elbows paired with a pearl necklace and matching earrings. Very old school Hollywood.

She's tanner, as if just returning from an island vacation. Her blue eyes, which have specks of green throughout, glow.

"Thanks, Noey!"

She blows a kiss to her best friend, and I'm tempted to lunge in front of Noah to steal it, but I stay where I am, peering over Lance's shoulder since Sage still hasn't spotted me.

I've been the Don of the QBM since I was twenty-two years old. Fourteen goddamn years killing and threatening and scaring men to the point they piss themselves.

Yet I'm hiding from the woman who walked out of my life after what had to be the best sex I've ever had.

"Sage, you've met Del before."

She says something, but I'm no longer listening. Because I'm freaking out. Because I've been searching for this woman for *weeks*, and she's finally back in my life.

Only this time, I won't let her go.

"And this is Elias—"

"Oh, fuck." Sage's cheeks pink, and she takes a step back.

"You," I growl.

Chapter 5

Sage

"I'm sorry," Noah begins. "Do you two know each other?"

"We fucked, and she disappeared," Elias bellows, garnering a few looks from people nearby.

"Tell the whole room, why don't you!" I huff. "And it's called a one-night stand for a reason."

"Do all your one-night stands give you multiple orgasms? Do they fuck you until your eyes cross and your brain stops working? Isn't that what you said to me after the fifth round?"

The shock of running into Elias battles with lust. My cunt remembers every inch of that man; the way it stretched around his cock as he pounded into me, his strong hands as they held my hips, and his greedy mouth on my lips, my throat, my clit.

"Is this the unbelievably earth-shattering mindless sex guy you told me about that you met at a club in Brooklyn a few weeks ago?" Noah asks.

I narrow my eyes at my best friend, and she counters with a raised brow.

She said that—out loud—on purpose.

I glance at Elias, and his chest puffs with pride. He smirks, the asshole.

"You mean the club *I* own? Underground Park Slope?"

"Yes! That's the one!" Noah giggles. "Oh, Sage... after what you told me... why would you ever deny yourself another night with The Boss?"

"The Boss?" Del asks, clearly amused by the drama.

"Yes, why, Sage?" Elias locks eyes on me, but I refuse to look at him because I know the moment I stare into those pools of blue, I'll want to fall into his arms and beg for forgiveness for leaving him.

Not to mention how fucking handsome he is tonight. He's wearing a black suit that fits his large chest and beefy arms like a glove. Underneath is a red dress shirt with a matching pocket square and a black tie. He's clean shaven, and his black hair is slicked back, except for the small strand that always seems to hang down over his forehead.

"Anyone going to address Sage calling Elias 'The Boss'?" Del reiterates.

"Because he owns the club, obviously," I say, eyeing Noah, begging my best friend to save me despite her being the one to throw me to the wolves.

Elias's smirk grows to a full-fledged smile. God, I hate him.

God, I want him.

"Or is it because I owned your pussy? Made that cunt sore and stretched to fit my cock that no other man will be able to live up to the job of pleasing you like I did."

This cocky mother fucker. I mean yeah, sure, it's true, but he doesn't need to know he's a sex god sent down to torture me. He doesn't need to know how much I've been thinking about him for the last three weeks, touching myself when I'm in bed, or in the shower, or in the stockroom at work.

I walk up to him, nose raised and chin high. The top of my head barely reaches his jawline. Crossing my arms, I say, "I've had better."

"Okay," Noah says, grabbing my arm. "While what's happening between you two is... interesting, the show's about to begin."

"What show?" I ask, scrunching my nose.

Noah takes my hands in hers. "I'm sorry I didn't get to tell you before. Please don't be mad." She turns to Elias. "Can you watch over her? She means the world to me."

I open my mouth to ask what the hell she's talking about but the next thing I know, my best friend is treating Elias like a doll and moves the massive man to stand next to me. She lifts his arm to snake it around my waist.

Seriously, Noah?

I try to wiggle out of his hold, but he clings to me tighter.

Goddamn it.

This was *not* supposed to happen tonight. All I wanted was to have fun... to hang out with my bestie who I've barely seen in the past few weeks because she's been pre-occupied with her neighbor. Also... she nearly died a little over two weeks ago when her apartment building blew up moments before her and Del were about to walk in.

They claim it was caused by a gas leak, but I can tell Noah is holding back information from me.

She has secrets. I've always felt there's something dark and dangerous about her. She constantly tells me she'll off my ex-husband, masking the offer as a joke, but her face tells me she's serious.

Not to mention her father sounds like an awful man based off the things she's told me, like sending her away after her mother died because he couldn't deal with raising a child on his own. Refusing to speak to her about what happened. That's all she's revealed to me about her past, and the fact that her father tries to control her life, even as an adult.

I didn't even want to come to the man's party, but Noah promised me we'd get to hang out.

She's never broken a promise to me.

We met at our job. I'm a part-time server at a bar in Midtown East and Noah walked in a few months ago needing a bartending gig. We clicked immediately. She's outgoing, confident, beautiful. She's also tough and doesn't take shit from anyone.

She's inspired me to be stronger, to stick up for myself.

I've been working to claim my freedom and individuality back since leaving my ex, and Noah has been my personal cheerleader.

And now my best friend is on stage, confessing to the crowd that her real name is Noemi Lenetti, and she's not dead.

What? Not dead? What does she mean?

Ok. Yeah, she definitely left out a shit ton of details about her past.

What the actual fuck is going on?

I need more booze, but the arm around me won't budge, even when I squirm and try to step away from the massive man who smells like mahogany, vanilla, and something roasted... like a cozy night by the fire, eating vanilla Christmas cookies.

The man's warm, too. I want to lean my head on his shoulder and close my eyes. I want to cuddle up to his side and fall asleep.

"Let's go," he says to me and releases his hold.

The freezing air of the ballroom washes over me at his absence, and I shiver.

Back to reality and pretending to hate this man so I can keep him at a distance.

It's really for the best.

"I'm not going anywhere with you," I spit out.

Elias grabs my hand and tugs. I attempt to use my weight to prevent us from moving, but my heels on the marble floor give me no traction.

"And *I'm* not leaving you here by yourself after the daughter of New York City's most powerful crime boss just announced she's engaged to the enforcer for a rival mob," Elias whispers next to my ear.

He maneuvers us through the crowd, his hands on my hips and his body near flush with my back.

"Wait, what? Noah's engaged? To who?"

"To my brother."

I whip my head back around to see Noah hugging Del's arm.

"Del?"

How did I miss that part?

Right, I was in shock from my bestie's confession.

And I was daydreaming about Elias.

"Wait. Del's your brother? Hold on. Did you say Noah's the daughter of a powerful crime boss? And what do you mean by rival mob? WHAT DO YOU MEAN BY EN-FORCER?"

I'm going to have an aneurysm.

"Who the fuck are you? I thought you were a night-club owner. Is your name even Elias? You know, when I Googled Underground Park Slope owner trying to find information on you, Elias didn't come up."

"You Googled me?"

"Who's Johnny Goode?"

"I'm Johnny Goode, owner of Underground Park Slope. I'm also Elias Carter."

"What? I don't understand. What the fuck is going on?"

Elias's grip around my waist tightens. We're the only ones leaving, not that anyone is paying us attention. They're all wide-eyed, staring at the drama unfolding on stage.

Holy shit, Noah is *engaged*.

I am going to kick her ass tomorrow.

I mean, I knew her and Del were spending a lot of time together, but fuck.

Engaged?

Mafia?

Oh, God, what have I gotten myself into?

"Don't act dumb, Reine. You're friends with Noah. You know exactly what's going on."

"I don't—"

My throat aches, and pressure builds behind my eyes. Goddamn it, here come the tears. I press my palm to my chest, my heart thumping frantically against it.

I'm about to lose my fucking shit.

"Elias," I say, a sob claiming my voice.

He stops walking, hearing the tears. I'm full-on crying now. We're out of the ballroom at this point, and the hallway leading back to the extravagant lobby is empty. Elias grabs me by the chin, his concerned blue eyes observing mine.

"You didn't know?"

Tears roll down my cheeks. God, I hate when people see me cry. I cried way too damn much because of my ex, and I promised to never let myself get so weak to do it again.

Then I remember crying isn't weak.

It's natural. It's needed.

Like right now because this is all too overwhelming.

"You didn't know?" Elias repeats when I don't answer.

I shake my head.

"Fuck, Sage."

He sighs and clenches his jaw. He seems hesitant about what to say next, maybe battling with telling me nothing... and telling me everything.

"Your best friend is the daughter of New York City's most powerful mob boss. I'm the leader of the QBM, a rival mob. My brother, Lance, is my enforcer. Noah announcing their engagement is going to shake up our world, and I want to get you out of here to somewhere safe."

My brows furrow as I process this information.

It doesn't seem real.

Elias is...

ELIAS IS A MOTHERFUCKING MAFIA BOSS?!

Not Johnny Goode, club owner.

Wait. Johnny Goode? Like *Johnny B. Goode*, the Chuck Berry song?

Seriously, Elias?

It's as if I've been dropped into the plot of a mafia movie. *Or a sexy mafia romance book.*

Okay, wow. I am clearly going insane.

How the hell do I always end up in these situations? First, I divorce Chase for turning to a life of crime. Now I've managed to fuck a mafia boss and become best friends with the daughter of another mafia boss?

I should go. I should be terrified and run away from this man.

But I'm not, especially with the way he pushes my hair away from my face and uses his thumbs to wipe my tears. Which only makes me want to cry more because it's been too long since a man has treated me so gently.

I won't let them. Chase went from loving to controlling. Now I push men away. *I'm* the one who needs to be controlling.

At least, I was until I met this infuriating man.

I bat Elias's hand to wipe my own damn cheeks and huff out a frustrated breath, which only makes him smile.

He's less intimidating when he smiles.

"I mean, I guess I always suspected Noah was hiding something. Some of the things she told me about her fat her…"

I chew on my lip, wondering if I'm officially done panicking. I'm sure reality will all come crashing back tomorrow when I remember I went to a Christmas party hosted by a mafia boss.

Wait… do all these people here know who Noah's father is?

We're at a freaking upscale hotel for fuck's sake.

"Are you sure we need to leave? I mean… certainly a mafia war isn't going to break out at this high-class party at a fancy hotel in the middle of Manhattan? And Noah just announced her engagement. I didn't even congratulate her… or Del… and I want to celebrate with her and—"

My rambling is interrupted by the door to the ballroom opening, causing me to jump. Sounds of music, conversation, and laughter spill out.

Guess the party has resumed.

Elias palms my cheek before dropping his hand to grab mine.

"We'll talk when there's fewer people around."

I breathe in and out slowly, trying to calm my racing heart as he leads us to the lobby.

How can a man who heads a fucking mafia be so sweet?

The way my stomach fluttered at his comforting touches while I had my short-lived breakdown…

Yeah, I can't let myself fall for this man—or fall any further than I already have. *What if he's just like Chase?* I shake the thought out of my head. Elias is *nothing* like Chase.

Still... I need to get away. But how? He's yet to let me out of his sight since our reunion.

I spot the restrooms to my right. Perfect. Maybe there's a window or extra door or... I could slip out when he's not paying attention.

"I need to pee," I say, attempting to veer us to the right. "I had a lot of champagne, and I'm not wearing underwear so if I piss myself, it's going down my leg."

It's a lie. I only had one glass of champagne, and I don't have to pee.

Elias stops in his tracks and slowly turns to face me. His eyes travel down my body.

"No underwear?"

His eyes light up with desire. The same look he gave me in his office at the club, seconds before I kissed him. I catch a small smirk before Elias leads us across the lobby to the restrooms.

He opens the first door and instead of waiting outside like a good guard dog, he tugs me over the threshold.

Wait. This is the men's restroom.

"What the fuck?" I whisper.

One man is at the sink, washing his hands. Two more are at the urinals.

"Get out," Elias barks at them.

They don't have to be told twice. The men taking a piss quickly zip up and bypass washing their hands before leaving. The door to one of the stalls opens and a young employee stumbles out, struggling to pull up his pants while he clamors out of the bathroom.

Elias checks the rest of the stalls, then locks the door.

"You have no right," I yell, planting my hands on my hips.

Elias extends his arm to the row of stalls.

"Go ahead."

"Why did you bring me to the men's restroom?"

"I'm a big scary man. I wasn't going to walk into the lady's room."

"You could have waited outside, you big oaf!"

"Did you really think I was going to leave you alone again after you ghosted me? Think again, Reine."

I stomp my foot and cross my arms.

"This is kidnapping!"

"Your best friend asked me to keep you safe."

I *did* hear Noah say that to him. But did she know the mafia boss was going to *kidnap* me?

Arguing with this stubborn fool is getting me nowhere. And I hate how turned on I am with this alphahole bull-shit.

Jesus, what a rollercoaster of emotions I'm experiencing tonight. How can I go from scared and confused to turned on and *willing*?

"I refuse to pee while you're in the same room as me," I say with a huff. Not to mention I don't need to pee at all. "Get out. Right now."

The command is weak, and Elias sees my fight waning. He takes off his jacket and hangs it on a hook on the door. Walking towards me, he smirks while folding up the sleeves of his red dress shirt, exposing his tattooed arms—God, why is a man exposing his forearms so freaking sexy?

Elias lifts his hand and wraps his fingers around my throat.

"You had a lot of champagne huh?"

"Yeah, like three glasses."

Lie number one. He's suspicious.

"So... you're drunk?"

"Wasted."

Lie number two. He sees right through it.

"Do you even need to pee?"

"Y-yes."

Lie number three. Busted.

"Fine. Then let me fuck it out of you."

My body betrays me, and I whimper. Elias squeezes my throat harder. I vaguely register the clink of my clutch hitting the floor.

"Mmm. Such a needy little liar, aren't you?"

I press my thighs together. He sees me squirm.

"What do you need? Is it consent? It's yours. Will you let me fuck you right now against the bathroom counter?"

I will my voice to speak up and say no. That I don't want to be fucked against the bathroom counter. The words are on the tip of my tongue.

But I'd be lying.

I do want this.

I want *him*.

And Elias sees it all over my face.

He backs us up until my ass hits the hard line of the counter. He leans in, brushing his lips over mine.

"Last chance, Ma Chérie."

Okay so he's definitely calling me something in French every time he says Reine.

I could look it up but then that would mean I care, which obviously I don't.

"Please," I say, the word barely a whisper.

Elias's mouth crashes down on mine. My hands grip his shirt, and I pull him closer. His tongue teases my lips, and I open them for him. He shoves his tongue inside and lashes it against my own.

Fuck, I forgot how amazing he is at kissing.

Without breaking the kiss, he slides his free hand down my front and through the slit of the dress—easy access to my heated core where he finds me soaked.

And panty-less, as promised.

I moan into his mouth when he slides one of his thick fingers inside me. The sound encourages him, and he adds a second finger. He starts pumping in and out casually while simultaneously choking me and masterfully moving his luscious lips over mine.

The more I whimper, groan, and moan, the faster his fingers fuck me.

My body remembers his touch. It's been deprived... n eglected... *needy.*

Which means it doesn't take long for me to reach my release. I'm sent over the edge when the heel of Elias's palm presses against my clit.

He waits until my clenching cunt stops before he pulls his fingers out and licks them clean.

"Good girl, Sage," he says and releases my neck to twist me around.

The sound of a zipper pierces the quiet air followed by the crackle of foil from a condom wrapper he just pulled from his pocket. *What the hell? Did he bring condoms expecting to get lucky tonight with someone*—you know what? It doesn't matter because I'm the one who's here now.

He folds my dress up to expose my ass and presses the tip of his cock against my slick opening.

"Now, watch in the mirror while I fuck your sweet pussy."

He slides into me in one rough thrust.

I scream, my hands clutching the counter to hold myself up.

My head drops, but Elias grips my hair and lifts my head. "I said watch, Reine. Eyes on us."

Fuck. This is hot.

My cleavage bounces with every pump of his hips. My chest and face have turned a dark shade of red, and I'm not sure if it's the adrenaline from everything that's happened tonight or because I'm being fucked by a mob boss... in front of a mirror... inside the bathroom... at the party of another mob boss.

I can't look away because Elias has a tight hold on my hair with one hand. With the other, he slips it behind my dress's bodice to cup my breast.

His fingertips take hold of my nipple, and he pinches and tugs it.

"Yes, Ma Chérie. You liked that, didn't you? The way your pussy walls choked my cock just now."

I close my eyes, and Elias immediately jerks my hair.

"Eyes. Open."

"Yes, sir," I wheeze, and Elias removes his hand from my front to slap my ass. Hard.

I scream again, not even caring if anyone passing by can hear us.

"Brat."

He rubs the stinging spot on my ass cheek, then he slows his thrusts to slide his palm up and down my spine.

His grip on my hair hasn't loosened one bit, and there's an ache on my scalp that's bordering pain—which only adds to my pleasure.

The tip of Elias's thumb slides between my crack until it presses my tight puckered hole. I watch as he looks down and spits. He smirks, clearly feeling my walls pulse around his cock when his spit slides over my asshole.

"Such a dirty girl, aren't you Sage?"

He inches his thumb inside me and starts moving his hips again. Once the thick digit is in as far as it will go, he picks up speed.

The extra pressure has me worked up again. And watching in the mirror as Elias's big body pounds into my big body, feeling his thumb pump in and out of me, seeing his eyes roll into the back of his head as pleasure takes over him... it's too much, and I'm shaking with a second orgasm.

And I'm not trying to be quiet about it.

Elias joins me with his release soon after.

He leans his head on my back to catch his breath. That lasts all of one minute before someone is banging on the door.

"Fuck, Sage. What are you doing to me?"

I should be asking him the same question.

Chapter 6

Elias

"I will be taking you home," I say, removing the condom and tossing it in the trash.

Sage scoffs while adjusting her dress and fixing her hair.

I'd much rather she leaves here disheveled, so everyone sees how well I fucked her, but Sage doesn't like to take orders and when she does, she fights every step of the way.

And I love the fight.

"Absolutely fucking not. I'm taking a cab."

"Do you think I will allow you to step inside a stranger's car?"

"Allow?"

Shit. That was the wrong thing to say.

"I do whatever the fuck I want and that includes taking a cab, which I do all the time. Just because you've had your dick inside me twice—"

"—it's far more than twice now."

"Doesn't mean you have claim over me. You're not my boss."

I bristle at the words. I'm not her boss, but she sure likes to call me *Boss*.

She picks her purse up off the floor and retrieves lipstick before applying it to her puffy lips. I stifle the urge to crush my mouth to hers and smear it all over again.

"This isn't up for debate. I will take you home."

"So you can stalk me? No. No way."

Another round of banging on the door cuts off my argument.

I snarl and turn away from Sage to unlock the deadbolt.

"What?" I growl.

It's Jax, my head of security. He's been staking out the lobby while I was inside the party, ready to move in if I needed backup.

"Lenetti found out you're here. Time to go."

I'm surprised it took this long. It's clear the soldiers checking invitations didn't run off to tell Gio I had arrived. Rumors have swirled for years that there's a mole in the Empire crew. A handful of his men can't stand him. That's the only explanation as to why I was let in. Which also makes me wonder if Lenetti didn't know I was here, who sent me the invite?

I open the door wider to scan the lobby, and Sage uses my distraction to push past me.

That's when two of Lenetti's men spot me. They're on the move in our direction, hands at their hips ready to grab their weapons, but me and my men are already heading for the exit.

I catch up to Sage, who's waiting with others to hail a taxi—the minx nearly got away again. I grab her wrist, pulling her flush against me.

I inhale her sweet strawberry and vanilla scent. My body has become obsessed with it—addicted—as my cock jerks with need despite blowing my load minutes ago.

"Please. Let me take you home."

She searches my eyes, and her defiant mask drops slightly to show me a hint of apprehension.

"No. I can't. Elias, please don't make me."

Please don't make me?

What the hell? Who makes her do things she doesn't want to do? I mean, sure, I dragged her into the bathroom and fucked her in front of the mirror, but I wouldn't have if she told me no.

I want to pull her into my arms and hold her. *Protect* her. She must see that I won't be that man.

It's the only explanation.

A man forced her to do things she didn't want to do.

Whoever he may be, I *will* find and kill him.

I release her because of course she doesn't see I'm not that man. She doesn't know me. We've fucked, but I'm still just a stranger. *She's* a stranger.

And she's running from me again, stepping away to flag a taxi.

"Your number then. I can't lose you this time."

Her brows furrow, and she chews on her bottom lip. My hand moves before I'm able to stop it, and I pull the plump kissable lip from her teeth and palm her cheek. Her breath hitches, and she closes her eyes.

Then she smacks my hand away, failing to hold back her smile.

"You know you could find me through Noah."

"And *you* know she wouldn't willingly give me your information."

She huffs and rolls her eyes.

"Fine." She holds out her hand, and I quickly retrieve my phone from my pocket. "Don't make me regret this, Elias. I will block your ass if you keep being this clingy."

She aggressively taps at the screen.

"Clingy, huh?"

"Yeah. Right now, you're at Level 10 Clinger status."

She hands my phone back, and I call the number. Her phone lights up, and she waves it at me, proving she entered her actual number.

Sage walks to the cab that just pulled up, and I swoop in to open the door for her.

"Let me be clear, Reine," I say, leaning down to whisper in her ear. "You keep fighting me, but that pussy of yours didn't get the message. She *loves* my cock. *Level 20 Clinger.*"

She sucks in a sharp breath, and I place a soft kiss on her cheek.

"Text me when you are home safe," I say and let my queen go.

I considered following Sage or sending one of my men to watch over her, but I just got her back, and I don't want to scare her away with my Level 10 Clinger behavior.

At least I have her number now. I send it to my tech guy, hoping to get an address with it. Or any information at all.

What are you hiding, Sage?

My phone vibrates with a text, as if my thoughts of her conjured it.

Reine

It's been less than fifteen minutes since she left Lenetti's party, which means she lives somewhere in Manhattan, somewhere close to Midtown.

I ignore the middle finger emoji that accompanies the text and start typing out a reply, promising punishment for virtually flipping me off, when my phone rings. My heart lurches in my chest, hopeful that it's Sage, before I see my uncle's name.

"What?" I growl upon answering.

"Got a tip about a shipment. Three a.m. Red Hook," he says, ignoring my moody behavior.

I glance at my watch. It's not even midnight.

Good. We need time to prepare.

"Send in a team to secure the place. I need to go home and change. I'll meet you at the port at two." I scrub my palm over my face and sigh. "Is this Moonlight?"

It's the dumbest fucking name. A name that got on my radar a month ago when I received a tip about a shipping container full of women and young girls at a port in Newark. Goddamn human traffickers. I will kill every last one of them including this asshole with the cheesy fucking name.

My tech guy has been tracking their movements. They've been making their way up the East Coast and now they're in Brooklyn.

"That's what I'm hearing, but we won't know for sure until we intercept the shipment and question the girls."

I clench my free hand into a fist. Anger rolls throughout my body. I'm really going to enjoy torturing this fucker.

"Call the mayor. Tell him to get apartments ready. He needs to send buses, counselors, clothes, and supplies."

It took me over a decade to work my way into New York City's political scene. The mayor is someone who owed me a favor. The DA is also in my grip. And now I'm slowly working my way through the NYPD. The department's been corrupt for years, but when you head a mafia and own a lot of elite night clubs where the rich and famous go to be discreet, you learn secrets, and secrets can be turned into blackmailing.

Lance is my enforcer. He's taken down dozens of high-profile businessmen and politicians for me, allowing me to replace their positions with people who owe me favors.

The newly elected mayor is a man with a strong political and community background. He came to me for help when his father became indebted to the Lords of Staten Island. I worked out a deal with Finn O'Connor to release the mayor's father into my authority. All it cost me was a few business connections that Finn used to start an underground gambling ring.

What O'Connor doesn't know is that I've had eyes on that gambling ring, keeping track of every transaction, every illegal misdeed. I plan to use it to take him down at some point.

Now's not the time. Lance and I are close to pinning Lenetti for our mother's murder.

And now I have to deal with this new human trafficker.

"Did your source have a number?"

"At least a dozen."

I clench the phone tighter and curse. *At least?* I will burn this city down trying to find Moonlight if there's more than a dozen young women in that shipping container.

"Should I call Lance?" Martin asks during my raging silence.

"No. He's useless to me tonight."

Martin chuckles. "I heard about his little stunt at Lenetti's Christmas party."

"Yeah, and I'm sure he's dealing with the aftermath of that. I'll worry about him later. I need to focus on this raid. Make sure there's enough soldiers planted around the terminal. Call Alex and put him on standby."

Alex is my backup enforcer. He's good, but not as good as my brother.

I hang up and lean my head back on the car seat. All I want to do is call Sage and beg her to let me come over so we can cuddle.

Is that too much to ask?

I open her text message and start typing.

> **Miss you already**

The corner of my mouth turns up when I see the three little dots dance. They disappear... then pop up again.

After at least a minute, her response comes through.

Reine

> **Level 100 Clinger**

Chapter 7

Sage

I jerk awake to someone banging on my door. Squinting an eye open, my palms pat around my bed for my phone. I find it underneath me. I must have fallen asleep with it in my hand.

Because you were waiting for Elias to text you back.

But he didn't. He didn't respond to me calling him a Level 100 Clinger.

I shouldn't have been disappointed. I don't need to be missing him and wanting him to text me.

I check my phone for the time—finding no new texts—and groan.

Six a.m.

"Who the fuck?" I mumble and roll out of bed.

I quietly walk to the door and hold my breath when the wooden floorboards creak.

"Open up, Sunshine," a familiar voice growls from the other side.

My heart plummets to my stomach, and I suck in a deep breath.

No. No fucking way.

"I know you're in there. I can hear you breathing."

How the hell did he find me?

There's a reason why I changed my name and hid in the most populous city in the country.

I should have gotten a restraining order.

"If you don't open the door, I'll break it down."

I wish I had a gun, not that I know how to use one. I consider pulling a knife from my utensil drawer, but I'm not strong—or brave—enough to use it.

I unlatch the chain lock followed by the deadbolt, then the doorknob lock and crack open the door.

"Chase?"

"Let me in."

"No."

He shoves the door and pushes me out of the way. The wall stops me from falling on my ass.

"What the fuck, Chase?"

"Shut up!"

"You have no right—"

Chase grabs me, his fingertips digging into my upper arm. I try to pull away from him, but he's too strong.

"How do you know Elias Carter?"

I stop struggling, my face falling. "What? I..."

"Don't even *think* about lying to me. My men saw you at Lenetti's party. They sent me pictures, Sunshine. You in a tight red dress, looking like a fucking slut."

"Your men? What are you—"

Chase cuts me off and grabs my hair to drag me over to my bed. My feet are barely able to keep up with the sudden move. He shoves me down onto the mattress and fear rips through my body, my throat drying.

Chase has never forced himself on me, but this is a different version of the man I was married to.

What if I left him before his true monster came out? What if that's who he is now?

Chase's hand strikes out and a sting blooms across my cheek.

Suddenly, I'm back to the first time he hit me. To the shock and betrayal I felt when he backhanded me for spending money on a new set of nails. He was pissed because I let him forget it was my birthday.

You should have reminded me.

You shouldn't have used your money to buy yourself a gift.

It was always my fault.

And I started to believe that I was the problem.

Which made leaving him the hardest thing I've ever done. I felt *guilty*.

It took years of therapy to finally accept that I did nothing wrong.

"You fucking bitch," he spits and pushes me back so he can straddle me. He clutches my throat with both hands. "I had eyes all over Gio Lenetti's Christmas party. My men saw him take you into the bathroom. Everyone heard you. They saw you walk out, you looking thoroughly fucked."

"You're hurting me," I wheeze out, clawing at his fingers.

"Good. Maybe that means you'll do what I say."

My vision begins to blur and right before I pass out from lack of air, Chase lets go.

He crawls off me, and I sit up, coughing and rubbing my neck. I try to wet my throat with a sip of water from the bottle I left on the table next to my bed.

"Why are you here, Chase? We're divorced, remember?"

He turns his back to me. He's such a small man compared to Elias, but he's not scrawny or weak. I'd say he's average size with a bit of a dad bod. He buries his hands in his light brown hair, tugging at the strands—something he does when he's stressed out.

"I need you to do something for me."

"No."

I flinch when he whips around and takes a step toward me.

"You *will* help me, or I'll pay a little visit to your parents."

My eyes widen, and I'm sure the blood has drained from my face. "You don't know where they live."

"You're my wife. I know everything about you and your family."

"*Ex* wife!"

Chase spits on me, and I protect myself from the spittle with my hands over my head, waiting for something harsher. He gets in my face, his mouth inches from mine. I hold my breath.

"You. Are. Still. Mine."

My attempt to hold back my tears fails, and they fall, one by one down my cheek. Chase shakes his head, appearing to almost pity me, and stands up straight. I let out a long stream of breath, relieved to have the space between us.

"Ready to comply?"

I give him a quick nod.

"I'm making a name for myself in New York City's crime syndicate. I've moved on from identity theft and drug dealing. I'm running shit now, and I'm aiming for the top."

"What the fuck are you talking about?"

He's fucking delusional.

Chase snarls, his dark blue, rage-filled eyes piercing through my soul. He huffs out a breath, booze stinging my nose. Something tells me he hasn't been to sleep yet if he smells like a bar at six in the morning.

"Elias took something from me. He's getting in the way of my... business ventures. I need him gone and since you're opening your legs for him like a desperate fucking whore, you're going to help me take him down."

"I don't know how—"

"You're going to be my spy. Listen in on conversations. Gather intel on the QBM and the Empire and bring it back to me."

"You're insane."

He kicks me in the shin, hard enough that I know it'll leave a bruise. I bite my lip to stop myself from crying out.

I can't show him how much he hurts me.

He cocks his arm back, preparing to back-hand me, then drops it. The moment I relax my shoulders; he lashes out and grabs a chunk of my hair.

"If you don't help me, I will go to your parents' place. The cute little green home on Willow Street in New Haven? In the suburbs?"

Oh, fuck. He wasn't lying. How did he find them? The entire time we were married, he never let me go see them. He's never been to their house, and I was confident he didn't even know their names. He met them once at our wedding, but he barely spoke to them. Plus, anytime I talked about my parents, I'd say Mom or Dad.

Not to mention that he'd tune me out during those conversations.

"I will torture them, cut off their fingers, let you hear their cries and begging until you comply. If you run to the cops or tell your boyfriend or the mafia princess bestie, Mommy and Daddy go bye-bye."

"I don't even know Noah that well."

"Don't lie to me! I told you; I've been keeping tabs on you for a while now. I watched your friendship with that woman grow. Then last night she reveals to the world that she's Noemi Lenetti, Empire heir? Imagine my surprise when you managed to land the QBM boss too. How lucky am I that my ex is a fucking slut?"

He releases me, and I fall off the bed, barely catching myself with my palms on the floor.

"And now Noemi is engaged to Lance Carter. I can't have the Empire and the QBM uniting. They'll be too powerful, especially if they dissolve the Lords of Staten Island."

The Lords of Staten Island? So there's a third mob in New York City? My head hurts. This is too much information. I want to go back to yesterday when I didn't know about New York City mafias. When my ex was just an idiot low-level criminal not some wannabe crime boss.

Chase shrugs. "Actually, this is good. If the Empire and the QBM take out Finn O'Connor, and I take down Lenetti and Carter, then I'll claim the mafia throne."

Fucking delusional.

"I'll call my crime syndicate, the Elite," Chase says, waving his hands in the air as if the name is flashing in neon lights in front of him. He points at me. "And you'll be my little rat, giving me all the intel. I need names: their associates, their law enforcement sources, safe houses, business dealings, everything."

"I don't have access to that type of information. I've never met Noah's father... I don't know anything about his organization. I swear. Noah and I met at work. She's always been Noah to me. I just learned about her secret life last night." Chase stares at me as if waiting for me to break and tell the truth. "My parents, Chase. I wouldn't lie."

His fists clench at his sides. He's seconds from taking out his anger on me again. Thankfully, his phone vibrates, and I'm saved. Chase curses and angrily taps at the screen, then shoves it back into his pocket.

"Then you better figure out how, for your parents' sake."

He gives me one more snarl before stalking out of my apartment.

I curl up into a ball on the ground and shut down.

I cried until I had no more tears left, then I showered, dressed, and put on makeup to cover my puffy eyes and the bruises Chase gave me.

They're not as bad as the ones he used to give me.

I call a ride share and head to Brooklyn where Noah is holed up.

After her building blew up a little over two weeks ago, and she nearly died, she grabbed my phone and installed an app that allows me to track her location. She installed the same app on her phone too. She asked that I only use it in an emergency situation, and I agreed.

Now is an emergency.

Kind of.

Noah isn't expecting me, likely already forgetting about the tracking app. Confusion riddles her face, then relief takes over as she pulls me into a hug.

"I'm sorry I didn't tell you. Please don't hate me."

My body melts into hers. "I could never hate you."

She releases me and scrunches her nose as if she doesn't believe that.

"Do you want something to drink?"

"Something hard, please."

I explore the loft while she's in the kitchen pouring us some whiskey.

The space is overtly manly. Blacks and grays and hardwood everywhere with brick walls and floor to ceiling windows. The loft has been renovated, and a wall has been put up to separate the living area and bedroom.

"So, this is Del's place?"

Noah nods.

"Is he here?"

Noah grimaces as she walks over to me carrying two glasses.

"He's in the bedroom recovering. My father, um, shot him."

She hands me a vodka soda, and I slam it back.

"Damn, Sage. Everything okay?"

I wince, desperately wanting to tell her about Chase. Thankfully, she starts talking before I make the mistake of revealing everything.

"Of course, it's not okay," she answers for me. "You're not okay. I kept a secret from you. I—"

"Your father shot Del?" I interrupt, my voice an octave higher.

"Yeah, well, you know... rival and all."

"Right..."

Noah takes my glass and refills it. I numbly sit on the couch trying to process... everything. This world my best friend belongs to—that I'm now a part of.

She returns with my second round of booze, but I stop myself from pouring this one down my throat and sip it slowly instead. It's top shelf vodka, that's for sure. I let the liquid coat my insides and relax my tense shoulders.

Closing my eyes, I sigh. "Why don't you start from the beginning?"

For the next hour, she talks, and I listen, asking questions when needing clarification. Noah tells me about the night before Christmas Eve twenty years ago when two men broke into her home. How she watched from the stairs, hiding behind the balusters of the staircase and watched them shoot her mom point blank. How she ran and hid because they planned to kill her too.

Her father then sent her away and changed her name to protect her. She was only eleven years old. I can't imagine witnessing something so horrible only to be abandoned by the man who was supposed to comfort her.

Noah returned to New York City for answers because not only was her mother killed, but the next night, the wife and daughter of Finn O'Connor, Lords of Staten Island Don, died in a mysterious fire.

Then Del was forced to kill his own mother.

Elias... he was the one who found her. I don't know how old he is, but I'm assuming he's in his thirties now. If his mother was killed twenty years ago, then that means he was probably only fifteen or sixteen. And for it to happen on Christmas Eve?

Noah didn't go into details about Del and Elias's mother's death, and I wasn't about to ask. I'm already sick to my stomach about everything that's happened to her. Especially now that she believes her father is the one who placed the kill order on all the mafia wives and children.

They just need more concrete proof.

"So you're not mad at me?" she asks.

I shake my head.

"Never. I'm honestly more upset that you kept this badass part of your life secret, but I understand why you had to."

A silence falls between us, and I'm not sure if Noah is waiting for me to ask her more questions.

I have a million, but instead, I blurt out, "I slept with Elias again."

She chokes on her drink, making her cough.

"In a bathroom at the party last night."

My cheeks heat, and I tell myself it's the vodka and not me remembering how hot it was watching Elias fuck me in the mirror's reflection.

"Sage, I've never seen you flustered over a man before," Noah says, amused.

"I'm not flustered."

"You definitely are."

"Fine, but it's because he's frustrating. I can't stand him."

"Are you sure about that?"

"Abso-fucking-lutely. I never want to see him again."

"Liar."

I groan. "Okayyyy, you win! He's the best fuck of my life, but he's controlling and *that's* what I hate. But at the same time, it's sexy as hell. I just... I want to tie him up. Blindfold him. Give him a few welts with my riding crop."

I need it more than ever after Chase's visit this morning. I could get on the Madam app, but it's solely virtual. Or I could go to the sex club. Spank a few subs and order them to lick my pumps.

It wouldn't be the same.

It wouldn't be Elias.

"Oh, you've got it bad for him."

"What?" I squeak, Noah's voice surprising me and pulling me from my thoughts. "No. I don't. He's a good lay. That's it."

"Sure. Keep lying to yourself." She points at my glass, and my eyes widen, not even realizing I drank it all. "Want another?"

I shake my head. "No. One more and I'll be tipsy, and I have a shift at the bar in an hour."

"Are you off on Saturday?"

I nod.

"Good. Come to dinner at my father's."

"Your father who's a mafia boss? The man who you suspect is responsible for ordering a hit on a bunch of people? The man who just shot your new fiancé? Congrats, by the way."

She waves off my accolade. "It's a fake engagement... kind of. And don't worry about my father. He was only pissed that I sprung the engagement on him in front of all his rich friends, but he's cooled off by now. I have a plan, and I need you there at dinner to act as sort of a mediator. Gio won't lose his cool with a civilian present."

"Um... are you sure?"

"I'm pretty sure."

I check my phone and groan. "Ugh, I'm going to be late, but yeah, I'll come to dinner. Not going to lie, I'm terrified."

"I'll make sure nothing happens to you."

Chapter 8

Elias

I've been in a foul mood all week, and I've barely slept.

It began with the shipment we busted.

Twenty.

Twenty women, girls, and boys were in the shipping container. Some as young as twelve. Some kidnapped right from their front yards in a small Midwest town. Brooklyn was their last stop where an auction was to be held for rich disgusting pricks to bid on them.

We're working to get the names on that auction list, but it's a long shot since the men taken into custody last night were mules, forced to transport the shipment to the pier. They were likely being blackmailed and won't know the names I need to pass on to the Marionette and Colpa Sicario.

My brother and Noah.

Two mafia brats who are also the country's top contract killers.

Anytime I get names from these sex trafficking busts, the FBI allows the assholes to be killed or to coincidentally disappear because the government doesn't want to admit this country has a human trafficking problem.

Most of the girls and women are on their way back home to their families. I made sure they were set up with funds for whatever they want or need, not that money will resolve their trauma. But hopefully unlimited access to counselors will help.

My sour attitude is also because of Sage. It's been nearly a week since I've seen her.

She hasn't responded to any of my texts either. Not that I'm being a *Level 100 Clinger*. I'm not. I've only sent her six texts. There's nothing wrong with wishing a person good morning every day.

I considered asking Noah for her address, but I knew she wouldn't give it to me without Sage's approval.

And reason number three I'm in a shitty mood: my goddamn brother.

Word quickly spread about Noah and Lance's engagement. Me being at the Christmas party didn't help. Tensions are high between the Empire and the QBM with speculations that I'm attempting to start a turf war by arranging my little brother to marry Lenetti's daughter.

Not that Lenetti is worried. He showed his fucking dominance by shooting my brother in the shoulder. He was also likely punishing Noah for getting engaged to a QBM heir. The only reason I found out Lance was shot was because Sage texted me—the only other text I received from her aside from the one telling me she was home. She found out after visiting Noah at Lance's Brooklyn safe house.

I stormed over to my brother's place to confront him about it, only to walk in on him fucking Noah's ass. Those fuckers enjoyed putting on a show, but I stayed because one: I wanted to piss off my brother and two: I needed answers.

What are these two up to with their fake engagement?

Noah has a plan.

Which is why my driver is now pulling up to Lenetti's Lower East Side townhouse.

Noah wants to convince her father to merge the Empire and the QBM.

I practically called her insane, because there's no way I'm giving over control to Lenetti, and he would rather kill me than let me rule. Noah explained that combining the organizations is temporary until we can uncover the truth about our mothers' murders.

Noah witnessed two men kill her mother the night before Lance was forced to slit our mother's throat. We believe Lenetti was behind both hits. If that's the case, then he dies, and I take over sole control of the combined organizations. If Finn O'Connor was responsible for the murders, then he dies and the plan to dismantle the Lords will continue. And if it was my father, Percy, then there's nothing left to do since he died fourteen years ago.

I step out of the SUV to cleaners dousing the sidewalk with sudsy water, washing away a puddle of blood. I'm going to guess my brother had something to do with this. Of course he'd be the one to start shit on Empire territory.

"Oh my God!" a familiar voice gasps. "What happened?"

Sage is walking up the sidewalk, her palm over her mouth.

Fuck she's beautiful.

Her hair is up in a messy blonde bun. She's wearing a red sweater, a flowing black skirt that falls mid-calf, and a pair of black ankle boots. Christmas tree earrings hang from her ears.

My heart flutters at the thought of spending the holiday with her. Which surprises me into silence because I haven't wanted to celebrate Christmas since before my mother's death.

"Nothing for you to worry about, sweetheart. Just an accident. You must be Sage."

One of Lenetti's guards is laying it on thick with the flirting and Sage is eating it up.

"I am. How did you know?"

"I was told to keep an eye out for the cute blonde."

Sage giggles like a fucking teenage girl with a schoolyard crush. "You're cute yourself," she coos, fluttering her eyes and biting her lip.

I want to murder this man. He's tall and built with brown hair shaved close to his head.

I walk toward them, and Sage spots me over his shoulder. She hadn't seen me before now, and her greenish blue eyes widen. She blushes and takes a step back to put some distance between her and the 'cute' guard.

"Elias," she says, her voice barely a whisper. "I didn't know you were going to be here."

The guard turns and snarls when he sees me.

"Carter," he says, hand hovering over the gun at his hip.

Two other Empire soldiers surround me, forming a triangle. I flash him my Beretta in the holster underneath my suit jacket.

"Don't try anything stupid, Big Guy. Not with the pretty lady here."

My eyes flick to Sage, and she stands there frozen and trembling, eyes like saucers.

She's terrified.

I almost lower my guard to go to her and bring her into my arms.

"Hand over your weapons."

"Not going to happen."

"Then you don't go in."

"Elias," Sage whisper shouts at me. "Give the man your weapons."

The desperation in her voice makes me pause. Is she urging me to go into my rival's headquarters unarmed because she's scared of what this man will do? Is she worried about me?

Or is she working with Noah? A trap? I may enjoy this woman's cunt... and lips... and... *everything*...

I shake my head.

She's not my enemy.

I'm just being paranoid.

"Please," she mouths, no sound coming from her pouty red lips.

Fuck.

It's this moment, on rival territory, that I realize I would do anything for this woman.

I unarm myself, handing over the two guns in my shoulder holsters, the one I stuffed in the back of my pants, and one in a holster on my ankle.

"The knives too," the guard says as I turn to walk into the townhouse.

"It's fine, Keith," a man says, appearing in the building's entrance. "He's not going to be a problem, are you, Carter?"

I recognize this twerp as one of Lenetti's top soldiers. Blond hair. Average height and build. Slightly older than me. Ruggedly handsome.

"Matthew. Lenetti's head of security," he says with a nod of his chin.

"I thought..." I begin.

"Recently promoted thanks to your brother. He shot Gio's main guy."

"He what?" Sage squeals, peering back at the sidewalk where the blood has been washed away.

Fuck.

I was right.

Lenetti's had the same asshole as his head of security for thirty years. Vershun was also the Empire's Caporegime—the fourth highest rank in a mafia behind the underboss and the consigliere. The caporegime leads soldiers, maintains order, and enforces rules.

If Lance killed him, then I'd be surprised if he was still—

"Don't worry, your brother is alive."

I silently curse because I clearly showed this fucker a hint of vulnerability. I'm typically good about hiding my emotions, but Lance fucked up, and he's lucky he wasn't killed.

"Come on, Sage," I say, taking her hand and tugging her inside.

Matthew holds up a hand before we walk through the doors.

"You try anything, and she's the first to die," he says, nodding at Sage who hugs my arm to her body.

My jerk reaction is to put a bullet through this fucker's brain, but Sage is still trembling next me.

I don't say anything and walk on, following one of Lenetti's staff members down the hallway to a sitting room. The woman says she'll notify Noah that we've arrived and leaves.

The moment we're alone, Sage pushes away from me and starts panicking. She paces the room, breathing in and out slowly, shaking her hands like they're covered in water, and she's trying to dry them off.

"Hey," I say, taking a step toward her. She backs away from me.

Fuck that hurts.

"I just need a minute to process..." she waves her hand around the space, "everything. You. Del killing a man in broad daylight in the middle of Manhattan."

"To be fair, this entire block is owned by Lenetti and only his soldiers and trusted circle live in these buildings. Only people he allows can walk down the sidewalk so there wouldn't be any witnesses, or a chance Lance would get caught. He must have had a good reason to shoot that man."

A manic laughter bursts out of Sage.

"Of course, right. How silly of me. Murder-schmurder."

"Sage," I sigh, trying to approach her again but the sharpness of her narrowed eyes stops me.

"If I had known you'd be here, I wouldn't have come."

Her defiant mask slips but only for a second.

She's lying.

"Is that so?"

She crosses her arms and nods.

"What was your plan? Never see me again? Forget I exist as if I haven't made you scream just by tasting that sweet cunt of yours?"

"Oh, fuck off, Elias!" she yells. "Is that all I am to you? A warm cunt?"

I step closer.

"Of course not," I bark. "You're a distraction, and I can't fucking stand it."

I grab her wrist and tug her against my body.

"Not just your cunt, but your smart-ass mouth that won't stop challenging me, which pisses me off because I *like* the fight. You haunt my thoughts, day and night. You're all I fucking think about! What did you have for breakfast? Did you sleep well? Are you safe? But you don't answer my texts, so I worry. And do you know how hard it's been not going to you?"

Her lips tremble. Not with fear... but with something I can't understand. Disbelief maybe? "You don't know where I live..."

"You don't think I couldn't have found out? Sage," I brush my lips over hers, "I'm a powerful man. I can get whatever I want."

"What do you want?"

"I want *you,* Reine," I growl and claim her mouth.

Chapter 9

Sage

Elias's tongue swoops past my lips and ravishes my mouth. I moan and grab hold of his suit jacket to hold myself up.

I never imagined a kiss would make me weak in the knees like some cheesy romance movie, but here I am, trying not to collapse to the floor because of Elias's talented mouth.

This big man has me pinned to the wall, his hands cupping my face, and I don't even care that we're in a townhome that belongs to a scary mafia man, I'm ready to let Elias fuck me right here.

Right *now*.

A throat clears.

Del and Noah have entered the room.

I tear myself away and, in a panic, I slap Elias across the cheek.

The sound ricochets throughout the small room. I wipe my mouth and walk over to where Noah stands, ducking behind her like a fucking coward.

I peek around her and see Elias has his back to us, his hand on his face where I hit him.

"Are you okay?" Noah asks.

"I'm fine," Elias answers.

"I was asking Sage," Noah says, her voice full of humor.

Elias turns enough that I see the moment his frustrated and somewhat embarrassed expression from my slap turns murderous. He balls up his fists at his sides.

"She's the one who slapped me," he growls.

"He kissed me without my permission," I counter.

It's a weak and childish argument but like I said, I PANICKED. I almost fucked up. If Elias's hands had been anywhere other than my face, he might have found the wire Chase forced me to wear.

"I haven't seen you in a week, and you didn't seem to mind when you moaned the moment I slipped my tongue inside your mouth."

"Okay," Noah says, breaking up our spat.

A woman appears at the open door letting us know that dinner is ready, and my frustration with this man and my feelings for him are put on the back burner.

My anxiety returns.

Time for dinner with Noah's father... who terrifies me.

Elias terrifies me... in a completely different way. Yet I keep poking the bear.

Maybe it's because I want him to devour me.

As we walk to the dining room, I hear Noah talking to Elias, but their voices are too low for me to make out the words.

All except Elias saying, "I'll keep her safe."

My stomach twists, my heart flutters, and tears burn the back of my eyes.

He could protect me.

I can't let him.

Chase said he'd kill my parents if I told Elias or Noah. And what if Chase hurts them too? I have no doubt Elias could demolish Chase and his newly formed crime organization, but I can't take that chance. Elias is a reactive man. If I ask for his help, he won't hesitate to hunt Chase down and murder him. It's clear this is what he does as a mafia boss, but if Chase gets wind that Elias is looking for him, he will have reassurances in place.

He knows where my parents live. He likely has eyes on them now. Men waiting outside my childhood home, waiting to go inside and kill them if I fuck up.

I'm traveling to Connecticut to see them for Christmas. I'll have to figure out a way to sneak them out. I could rent a hotel room for them, maybe somewhere a couple towns over. I have enough money saved up.

I'd have to explain *why* I want them to go into hiding, but I'd rather do that than have them die.

I push my overactive thoughts aside as we enter a large dining room, lit only by a dim crystal chandelier above the long table. We sit at the end. Noah and Del on one side, me and Elias on the other with Noah's father at the head. A server comes around to get our drink order, then disappears.

"Who is this?" The scary mafia boss asks, pointing his chin at me.

"My best friend. I told you she was coming, remember?" Noah says with a sigh.

She told me he's not a fan of bringing 'civilians' into their world, but she basically named me her associate so he wouldn't see me as a threat.

Noah's father looks at me again and gives an approving nod.

His brown eyes slide to Elias, and they narrow.

"Elias Carter. Never in my life did I think I'd be serving QBM swine in my own home."

Elias goes rigid beside me. I swear I can *feel* the anger radiating from him, boiling within and ready to blow.

I slip my hand under the table and find his knee, squeezing gently. He jerks slightly at my touch before his body relaxes, even if I'm the only one who notices.

"You can thank your daughter for that, Lenetti."

Noah's father takes a sip of his whiskey and turns his head to her. "Yes, what is my daughter up to?"

"Well," Noah begins, gulping hard enough I can see her throat working. She's anxious, but she would never admit it. "As you know, Lance and I are getting married."

Elias and Noah's father scoff at the same time.

"Oh, fuck off, the both of you," Noah says. "It's happening and when we're married, our organizations will be connected. We should take advantage of that. We need to work together."

"You betray the Empire to sleep with the enemy. Now you want me to do business with QBM rats?"

Elias tries to stand, but I grab his forearm, stopping him. I take his hand in mine, and he turns his head, locking eyes with me. The murderous expression he'd been giving Noah's father falls. His brows pinch, seeing my concern.

I don't want Elias to die and if he keeps trying to lash out at his rival, I fear dinner will end with a bullet in his head.

I squeeze his hand, and he lets out a puff of breath, the corner of his mouth turning up.

I always want to be the reason he smiles. I bet he has a hearty laugh too.

The server returns with drinks, pulling Elias's attention away from me. I already miss his intense stare.

Damn it.

Once again Elias is distracting me. Chase told me to be listening for information just in case the wire doesn't pick everything up. Information that will betray Elias and Noah. But what other options do I have?

Tell Elias. He'll protect you.

"Look, the Lords need to go," Noah continues. "They're beginning to gain the attention of the FBI. It's a matter of time before Finn O'Connor is arrested on RICO charges. You know he'll sing once he's in custody to get a plea deal. Then the government will target us. Your FBI sources can't protect you forever. So, let's unite and take control now before that happens."

Elias has zoned out while listening to Noah, not saying a word.

She continues. "The Empire runs guns. QBM handles drugs. QBM also takes down sex trafficking rings. The Lords are the biggest offenders when it comes to exploiting sex workers. Lance has recently come into information that they're recruiting teenagers. Babbo, we could help the QBM shut it down. We merge our organizations and become powerful enough to dismantle the Lords."

"And who will be in charge?" Elias asks, twirling a fork between his fingers.

"You still have Queens and Brooklyn. My father will maintain control of Manhattan and the Bronx. And..." Noah takes a deep breath. "Del and I will control Staten Island."

Del leans over to whisper something in Noah's ear, but it's not loud enough for any of us to hear.

"Big decisions will be made by the four of us. Like a counsel," Noah adds.

"You don't know anything about running a mafia," her father says after a few moments of silence.

"You're right," Noah responds, head high. At least she's not intimidated by him. "But you want me to learn the business. Here's my chance. Let me shadow you over the next few weeks or months. Show me what I need to know."

Lenetti takes another sip of his whisky, then smooths his fingers over his clean-shaven face.

"We need a plan," Noah begins, only stopping when three servers enter, carrying large bowls of salad and baskets of bread. They set them down on the table in front of us. A woman dishes out Gio's salad.

My stomach is in knots, and I'm slightly nauseous from my nerves, so I don't move a muscle. I'm also sweaty as fuck because I'm worried about this goddamn wire.

I am *not* meant for a life of crime.

"We work together—all of us—to form this plan to take down the Lords," Noah says after plating her food. "You, me, and Elias. You know, teamwork? One big, merged mafia? A mighty mafia?"

I hold back a giggle. I love that name, but Elias apparently doesn't and sighs beside me.

The silly mafia name settles my nerves enough that I bravely reach for the salad bowl... only for Elias to snatch the utensil away and scoop a helping onto my plate.

I open my mouth to tell him I'm not a fucking child, and I can do it myself, but I snap my mouth shut after glancing at Noah's father who somehow manages to keep his eyes on us while devouring his food.

Gio takes another bite of his salad. He chews for what had to be minutes before breaking the silence.

"Fine."

"Really?" Noah asks.

"I agree to work together to destroy the Lords. We will not combine our organizations. That will never happen, mio angelo."

My best friend does a little celebration in her seat, which is interrupted by her father leaning over and stabbing his fork through Del's left hand, nailing it to the table.

"What the fuck, Giovanni?" Noah screams, standing abruptly enough her chair topples to the floor.

I yelp, also standing to back away. Elias moves in front of me, but I can still see the action at the table.

Del grunts and rips the fork out of his hand. Blood pours out of the top and bottom, soaking the white table-cloth red.

Ugh. I don't mind a little blood, but that? No, thank you! I bury my face into Elias's back, gripping the fabric of his suit jacket.

"That's for killing my head of security," Gio says.

Then I hear the chair creak as he sits down and the silverware clink on the plate when he resumes eating.

Chapter 10

Elias

I should go to my brother, make sure he's okay. I should. But Sage's body is flush with my back and she's shaking.

I turn to her and palm her cheek. "Are you okay?"

She looks up into my eyes, her tanned face pale and tears pooling in her eyes.

"I'm fine," she whispers. "I just need to get out of here."

I glance at Noah, and she gives me a nod, letting me know she can take care of Lance. I grab Sage's hand and pull her out of the room.

She looks like she's seconds away from throwing up.

I call my driver as we walk down the hallway and by the time we make it outside, he's pulling up. I don't even care to retrieve the weapons I handed over to Lenetti's security and open the door for Sage.

After helping her inside the tall SUV, I walk around and get in.

"Where do you live?" I ask as the driver pulls away.

She stares out the window, hands twisting in her lap.

"Sage," I say a little more forcefully this time.

She sucks in a quick but shaken breath. "Take me to your place."

I want to question her, ask her why she's *still* refusing to tell me where she lives, but she's shutting down on me, and I'm desperate not to lose her again.

I nod to my driver, and we head to Brooklyn Heights. I bought an apartment building there last year and moved into the penthouse. It's one of the many homes or apartments I have throughout Queens and Brooklyn but it's my favorite by far. The building sits on the New York Harbor waterfront with views of the Manhattan skyline and the Brooklyn Bridge.

After a fifteen-minute drive, we pull up to the front of a thirty-story building. One of my soldiers is there waiting to open the door.

I take Sage's hand in mine and walk toward the building's entrance.

When I bought this place, I increased security measures. I hired ex-military as guards, installed cameras throughout the building, and added a key card scanner for my penthouse that only my most trusted men have access to.

The tenants have been vetted by my head of security and my tech guy. A handful of my soldiers also live in units so I can have them close when needed.

If Sage notices the big men in suits at the entrance, she doesn't say anything. We enter my private elevator, and it starts moving after I tap a card on the reader.

Sage snorts, and it's the first emotion to come out of her since witnessing Lenetti stab my brother with a fork and shutting down.

"Something funny?" I tease, squeezing her hand.

Does she realize we're still holding hands?

"How rich are you?"

"Very."

"That's a non-answer."

"You want a number?"

"Yeah. Tell me, you snob."

I chuckle this time, and Sage perks up at the sound of my laugh.

"My net worth is somewhere around $900 million."

"900 fucking million?" Her eyes bug out, mouth open in awe.

"Yes. But half of that is assets—businesses or homes I own. And a portion of that money was obtained... not so legally."

The elevator dings and the doors open to the foyer. The space is small, housing a thin table with a blue and gold vase full of daisies on top and an abstract painting on the wall.

My entire apartment is full of items I know nothing about, including their value because I hired an interior designer to make the place feel homey.

To the right is a set of metal double doors. I enter a passcode into the pad and the locks unlatch.

"You sure have a lot of security measures," Sage whispers.

"Because I have a lot of enemies," I say, opening the door and waving her inside.

She doesn't move, and I realize my mistake.

I take her face in my hands.

"We're safe here. I won't let anything happen to you."

She winces, and I'm prepared to question her hesitation. Something's telling me that her distress goes beyond what just happened at Lenetti's. But before I can offer her assurances, tell her that whatever it is, I can protect her, Sage's stomach growls. Her face flushes red, and she hides her embarrassment with her hands.

"Sorry, I haven't had anything to eat since breakfast and dinner was ruined by... well, you know."

I pull her hands down and grab her chin. "Don't be sorry, Reine. Don't *ever* be sorry."

She lets out another shaky breath, and my heart pinches with anguish again. I can't stand seeing her like this. Someone has shaken this beautiful woman's confidence, and I vow to burn this city to the ground to find out who.

After asking Sage what she wanted for dinner five times and getting the answer 'I don't care,' her stubborn ass finally decided on Thai food.

Well, she technically didn't decide. I was naming some of my favorite restaurants and cuisines in the area and when I mentioned Thai Villa, her eyes lit up and she let out a quiet 'ooo.'

Thai Villa is one of the few restaurants in Brooklyn that are completely nut free.

I sent one of my men to pick up our order, and while we wait, Sage wanders around the penthouse. I follow silently as she takes it all in.

Everything excites her, like the baby grand piano sitting in the corner that I never play because it reminds me of my mother. She taught me and my brother but after she was murdered, my heart couldn't handle playing anymore.

Sage's fingertips skim over the closed lid, and I expect her to ask me if I can play, but she doesn't. Maybe she sees the pain in my eyes—the fear of talking about my past.

The rest of the living room is cozy—Sage's words—with an oversized dark blue cotton couch and loveseat. A modern fireplace sits within one wall, and another wall has a row of bookcases full of either books I don't read or random crap the interior designer added.

Sage doesn't ask why I have no photographs or personal items. Again, I'm relieved, but at the same time, I *want* to tell her about my life. I *want* to share my pain with her. But I can't scare her away. Not when she let me bring her to my home instead of trying to run away.

We head down the hallway, and she pokes her head in the guest bedroom. After finding nothing of interest, she moves on to my office that I rarely work out of because I'm hardly ever home. Finding nothing interesting in the office either, we move on to the main bedroom.

Sage's eyes light up. She immediately goes to the king-sized bed and falls back, testing its firmness. She spreads out her legs and arms and does a 'snow angel' on top of the red comforter.

She looks perfectly at home in this room.

She lets out an adorable giggle before standing and walking to one of two floor-to-ceiling windows. With her hands flat and nose smashed against the glass, she watches the rest of the sunset over the Brooklyn Bridge. I don't even care that she's leaving smudges. It only makes my cock jerk with thoughts of fucking her against that glass, leaving more smudges with her ass.

Once the food arrives, we bring it into the living room and sit on the floor. I lay out spring rolls, dumplings, pad

Thai, drunken noodles, and fried rice on the coffee table in front of us.

Sage's eyes widen when I lower the TV screen from the ceiling, covering the window wall that overlooks Lower Manhattan. I hand the remote to Sage, and she picks out some reality baking show on one of the many streaming apps I have but never use.

We eat in silence, aside from the chatter on TV, and by the time we finish our food, Sage is relaxed and on her second glass of the red wine I chose to pair with the Thai.

I can't remember the last time I sat down and watched anything. But now, hearing this beautiful woman snort when the contestants reveal their poorly made cakes, yelling 'nailed it' when they didn't, in fact, nail it makes me want to steal her away and forget about this life of crime.

While the episode is in its final round, I clear off the plates and takeout containers from the coffee table, storing the leftovers in my near-empty fridge.

I fill up a glass of ice water and return to the living room. Sage has moved up to the couch and has her long, thick legs tucked underneath her. She scrunches her nose when I hand her the glass, letting me know she'd rather have more wine, but she drinks it anyway.

Good.

I can't have her getting drunk when I plan to properly bed her.

We've fucked in my office and in a hotel lobby's bath-room, but Sage deserves better than that.

When the show finally ends, and she's had her second glass of water, she picks up the remote and shuts off the TV.

I'm sitting on the other end of the couch, and she turns to me.

And stares.

I'm nursing a glass of whiskey on the rocks and raise a brow before taking a sip.

She rolls her eyes.

"How did you become..." She waves her hand up and down my body.

"Sexy?"

She scoffs, her hand flails around the living room getting more dramatic.

"Rich?" I offer.

She huffs and I laugh, the sound rattling deep within my chest. It almost startles me because I can't remember the last time I'd been so amused by anything let alone anyone.

"A mafia boss?"

"Yes, you big oaf!"

I laugh again and Sage smiles with me. It lights up her soft, tanned face. My eyes fall to her pouty red lips before returning to her inquisitive gaze.

I shoot back the rest of the whiskey before setting the glass on the table beside me.

Inhaling deeply, I prepare myself for these memories. The ones that haunt me when I sleep. The ones that remind me how dangerous my life is and how I brought this woman into a world she doesn't belong in. But maybe Sage *does belong*. She has secrets. I need to know why she's hiding behind a false identity.

Does Noah not know her best friend is lying?

Chapter 11

Sage

Watching this massive, scary man transform into a puddle of vulnerability has me fighting the urge to pull him into my arms and cradle him like a baby.

"I took over the QBM when my father died. I was twenty-two," Elias says.

"How did he...?"

"Cancer."

Elias clears his throat, but he doesn't expand on his father's illness.

Which reminds me of what Noah had said when I went to Del's safe house.

"Noah told me about your mother."

His head jerks up at my words. His jaw tightens.

"She did, did she?"

I purse my lips. I shouldn't have said anything. This is his story to tell, and I can understand him being angry that someone else shared it with me.

But I can't take it back. Now I can only offer him my sympathy.

"I'm sorry you were the one—" my voice cracks.

Fuck, I'm tearing up. He's barely told me anything, and I'm already so heartbroken. Why does this man make me so... passionate about *everything*?

"I'm sorry, Elias," I say, my voice barely a whisper.

His anger softens slightly, and we sit in silence for a few minutes before he starts speaking again.

"It was my fault."

"What? But I thought—"

"Lance was the one who was forced to slit her throat, but I should have been there to protect them." He ends the sentence on a growl, voice raised.

"Explain it to me," I say. I understand why he thinks he should blame himself, but I need to hear him say it out loud. Does he have anyone to talk about this with? A therapist? His brother? It doesn't matter. Right now, he has me. "You were just a kid. It shouldn't have been your responsibility to protect them."

His jaw is clenched so tightly, I'm surprised I can't hear his teeth grinding.

"Start at the beginning. I've got nowhere to be."

That's not entirely true. Chase has been blowing up my phone with calls, likely because I took the wire off and shoved it into my purse earlier when I went to the bathroom after first arriving at the penthouse. I couldn't risk answering, so I sent him a text saying that I couldn't talk, and I'd give him the rundown tomorrow. I could lie and say I was stuck at Lenetti's, but I don't want to risk it. If he has spies... if he saw me leave with Elias... he might punish me for lying by harming my parents.

I wait for Elias to continue talking, and I almost think he's going to refuse when he forces an agitated stream of air through his nose.

"My father had always been on the wrong side of the law. When I was learning the business, he'd tell me stories about how he'd steal cars as a teenager and deal drugs to people far too young to be ingesting that shit. By the time he was in his twenties, he had a following. A crew. Men who'd help him with elaborate schemes, usually dealing with illegal drugs but nothing was off limits. He had chop shops, money laundering operations, and whatever else he could make money from.

"He dealt dirty. A lot of deaths resulted from the drugs he ran. A lot of people were murdered for speaking a single wrong thing in front of him."

Elias picks up his empty glass and swirls the melting ice, staring numbly as it clanks around.

"He met my mother when she was fifteen and he was twenty-five. She was *given* to him to clear a debt. Fucked up shit, but my mother didn't fight it. She always told us that it was a sacrifice she had to make to protect her family, mostly her younger brother and sister.

"Anyway, Mom said Dad didn't touch her until she was eighteen when they got married. How honorable of him, right? Nine months after their wedding day, I was born. I was her saving grace because Percy—that was my father's name—abused her physically and mentally, but that stopped when I arrived. She stayed busy raising me, and my father left her alone to do so."

I reach out for Elias's hand. He hesitates for only a second before taking it.

"But then he started beating me when I was six. I remember getting backhanded for talking back to him. Then again for acting out at school. Anything, really. My mother was my escape from my father and his harsh punishments. She loved me and did everything she could to protect me. But she wasn't safe from him either. He may have stopped harming her while she was pregnant with me and for the first five or so years of my life, but if he couldn't get to me, he'd get to her. When Lance was born, it got worse. I was the big brother. The role model. The one who had to lead by example. Especially once we both got older.

"When I turned thirteen, my father stopped letting me hang out with my friends or do anything fun in general. I had to sneak around a lot, but he had eyes everywhere. He caught me a few times, and I paid for it.

"Then I got smart and convinced my father to let me go to parties, clubs, and concerts where I could recruit QBM soldiers. My father liked to sign them up young so he could manipulate them into doing his bidding. He would teach them to love violence and enjoy killing."

Elias shakes his head; his eyes darken as he relives these memories. The pain in his face almost has me begging him to stop. I should tell him I no longer want to hear about how he became a mafia boss.

But when I lift his hand to my mouth and press my lips gently to his knuckles, his entire body seems to exhale.

"On Christmas Eve, when I was sixteen, I went to a party. My brother and mother tried to convince me to stay home. They were going to bake cookies and watch Christmas movies all night. My mother loved Christmas. She'd decorate the entire house, inside and out."

The corner of his mouth tilts up briefly before he frowns.

"I wanted to stay home with Lance and my mother so badly, but I worried my father would return home and catch me and punish me..." Elias swallows hard. "So, I acted like I was too old for that shit and left.

"At least with the party, I could make up the excuse that I was there for recruitment. I wasn't though. I just wanted one night of fun. No mafia. No crime or violence or my father's strict rules. I got wasted. I drank a lot of booze, took whatever drug was handed to me, and fucked any pussy that was put in front of me."

I dig my nails into the top of Elias's hand, then I realize it's dumb to be jealous over a young Elias and release my claws. If he notices my reaction, he doesn't let on as he lifts his cup to fish out a piece of ice. He chews on it forever. I know it's to prepare himself for what's next.

"It had to have been one in the morning when I got home. The moment I walked through the front door, I was immediately hit with a coppery metal scent. I froze when I saw her. My mother. She was on the floor of the living room with her throat slit.

"I couldn't blame the drugs or booze on what I was seeing. I'd sobered up enough... it felt like hours before I dropped to the floor at her side. She felt so light and fragile in my arms. I begged her to wake up—"

Elias stops talking and looks away from me.

I want to say something. Anything, but what? How can I make this moment better? Words are useless. He doesn't need words.

He needs comfort.

I crawl into his lap and wrap my arms around his head, cradling him to my chest. His long, strong arms cage me into a near-suffocating hug. He doesn't cry. He just sits there. Breathing me in. Rubbing his hands up and down my back.

"If I hadn't gone to that party… If I had just spent Christmas Eve with my mom and brother… I could have been there when those men arrived. I could have killed them, saved my mother, and prevented my brother from having to do such a horrible thing."

"You couldn't have known. And say you had been home. What if those men had killed you first? You can't blame yourself. You blame those men."

"I do and those men are dead for what they did. Lance killed them."

"Good," I say and kiss the top of Elias's head.

My eyes widen at the move. Did I really just kiss the top of his head? He doesn't react to it or say anything. Instead, he sighs and buries his face between my breasts.

I'm glad I took the wire off earlier. Otherwise, Elias would have felt it by now and instead of sharing this heartbreaking memory with me, he'd be kicking me out—or worse—for betraying him.

"I'm sorry I brought you into this life," he says, his voice muffled.

"You didn't," I murmur and rest my cheek against the top of his head.

"Me, Noah… either way, I know you're too good for it. For me."

I open my mouth to protest but he keeps talking.

"You shut down after Lenetti stabbed my brother."

"I…"

He releases me from the hug so he can look me in the eyes.

"You were scared."

I purse my lips, and he raises a brow, daring me to lie.

"Fine. Yes. I was. I've never witnessed someone get stabbed before. But you were there. You protected me."

"Noah asked me to."

"You would have even if she hadn't."

He pulls back and wraps his fingers around my wrists, and in a swift move that makes me yelp, he clutches them behind my back.

"What the hell, Elias?"

"Here's what's going to happen."

I roll my eyes because the sweet moment of sharing is gone.

The Boss is back.

"First, I'm going to spank you for rolling your eyes at me just now. Not just once. I'm going to spank you until your ass is red, and you won't be able to sit right for days."

I suck in a sharp breath. My nipples harden through the soft fabric of my sweater and scrape against Elias's chest. He glances down and smirks.

"You little slut. You like the sound of that, don't you?"

"Not as much as *me* tying you to a chair backwards and putting a gag in your mouth so *I* can be the one to spank you."

Elias groans, and he frees a hand to pinch one of my nipples. I buck in his lap and grind my pussy over his hardening cock beneath me.

"Second, I'm not going to fuck you tonight."

"What?"

"We've fucked plenty. Tonight? I'm going to make love to you. Worship you like the queen that you are. You are mine. My Reine. My queen."

"That's what Reine means? Queen?"

"It does, and I knew you were a queen ever since I saw you punch the man who groped you without an ounce of remorse."

"So, you speak French?"

"Some. Bare minimum. What's needed for business dealings."

Elias skims his mouth over my neck while continuing to pinch and pull my nipple through my top. Thankfully, the bruises from Chase choking me weren't too bad and have already faded. Same with the mark on my cheek when he backhanded me.

"Stop distracting me, Ma Chérie," he says, moving his hand to my hair.

He clutches the strands and tugs, allowing him to suck on my neck. I squirm in his lap because I do *not* want a hickey. Especially when I leave for my parents' place the day after tomorrow. But my attempt to break free of this man fails and it only causes him to suck harder.

Marking me.

The fucker.

"After I've made you come, I'll make you come again. And again. That pussy is going to hurt tomorrow, and it'll remind you to never lie to me again. Because once I've fucked the last orgasm out of you, when you're near comatose from pleasure, you're going to tell me why you're using a fake name and who you're running from."

Oh. Shit.

I don't have time to panic because Elias lifts me off his lap and we stand. He wraps his hand around my wrist and leads me to his bedroom.

"Elias..."

"No, Reine. After," he says. "All I want to hear from that dirty little mouth are moans and whimpers or the words 'yes,' 'sir,' or 'fuck me harder, Boss.'"

Boss.

He hated the nickname when I first called him that. Now he's begging me to use it.

This man infuriates me. He takes control, something I've refused to let another man do to me since leaving Chase. But this is different. Elias... cares. About my safety. My *pleasure*.

That first night we fucked, I came five times. He only came once.

Elias is demanding, but in the way I *need* him to be.

The way that doesn't leave unwanted injuries or holes in my fragile self-confidence.

No. It's no longer fragile.

I've been building my walls, strengthening my armor. I've finally figured out what I want when it comes to my life and my body.

And I want Elias.

I just can't keep him.

I'll give him tonight. Then I have to put some distance between us. At least until I make sure my parents are safe. After that, I'll tell Elias everything.

And ask him to kill Chase.

Chapter 12

Elias

This woman is going to be the end of me.

I'm struggling not to blow my load just by how obedient she's being.

I know Sage is the type of woman who likes to give men orders. Fuck, I want that too. But not tonight. Tonight she needs to let go. To forget about whatever has her shaken. Whatever caused her to hide into herself.

Once inside my bedroom, I back Sage up to my king-size bed and release her.

"I'm going to undress you now. Okay?"

She nods.

"Say it out loud, Reine."

"Yes, sir."

I palm her cheek, grazing my thumb over her lips. "That's my good girl."

She rolls her eyes but smiles.

"Careful." Her amusement fades to defiance.

Brat.

I move my hand to her right ear and remove the Christmas tree earring, holding it up in front of her face.

"Cute."

She shrugs in her adorably playful way that drives me crazy.

After removing the other earring, I place the jewelry on my dresser.

I start on her sweater next, untucking it from the skirt. My hands slide underneath, and she sucks in a breath when my palms flatten over her sides and move around to her back.

I unlatch her bra and pause.

She huffs.

"What?" I ask, even though I know what's annoying her.

"Could you *be* any slower?"

I ignore the reference to the TV show *Friends* and skim my hands back to her front. My thumbs graze the bottom of her breasts which are now falling out of her unclasped bra. She shivers.

"Patience, my needy girl."

I lift the sweater, and her arms extend over her head expectedly, but I stop when the tangled material covers her eyes. I tighten my grip, trapping her arms in the process.

"Elias," she whispers.

With one hand, I hold the makeshift blindfold in place, then graze my fingertips over her uncovered mouth, down her chin and neck. Goosebumps rise across her skin, her breathing picking up with every inch of skin I touch. Once I get to her full breasts, I move the bra aside and let her tits fall out. I take one of her hard nipples between my fingers and pinch... then pull.

She arches her body against me and moans.

"What did I say to call me?"

"B-boss," she breathes.

"Good girl."

I lean down to replace my fingers with my mouth, sucking her nipple and lapping my tongue over the hardened peak.

"Fuck, Boss. Yes."

My cock jerks at how reactive she is to my touch.

Keeping the blindfold in place, I move my hand to the stretchy waistband of her skirt and hook my fingers to pull it down. Not all the way off, though. I leave it mid-thigh, confining her even more.

She whimpers when I push her lacy underwear aside and tease her opening.

"Always so wet for me, Chérie."

She tries to part her legs, but the skirt won't allow much give. Just enough that I'm able to sink one finger inside her with ease.

Her pussy clenches around me.

"Oh, God," she moans and squirms because I'm not moving. "Boss, please."

My thumb grazes over her clit, and she nearly buckles to the floor, but I keep her upright.

"Please, what? Use your words," I provoke.

"Please. Fuck me."

"Hmm. So needy."

I slide my finger out enough to add a second and thrust the two back in, down to the last knuckle. Sage's pussy flutters around the digits.

She's panting and on edge as I play with her.

"Did you think I'd let you come so easily when you've been keeping secrets from me?"

I withdraw my fingers, then slam them back inside. My thumb presses against her clit again, and she lets out a sob of pleasure.

"You s-said... we-we were going... oh fuck... m-make love."

Her words are broken as I pump my fingers.

I lean over to scrape my teeth over her neck. She gasps and the sound is quickly followed by moans.

She's getting close.

When I move my mouth to hover over hers, I whisper, "I lied."

Right as she's about to come, I remove my fingers and lift her sweater and bra the rest of the way over her head.

She stands there with her mouth wide open, so I stick my fingers inside—the ones that were just in her sweet heat. She gags, not expecting the move, then closes her lips over them and licks them clean.

"See how good you taste?"

She nods, and I remove my fingers.

I finish undressing her, sliding her skirt and panties down to the floor. She steps out of the clothing and stands there, waiting for my orders like the submissive brat she's fighting so hard not to be.

Fuck she's beautiful. I let my eyes travel over her body from her hair that's a rat's nest because of me, to her blue-green eyes and plump lips, down to her kissable neck and heavy breasts, to her soft stomach and groomed pussy, and to her thick thighs that I desperately need around my head.

"Like what you see?" she teases.

I've seen her naked before—the first night we met. I memorized this body. I fucked my hand to what I remembered.

My memories do not do her justice.

"Come here, Reine," I order.

She takes a step... and another... slowly, so painfully slow.

She's testing me.

She wants me to punish her.

Oh, I will.

But first...

I grab her by the throat once she's within reach, and I slant my mouth against hers. She immediately opens for me, and I plunge my tongue in, tasting the salty pleasure she sucked off my fingers.

The kiss doesn't last long, and she whines when I pull away.

I sit down on the edge of the bed.

"Over my lap, ass in the air."

She frowns and scrunches her nose but does as I say.

Once she's in place, I crash my hand down on her plump cheeks.

"Fuck," she groans.

I do it again without warning, and she screams a little louder.

Music to my ears.

"Tell me to stop," I say.

"Don't fucking stop."

I spank her again, relishing the recoil and the beautiful sound of Sage's moans.

"More, sir, please."

I oblige, whipping her ass over and over until my palm stings and Sage's ass is burning red.

I slide my finger into her dripping cunt, lathering it up so I can sink it into her asshole. While massaging her aching skin, I pump the digit in and out of the tight ring of muscles.

"Yes, Elias, like that," she huffs.

I pick up speed and move my other hand to her clit, pressing my thumb down and caressing it in circles.

When I sense Sage is close, I stop.

"No!" Sage whines.

"On the bed," I say, removing my fingers from her ass and helping her off my lap.

"I thought you said we weren't going to make love."

"I lied about lying."

She rolls her eyes. "So we *are* going to make love? And who says making love anyway? Just say we're going to fuck."

I laugh, slightly deranged sounding, but it only causes her to roll her eyes *again*.

I gently push her, and she falls onto the bed. "We're going to go slow. I'm going to make sure you have no doubt that I will be the last man whose cock gets milked by that sweet pussy. Do you understand me, Ma Chérie?"

She adjusts herself until she's in the middle of the mattress, shaking her head.

"You're insane."

I crawl in between her legs, tearing open the condom I grabbed from the drawer of the bedside table.

"*You* make me insane," I say.

Once protection is on, I line the head of my cock to her opening.

"You can't be saying shit that sounds like a proposal."

I thrust into her, and she throws her head back and screams.

"Is that what you want? For me to propose to you?"

"No," she says on a grunt.

I pump into her casually, grabbing her hips and holding her down.

"Give me a couple months, and I'll change your mind."

"Shut up," she groans, and I chuckle.

I pause my pumping, which angers her even more.

"Stop torturing me, asshole!"

Bending so my body covers hers, I hook my arms under her armpits, allowing us to be face to face.

She kisses me out of fury, biting down hard enough to break skin and make my lip bleed. But she doesn't pull away. She kisses me aggressively, and that's my cue to resume fucking her. Slow but rough to start as we explore each other's mouths.

Then I pick up speed, and she ends the kiss to scream her pleasure. I use the moment to trail my lips down her neck and across her chest, taking a nipple into my mouth and grazing my teeth over the sensitive peak.

Sage arches off the bed and claws her nails down my back. I don't like being touched on my back—or my front, really—because of the scars my father left, but the urge to push her hands away isn't there right now.

Maybe it's because those beautifully manicured *sharp* nails definitely broke skin. Instead of scars from my father, I can have scars from my lover.

The pain is drowned by my pleasure and all thoughts of Sage feeling the scars on my back are gone. Her hands make their way down to my ass, and she squeezes my cheeks not-so-gently. I almost blow right then.

"Let me on top."

"No."

"Then fuck me faster."

I growl and take her arms by the wrists, securing them above her head.

I don't fuck her faster. I go slower, slamming into her and pausing as I let her pulsing pussy flutter around me.

Then I repeat, edging her release.

The brat.

Holding her wrists with one hand, I move the other down to her clit and start massaging, slow but deep circles.

"My cock was made for you, Sage," I say, watching her flushed body bounce beneath me. "You stretch so perfectly around me."

I pull out and slam back in.

She whimpers, her breathing erratic.

My thrusts pick up, no longer able to hold back. The brutal slam of my hips, combined with me massaging her clit, sends her over the edge.

I wait until she's done shaking and her pussy isn't choking my cock before I start moving inside her again.

"Give me another one," I say, lifting her off the bed slightly to put a pillow underneath her ass. This gives me a new angle, reaching parts deep within her.

She screams, letting me know I've hit that perfect spot, and her walls are already pulsing around me.

"That's it, my good girl. Come for me. Show me how well I fuck you."

She fists the sheets, arching her back as I drive into her.

I slap her tits, the sting on her aching nipples coaxing her third orgasm out of her.

And this time, I join her.

Chapter 13

Sage

Ive simply died and gone to heaven, meeting God aka Elias's cock.

He fucked me all night. I lost count with how many orgasms rocked my body.

I ache... *everywhere*.

Every place he marked me with his teeth, sinking down to break skin on my neck, my breasts, my inner thighs.

I've never been bitten during sex, and I never knew how much I wanted it... needed it.

My cunt hurts most of all. The type of ache that makes me wet by moving because it reminds me of his dick pounding me over and over and over...

Elias took care of me too.

Cleaning me up and applying ointment to his bites. Chase never did that with me, not even when he wasn't a psychopath.

I fell asleep in Elias's arms but woke an hour later when the sun started rising. Elias's cubicle room is encased in floor to ceiling windows, and he has black out shades, but a sliver of sun managed to peek through, right into my eye.

Plus, the man talks in his sleep. Some words were unintelligible as he jerked around. A few words I made out like, 'No. Mom. Wake.'

He dreams about the night he found his mother dead on the living room floor.

Not a dream. A *nightmare*.

I carefully get out of bed, thankful he's no longer spooning me, and rush to the bathroom to relieve myself.

I pause at the mirror, taking in my disheveled appearance. As much as I would love to show the world the marks Elias gave me, I'll have to cover them up before going to my parents' for Christmas. Except I'm not ashamed of these marks. They weren't left in malice. They were given with consent. For me and my pleasure.

Elias said we'd talk this morning about what I'm hiding from him, but I can't. Not yet. Not until I can get my parents to safety.

I know I should let Elias help me, maybe even Noah, but I'm too scared. What if Chase hurts or kills them, because of me? I know they're all tough and scary or whatever but there's just too much at stake here.

I have to at least try and do this on my own first.

I quietly find my clothes around his bedroom floor and get dressed.

I give the peaceful bear of a man one more look, then walk out of his bedroom.

He's going to be so pissed.

Grabbing my purse, I open the front door to his penthouse just a crack. When I'm sure the coast is clear, I step out and push the button to the elevator.

Nothing happens.

Shit. He used a card to work it last night.

"Can I help you ma'am?"

The deep voice makes me jump, and I stumble back slightly.

"Just trying to leave." I wave my phone at the massive man dressed in a suit. "My car is here."

"Let me get Mr. Carter."

"No!"

The man, who towers over me by half a foot, and with muscles all over in places I didn't know could have muscles, raises a brow.

"He's asleep. Please, I just... need to go."

The man purses his full lips. I've seen him before. He's almost always with Elias. He must be his head bodyguard or something. He's quite gorgeous—tall, dark, and handsome. If I were... available, I'd flirt my way out of this situation.

"Am I a prisoner here?"

He shakes his head.

"Then you have to let me go."

"With all due respect, ma'am—"

I swear if he calls me ma'am one more time, I'll kick him in the nuts.

Wait... maybe I should do that.

"If I let you leave, Mr. Carter will kill me."

"He wouldn't," I say, laughing. The man isn't humored. My smile drops, and my heart races. "Would he?"

"I'll go get him."

Shit.

I panic and when he turns, about to open the penthouse door, I grab the vase from the foyer table and smash it over his head.

I must have hit a sweet spot because he stumbles and falls to the ground, unmoving.

"Shit. Shit. Shit. I'm sorry. Please don't be dead."

I check for his breath underneath his nose and sigh with relief when air hits my hand.

God, I'm a horrible person. I'd rather injure a man than talk to Elias... who probably heard the vase breaking and is going to be out here in seconds.

I search the unconscious man's pants for a key card and whisper scream 'yes' when I find it in the first pocket. I tap it to the pad next to the elevator and the doors open. I rush inside and tap the card again before pressing the button for the lobby.

The doors shut, and I let out one long breath of relief.

Less than a minute later, the doors are opening. I lift my head high as if I didn't just knock a man unconscious and start walking. The suited men in the lobby give me an odd look, but they don't stop me. Maybe they assume if I got past beefy man number one, then I'm allowed to leave.

This sure feels like a prisoner situation.

Would Elias have let me leave? Should I have woken him up? He may be bossy, but he listens to the word no. He doesn't force me to do anything I don't want to.

I can't think about that right now. I accept that I likely overreacted, and Elias is probably going to hate me.

It's for the best.

I hop in the cab waiting out front of Elias's luxurious building and give the driver my address.

As we're pulling away, four security guards run out of the building. I turn in my seat and watch them stop at the curb, failing to catch me. The lead guy takes out his phone, I assume speaking to Elias.

Seconds later, my phone vibrates with a text message.

Boss

Stop running from me.

I stare at the text message the entire ride back to my apartment building. He even added a crying emoji.

The big scary mafia boss sending emojis? It's too cute.

My stomach spurs with regret. I should have woken him. At least made up a reason to leave. A doctor's appointment... a lunch shift at the bar—which is somewhat true except I work tonight. But I know Elias would have demanded he drive me or sent bodyguards with me. And I have a feeling he's pretty good at catching liars. He already suspects I'm hiding stuff from him.

Because I am.

I instruct the driver to drop me off on a different street, knowing Chase or one of his goons will be waiting for me out front. By the time I woke up this morning, I had dozens of missed calls and text messages.

Where are you?

It's morning. Time to talk.

You better not be at Carter's, you slut!

I stopped reading them after that. I responded that I'd be home around noon, and we could talk then. I desperately need sleep before dealing with him.

I make my way inside my building through the back trash area and take two flights of stairs to my apartment. The sun is starting to rise, filtering in through the windows in my kitchen and living room. It's enough light to see as I toss my purse on the table next to the door and slip off my shoes.

When I turn toward my living area, I scream and jump back, hitting my hip on the edge of a table and nearly falling to the ground.

"Caught in a lie, Sunshine," Chase growls and stands.

"How the hell did you get into my apartment?"

"Why have you been ignoring my texts?"

He stalks toward me, his eyes wide and bloodshot. He looks strung the fuck out.

"I stayed at Noah's father's house. It wasn't safe to talk there. We were up late so I barely got any sleep. I just wanted a few hours before we talked. I kept the wire's power on through dinner. Didn't you hear everything?"

He stops inches in front of me, his breath reeking, likely forgetting to brush his teeth while high on whatever drug he's on. He clenches his teeth, his nostrils flaring.

"It stopped working shortly after you arrived."

Oh, thank fuck. That means he didn't hear me with Elias. He didn't hear *anything*. I attempt to hide my relief with a wince.

"I'm sorry. I didn't know."

He also didn't tell me the wire failed in any of the frantic texts to me.

"Did they have a jammer?" he asks.

"Wouldn't a jammer cause my phone not to work too?"

His hand shoots out and grabs me by the throat. "Did you fuck with the wire?"

Typically, I'd be struggling for breath, but he's too strung out and his grip is lax.

"No, of course not."

"What. Happened?"

"I... I don't know. Maybe your lackey put it on wrong."

I wonder if it was because I sweated too much, and it shorted out. I won't ask him if that's a possibility because he might just kill me.

Chase drops his hand from my throat, mumbling something about dumbass Dante. His phone rings, and he turns away to answer it. My entire body relaxes. While he's barking orders at whoever called, I take the wire out of my purse and set it on the table next to the door.

I cautiously watch Chase, noticing him getting angrier the longer he's on the phone. When he hangs up, he shoves the phone in his jacket pocket and glares at me.

"We're not done here. I'll be back in a couple days to talk about what happened at that dinner."

"I won't be here. Christmas is next week, and I took time off to spend it with my parents. I leave tomorrow afternoon."

He smiles, a smile that I once found handsome, but now sends chills down my spine.

"Then I guess we're having a little family reunion."

"What? No. I can just head up there after we talk."

Chase stands there staring at me with narrowed eyes, considering my ultimatum. "Fuck no. I don't trust you. I'll just go with you. Don't think about leaving early either. My men will be watching your every move."

He doesn't give me a chance to respond and storms out of my apartment.

Goddamn it.

My parents knew my marriage to Chase was bad, but they didn't know it was *this* bad. They don't know this new version of Chase. They knew he wasn't a good guy, but now? They'll want me to go to the cops. They won't understand why I'm not.

I'm also terrible at lying to them. They're going to know something's wrong, especially when Chase shows up at their home for a visit—which he never did when we were together.

But I have no choice. I can't defy Chase.

Hopefully he won't want to stay the entire week. The moment he's gone, I'll figure out a way to escape his goons and take my parents somewhere safe.

"You're not eating."

I jump at the sound of Chase's voice.

It's Christmas Day, and Chase got in late last night after he had quote, 'business to take care of' the past few days. He sent his goons with me to my parents. At least the two creepy men drove in their own vehicle. They barely speak and tend to stare at me as if I'm meat on a stick and they haven't had a meal in days.

I have no doubt that the word 'no' means shit to them.

I push the green bean casserole around my plate with my fork and shrug.

"You're always hungry. Eat."

My grip on the utensil tightens, and I stifle the urge to stab him in the eye.

I force myself to take a bite, not because he 'ordered' me to, but because I can feel my mother's questioning stare our way.

"So, Chase," she says, giving him her infamous icy stare down.

She's hated him since the moment they met the day before our wedding. She hated him because he refused to 'allow' me to come visit them. She hated him because she knew he was controlling me, but she couldn't convince me to leave him. When we got divorced, she just had to throw it in my face that she 'always knew something was off with him.'

I love my mother, I really do, but she's not one to hold back her opinions. She's vocal about *everything*. But she also supported me in all my life decisions, even if they weren't the best options for me. Then she was there when I'd run back to them with my tail between my legs because something didn't work out the way I planned.

Like my marriage.

I met Chase when I was twenty-one and he was thirty. I moved to New York City to 'find myself' and was bartending at a hole in the wall dive bar in the East Village. Chase's band had booked a gig there. We immediately clicked and hooked up, and the next morning he asked me to go on tour with him. I was young and restless and had no real responsibilities. I was renting a dump of an apartment on a monthly basis and had enough money saved to fuck around for a few years, so I went with him. I followed him around the country with his band for two years until his mom got sick, and he left the band to take care of her.

I went with him to New Jersey because I convinced myself I was in love.

He proposed to me a year later, and after a year-long engagement, we got married. Six months after the ceremony, his mother passed away.

Things went downhill after that.

I missed all the signs of him being a narcissist. It was always me taking care of him. He constantly demanded my attention, my company. I always thought it was because he was stressed about his mother and needed an escape. It got to a point where he'd get angry when I tried to go to the grocery store without him or when I wanted to hang out with a friend for a movie night. He dismissed my feelings, especially when I expressed how much I missed my parents and wanted to go visit them.

The final straw was when he lost his job at the mechanic shop. He didn't tell me we were struggling for money because he'd spent our paychecks on drugs, anything to numb the pain of his mother's death. Bills went unpaid, and I had to get a second job just to keep the lights on. Then I found out he used my identity and applied for five credit cards, maxing out each one.

He didn't stop with me. He realized he could make a lot of money stealing identities, especially those of elderly people. I told Noah he went to jail, but I lied. He never got caught. He just kept doing worse and worse things.

And I never turned him in.

I was too afraid of what he'd do to me.

What if I turned him in and he made bail? He would have killed me.

Instead, I served him divorce papers. I was surprised he signed them. He didn't even put up a fight. Turns out, he was cheating on me. He was more than willing to leave me for this other woman.

Once everything was finalized, I moved back to New York City and assumed a new identity in hopes to never see the asshole again. Sage Morgan no longer existed as far as I was concerned.

It didn't matter how big New York City is... Chase still found me.

"What are you doing for work these days?" Mom asks.

My throat dries out, and I choke on the bite of green bean casserole I just shoved into my mouth. I wash the food down with a sip of wine.

Okay, it wasn't a sip. I gulped down the entire glass and refilled it to the brim.

I can't be sober for this.

Chase slaps on that charming smile that most people fall for. Like my father. At our wedding reception, they talked sports and action movies and whatever else men find pleasure in.

It was all an act.

Chase hated sports.

He never watched movies with me.

"I'm actually running my own business."

Chase's spell doesn't work on my mom, though. She raises a brow, waiting for him to elaborate.

"International shipping, mostly. I make sure my clients' cargo is delivered on time and with no issues."

My stomach sours and the green beans are threatening to make a reappearance.

"Hmm," my mom says.

I hold my breath, waiting for her to ask him exactly *what* he ships, but thankfully she doesn't.

However, she's not done grilling us.

"So, are you two back together?"

"No," I immediately bark out the same time Chase says, "yes."

Mom startles at my outburst, her hand over her chest. I glance at my dad, and he's peering over the top of the book he's reading in one hand with a fork full of food in the other. He's never been much to talk during family dinners. My mother is the outgoing one whereas my father would prefer quiet. He never voiced his dislike for Chase after the divorce, but Mom told me he was furious.

If only he knew how bad it was.

Chase's hand falls to my leg, and he squeezes my thigh hard enough that I'm sure more bruises will be left.

"We're not back together... yet," he says through gritted teeth.

Before I can risk more bruises and vehemently deny that we aren't, and never will be, getting back together, Chase's phone rings.

He's been getting calls all day, ever since I finally told him what went down at Lenetti's dinner.

Since Chase already knew that the Empire and the QBM wanted to bring the Lords of Staten Island down, I told him they were planning to make their move soon. I didn't know the exact date or the details of that plan, and thankfully Chase didn't push me for that information.

He probably wants to warn the Lords so a gun fight can break out since his goal is to be New York City's top crime boss.

If the Lords kill Carter and Lenetti, then that's two mafias down for the count, he'd said.

I also remembered Noah talking about sex trafficking and lied about a shipment interception taking place this weekend. I didn't say where or what was in the shipment.

Chase was sent into full blown panic, and he's been on the phone barking orders at people ever since. His reaction only confirms he's dealing in something much worse than guns and drugs.

I have no doubt now that he was behind the sex trafficking rings the news has been reporting about lately. I just saw one was busted on Long Island the other day.

"If you'll excuse me, I need to take this call," Chase says and leaves the table.

I should follow him. I may have lied about Elias busting a shipment, but if Chase really does have one coming in, I can find out where.

Then once Chase leaves, I'll call Elias to tell him *everything*.

I just hope he doesn't think I'm playing both sides.

Chapter 14

Elias

Is she fucking playing me?

Who the hell are these two assholes?

I've been sitting outside Sage's parents' house for an hour, watching and waiting. The moment I pulled onto the street, I spotted two black SUVs with tinted windows. The idiots inside both vehicles didn't notice me parking nearby.

Fucking amateurs.

I pick up my phone from the dock and call my tech guy.

"Run a couple plates," I bark when he answers, and I list out the letters and numbers.

I ignore his grumbling at me being so brash. I don't have time for pleasantries.

"Both belong to a Chase Henley," Phil says after about two minutes and rattles off an address. My phone buzzes a few seconds later with a photo of a guy, but I can't be sure if it's any of the men in either SUV.

I sigh and tell Phil to have one of his fancy tech programs scan traffic cameras to find out all the places both vehicles have been so I can figure who this Chase is and if he's working for someone. I have no fucking clue how it works, but Phil has never failed me anytime I ask for a favor.

Movement from the front door of the home catches my eye and a man on the phone angrily walks out. *That's* the man from the photo. He's not too tall, five nine at my guess, and he's got light brown hair that appears greasy in the porch light's beam. I've easily got 150 pounds on him. He's pale, too, his skin covered in a sheen of sweat.

His movements are jittery. He's got to be high on some sort of drug. I've seen it too often busting addicts, hoping they'll narc on their dealer so I can chase down the boss moving drugs throughout New York City.

The man cradles the phone to his shoulder so he can light a cigarette—like he's the star of some shitty crime movie—then takes out his gun to check the bullets.

Movement again from the front door alerts me to Sage's presence, listening in on this man's conversation.

My instinct is to get out and run to her. Protect her.

I can't. Not yet. I need to see if she's playing me.

She must have made a noise because the man turns. He lunges, and I watch as he drags Sage outside. He throws her to the ground and kicks her in the stomach.

My hand is on the car door, ready to kill this mother fucker, but he's already walking off.

Fuck.

That was close.

If I had acted on my impulse to get out, guns blazing in this quiet suburban neighborhood, Sage could have been caught in the crossfire. Not to mention that would have been a huge mess to clean up.

The asshole gets inside one of the SUVs and drives off.

My eyes move back to Sage. She picks herself up off the ground, then flips off the departing SUV. She flips off the two men in the remaining SUV as well.

I smirk at my feisty little queen.

What have you gotten yourself into?

Lance told me about her ex, warning me to be careful with her because he was a piece of shit. He didn't go into detail but if the man who just left is her ex, I have a feeling he's back in her life for a reason.

And not a good one.

I call my uncle and tell him to get soldiers ready. As soon as Phil gives me locations, my men will move in.

I wait in my car for another hour until the lights in the house go out, letting me know Sage's parents have gone to sleep.

Time for answers.

I send her a text.

> **What are you wearing?**

She's been ignoring me, of course, but that hasn't stopped me from sending them.

Level 100 Clinger, and all.

I stuff the phone in my coat pocket and get out.

Walking over to the SUV with the two goons left behind to babysit Sage, I knock on the window. The man in the driver's seat startles.

Look... if you're going to be a criminal, you gotta have situational awareness. These two idiots are highly lacking in that area.

He rolls down the window.

"The fuck you want?" he grumbles, attempting to be intimidating.

I throw on a smile and prepare a stereotypical suburban dad voice. Never mind that I'm in a suit and look nothing like a suburban dad.

"Hi there. Neighborhood Watch. I've noticed you've been parked in front of this house for a while." I wave my hand around for emphasis. "Can I ask who you're here to see?"

The man turns his head to look at his friend in the passenger seat and that's when I attack.

I sink a knife into his temple with my right hand and with my left hand, shoot goon number two. The silencer muffles the sound to an extent, and I can only hope no one peeks out their window or opens their door to investigate the noise.

Not that I'm worried. I have credentials for instances like this. I've had to fake being a cop or FBI agent too many times to cover up a crime scene and reassure the public that they are safe from the bad guys.

Lying about one gunshot is better than cleaning up an entire shootout scene.

I considered letting one of these men live to torture information out of him, but then I'd have to store him somewhere until my backup arrives. It's not worth it, especially since I know Phil will get me what I need.

And Sage is about to tell me everything too.

I tuck my weapons away and pull out my phone.

My heart skips a beat at Sage's text on the screen.

Reine

I'm not wearing anything. Want to see?

I curse and readjust my twitching cock.

She's awake. And horny, apparently. Good. Time to confront my deceitful little queen.

Yes. I'll be right there

Reine

Huh? What do you mean?

I make a call for a cleanup crew to get rid of the bodies, and the SUV, then walk to the home's front door.

It's locked, which is good—not that it would have stopped those two idiots I just killed from getting inside—but it might have given Sage and her parents enough time to hide or escape.

Doesn't matter. The men are dead now.

Using lock picking tools that I keep in my car, I get the front door open and make my way inside.

It smells like Sage in here. Strawberries and vanilla.

I follow her scent to a room; one that's on the opposite side of the house from her parents' room.

I hope it's the right room.

I send Sage a text.

Don't scream

She answers almost immediately.

Reine

Are you drunk? What are you even talking about?

When I open the door—thank fuck it's her bedroom—she does, in fact, scream.

I rush over to where she's lying down on her bed, reading a book, and cover her mouth with my palm. Her eyes flare with fear before narrowing.

"What are you doing here?" she asks against my palm. Her nails dig into my arm. "Let me go, you dick."

I smirk at her feistiness that I find way too cute.

"You won't scream again?" I ask, my voice low. She shakes her head.

Not sure if I believe her, but I release her anyway. She stands hastily, glaring at me when she closes and locks her door.

The moment she turns to face me; a fist meets my right eye.

Okay, fine, I deserved that.

"Fuck," she hisses, holding her hand against her chest. "Is your big head made of rocks or something?"

"You need ice for that," I say and pivot towards the door.

"Stop," she snarls. "Lord forbid my parents wake up and catch a massive dude in the kitchen."

"You're the one who screamed when I told you not to."

"You shouldn't be here, Elias. How the fuck did you find me?"

"Go get ice for your hand and we'll talk."

She gives an exasperated sigh, and I grin ear to ear. She rolls her eyes and leaves.

While she's gone, I snoop.

Pictures are hung up around the room of a young Sage in high school. Her posing with a flute in a marching band uniform. Her on stage performing with that flute. Her with crossed eyes, sticking her tongue out. Her with a group of girls I assume to be her friends. Over the years, her style changed. So did her body. She gained some weight, her hips became more defined, rounder, her stomach softer. She went from dressing in baggy clothes to form-fitting ones to show off her new-found curves.

Her confidence... the way her eyes light up in photos after finding love for herself. Her smile became brighter.

I move on to photos of her traveling across the country: Chicago, St. Louis, Memphis, Austin, The Grand Canyon, Los Angeles, the Pacific Northwest.

Some photos have been torn in half—someone she ripped out of her life.

This awful ex, if I were to guess.

The rest of her room has been immortalized in nostalgia. Posters of rock bands and celebrities I couldn't name. A few marching band trophies line her bookcase along with stacks of books—all romance from what I can tell.

Her queen-sized bed is decked out in light pink to match the pale pink walls. Across from the bed is a vanity where I imagine this beautiful woman sitting to put on makeup or style her hair.

Sage has clearly lived a normal life. She has two loving parents, she went to high school and played in the band, she traveled and smiled all the time.

She was happy.

Loved.

I'm sitting on her bed, flipping through one of her photo albums when she returns. She pauses for a second before closing the door and walking to stand in front of me.

She holds out an ice pack. I close the photo album and set it down before taking the pack and covering my aching right eye that will definitely be bruised by tomorrow.

It matches the blossoming bruise on my left cheekbone that Lance gave me from earlier today when we brawled. The fucker taunted me at Lenetti's before the Christmas lunch.

I won though so I'm not mad.

It was like old times. As a kid, I permanently wore a black eye from wrestling with Lance in the living room until our mom would yell at us for breaking a lamp or knocking over a coffee table. Except now Lance and I are both adults and our punches have bigger consequences.

Sage sits next to me, a second ice pack resting on her knuckles.

"Who taught you to throw a right hook like that?"

She huffs and a burst of air rushes out of her nose.

"I took a self-defense class a few months ago."

"Impressive."

"I guess."

"Were you learning to protect yourself from the man I saw leave earlier? The one who kicked you?"

She nods.

"He's the reason you're running."

"Yes."

Her voice is so small and quiet. I remove my ice pack and pivot on the bed to face her. She matches my position.

I reach up my hand and brush my thumb over a make-up-covered cut along her bottom lip.

"He did this to you?"

She nods again, her eyes filling with tears. "When I refused to let him sleep here in my room with me."

The fury within me builds and Sage places her palm on my forearm.

"Don't worry, my mother stepped in and told him to take the guest room. I kept my door locked all night."

"Tell me everything, Sage. Let me protect you."

Her eyes widen, those pooling tears now falling. She jumps up off the bed suddenly.

"You have to leave... they'll... they'll see you. Those guys out there... Chase's guys and... Elias, please... I can't let them hurt you too."

I stand and pull her into my arms.

"Hey, it's okay," I say, cradling her head to my chest. She's sobbing now, and I rub my hand up and down her back, hoping the move soothes her. "You don't have to worry about those men again."

She hiccups and lifts her head.

"What do you mean?"

"I killed them."

"You did?"

Her bottom lip shakes and more tears fall.

"I did."

"I'm so sorry, Elias. He threatened to kill my parents if I didn't..."

I hold her head in my hands and wipe her wet cheeks with my thumbs.

"Didn't what? What was he forcing you to do?"

She searches my eyes, as if gauging how angry I am. As if she thinks I'll harm her after she tells me.

"He... he made me spy on you."

I drop my hands and step back. My heart falls to my stomach. I feared this was the reason. I knew she was too good to be true—that fate didn't bring her to me when I was so desperately lost.

Sage has given me purpose. She challenges me and stands up to me. I've become addicted to her.

But she's working with the enemy.

She shrinks into herself seeing my reaction, cowering as if I'm about to strike out.

I'm going to kill that fucker for making her feel this way.

The fact that my anger is not with her is a good sign. If she were anyone else, she'd already be dead for her betrayal—forced or not.

But I can't kill her.

I could never.

"Who is he, Sage?"

It's clear he's her ex; I just need the details of what he did to her.

Sage sits back on the bed, ice pack on her knuckles. She stares down at the floor and avoids my questioning eyes.

"I left him a few years ago after he used my social security number to apply for as many credit cards as he could get. He maxed them out, then targeted other people. Vulnerable people. That wasn't enough. He started stealing cars for a chop shop. He lost his job and needed money, and it just got worse from there. He went on to deal drugs, first in New Jersey, but obviously he made his way here to New York City. Chase has always been charming, manipulative, and it sounds like that's how he worked his way up to a leadership role.

"He found me the morning after the Christmas party. He told me how he was wanting to take out the local mobs. He wants to take over..." she waves her hand around in front of me, "...whatever the hell you do."

I frown. I don't think she knows exactly *what* the Queensboro Mob does.

"I assume gun running and drug dealing, but I think he's doing more... something worse... like human trafficking."

My head shoots up.

"Human trafficking?"

"I wasn't sure, but I've seen on the news about recent sex trafficking rings being busted, and I put two and two together."

"Does the name Moonlight mean anything to you?"

Her eyes widen, and she nods. "When we were married, Chase would call me his sunshine, and I'd call him moonlight."

I raise my hand to push away a piece of her hair, and she flinches. When she relaxes, I cup her cheek. She closes her eyes and inhales deeply. She's trying so hard not to break down in front of me.

She's being so fucking strong.

"The night we met..." Her bottom lip shakes again, and I refrain from pulling her into my arms again. I can't. Not yet. I need to hear the rest. "I promise I didn't know who you were. Chase had nothing to do with us meeting. He had men at the Christmas party who saw me talking to Noah. He found out we fucked in the bathroom and he..."

"What did he do?"

I drop my hand from her face and fist it next to my thigh. I'm going to fucking murder him.

"He, um... he..."

"Did he put his hands on you? Hurt you like he did tonight?"

She nods, swallowing hard.

"Did he *rape* you?"

Her eyes widen. "No!"

My tense shoulders sag, but anger prevents my body from relaxing completely.

"He was super controlling when we were married, and he'd hit me if I angered him, but he never forced himself on me. But that was then. Now... he's changed. He's even more unpredictable than when we were married. I never feared him then like I do now." She swallows hard, her bottom lip still shaking. "He threatened to kill my parents if I didn't help him. When I told you I didn't know about Noah's life and her involvement with the Empire, I meant it. Us meeting was truly a coincidence, but when Chase found out I was friends with Noah and that you and I were... you know... he made me wear a wire to that dinner."

I curse but Sage's palm on my chest immediately pushes the boiling rage to a simmering point.

"Don't worry. It didn't work. I think it malfunctioned or something."

We sit in silence for a minute or two while I process everything she's told me.

"Why didn't you come to me... or Noah? Either one of us could have helped."

She shakes her head.

"I couldn't take any chances. Chase had men here watching my parents. One call from him and they would have come inside and harmed them... or worse. I wanted to try and figure this out for myself first."

"And did you?"

"I was waiting on my parents to fall asleep, then I was going to take leftovers to those men outside. My mom has some old sleeping pills that I was going to crush and put in the food. Then, when they passed out, I was going to take my parents away and hide them."

I rub my palms over my face.

"I'm sorry, Elias. I never meant to lie to you or deceive you. I did what I had to, even if it wasn't the right thing. Fear led me to make irrational decisions. I realize that now."

Her palm is still flat against my chest. Surely, she can feel how fast my heart is beating.

"Why did you leave me the night we met?"

"Because I was scared. Not of you," she adds quickly. "I was scared to put myself back out there again after giving my heart to someone who didn't deserve me. I was scared because you did more to take care of me than Chase ever did. You protected me without a question. I mean, you killed that man who groped me for fuck's sake. No one's ever done that for me."

I bark a laugh, and she smiles, her watery eyes staring up into mine.

"No one's ever killed someone for you?"

She laughs, and it's the best sound I've heard all night.

"Surprisingly, you're the first. But you know what I mean. No one's ever put me first. No one's ever looked at me the way you did that night... the way you are right now."

"And how am I looking at you, Reine?"

"Like I'm the one who can save you."

Fuck. I'm falling hard and fast for this woman. I knew I was going to fall in love with her from the moment she grabbed the balls of the man who groped her. I just didn't realize loving her would happen so fast.

I won't share my feelings with her just yet. It's too soon, and I need her to see more of the man I am. The dangerous mafia boss who would kill a hundred more men if she asked me to without a second thought.

"I'm going to take care of this, Sage. I have a place your parents can go. They'll be protected."

"What about me?"

"I want you by my side. I'm never letting you go again."

She sucks in a sharp breath. Tears once again threatening to fall down her rosy cheeks.

"Promise you won't tell Noah? Not yet. I need to do it, but I can't put this on her right now. She's got enough on her plate, trying to figure out who's responsible for her mother's murder."

My phone vibrates with a text, and I pull it out of my jacket pocket. It's from Phil letting me know he's tracked down a few of Chase's men in Manhattan. I forward the information to Martin and instruct him to send in some soldiers to grab them.

If Moonlight is heading back to Manhattan now, he'll find out soon that he's been compromised.

Who is this fucker? He seems to have come out of nowhere which has me thinking he's partnered with, or reporting to, someone else.

Someone rich and powerful.

"I won't tell Noah," I say and palm her cheek one more time, because I can't get enough of her.

I'd fuck her right here in her childhood room, while covering her mouth to muffle her moans, but I'm too eager to return to the city and track down her ex to kill him. She's also too vulnerable right now. I can't imagine how hard it was to confess everything.

Did she worry I was going to hurt her? I never want her to think that of me.

I point around her room. "Grab everything that's of value to you. Then wake your parents and have them pack essentials. I can send some men for the rest later. We leave in an hour."

"Where are we going?"

"After I send your parents to a safe house, I'm going to find Chase and kill him."

Chapter 15

Sage

Telling my parents the truth about Chase was probably the hardest thing I've ever had to do. My mom cried, and she's not much of an emotional person so, of course, her crying only made me cry. Meanwhile, Elias had to talk my father down. He was ready to take his hunting rifle off the wall and find Chase to kill him himself.

We told them Elias was an undercover FBI agent who was working to bring Chase and his newfound criminal organization down.

It was close enough to the truth. Elias is going to take Chase down, and he does have connections with the FBI. After knowing Elias could keep me safe, my dad bonded with him. It helped that the two love wrestling. They talked about it during the drive to a small airport outside of New Haven where they boarded Elias's private plane, along with the two QBM soldiers who will be protecting them.

Elias is sending them to a tropical island THAT HE OWNS for safe keeping.

Who even owns a freaking island anyway?

I got it as a gift, he'd said.

Of course. How silly of me.

Thankfully my parents are retired, and they've been eager to travel so they didn't protest being sent away.

We told my parents the men escorting them were also FBI agents. I'm still not sure if they entirely believe the story we told them. Elias does not look like law enforcement. Still, my parents are a good judge of character, and they didn't put up much of a fight when I told them I wouldn't be going with them because I have to help with Chase's capture.

Never mind that Elias is a criminal and killer. My parents must see what I see in him: a good man who will do everything he can to protect me.

I also told Elias what I overheard about Chase's next shipment, and he already has a team prepared to bust it.

Now we're heading back to the city. We've been on the road for an hour and traffic is insane, so we still have another hour to go. I glance over at Elias who's been on the phone most of the ride, barking commands at people.

I admit, it's fucking hot seeing him in full 'boss' mode.

And I shouldn't find all his scrapes and bruises sexy.

He seems to have a new one every time I see him. Like his busted lip and the small cuts on his face that he got during a brawl with his brother.

Noah told me about it and texted me photos of the aftermath. She watched them duke it out, not caring to stop them. She says they have a lot of animosity toward each other that they need to work out on their own.

Now Elias is forming a nice blue and purple bruise underneath his eye where I punched him. I snort, and he glances over at me.

"I'll call you back," he says to whoever he's talking to. "What's so funny, Chérie?"

"I really fucked up your face."

He raises a brow my way. "You're stronger than you think. I watched the surveillance video of you attacking my head of security last week. You know he's dead, right?"

"What? No! I checked to make sure he was alive before I left." I worry my lip and force back the panic crawling up my throat. "Did I really kill him?"

"No, but you could have. You hit him in the temple. He has brain damage now."

"Elias, fuck off and be for real."

"Fine, he doesn't, but you could have seriously injured him."

"You're not funny."

"I'm a little funny." He laughs at his mean joke and reaches his hand out to rest it on my thigh. I'm wearing thick, plush leggings, but I can still feel the heat of his touch.

I resist the urge to squeeze my legs together because the man is making me horny by just existing. If he notices my sudden blush and my heavy breathing, he doesn't act on it.

"What's your real name?"

"Sage."

He slowly rubs his palm from my knee up until he's just inches from my pussy. I've instinctively spread my legs for him.

"Last name, Sage. I know it's not Manilow."

His fingertips graze over the seam of my leggings, and I inhale sharply. My nipples harden underneath the over-sized sweater I'm wearing.

"How do you know that? Did you Google me?"

I yelp when he cups my pussy, the action fast and unexpected.

"I have a guy who does a lot more than Google. Tell me."

He moves his hand up until reaching the waistband of my leggings, still managing to keep his eyes on the road while he slips his fingers behind the material and down until he finds me soaked for him.

"I changed it so Chase couldn't find me."

Ugh. And I'm just now realizing that my parents are still easily searchable. Chase never went to their Connecticut home, but he found them because I did nothing to hide *their* identities. Maybe that's how he found me? He could have called them posing as an old friend and my dad, none the wiser, gave him my Manhattan address.

God, I'm an idiot.

To be fair, I thought Chase would be dumber.

"Real. Name," Elias says and slips a finger inside me. I moan and arch away from the seat as far as the seatbelt will allow me.

"Morgan. Sage Morgan."

Elias pumps his finger in and out of me so slowly, I groan with need for more.

"Nice to meet you Sage Morgan," he says and removes his fingers.

"What the fuck!"

He licks the tips, smiles, then winks.

The fucking audacity of this man.

"What was that for?" I whine.

"Oh, you want to come?" He tsks at me. "You've been a bad girl, Sage. Hiding things, running, not letting me protect you. You don't get to come."

Like the brat that I am, I proceed to slide my own fingers down my pants to finish what he started.

"Sage," Elias warns.

I ignore him and groan when I press down on my clit.

"Don't take what's mine. Don't you dare make yourself come."

"Fuck you," I growl and rub my clit in small circles.

I close my eyes and slip my other hand underneath my sweater to pinch my nipples. I'm moaning and whimpering and slowly reaching the cusp of orgasm when my passenger side door opens.

Oh shit, we've stopped.

On the side of the road.

Elias unlatches my seatbelt and twists me around.

He tugs down my underwear and leggings.

"Elias." His name was meant to be a protest, but it comes out breathy. *Needy.* "The cars... someone could see..."

He slides two fingers inside me, and my head falls back with a moan.

Elias hums. "Your words are saying one thing, but this pussy is saying another. This is turning you on, isn't it? The risk of getting caught?"

He removes his fingers and undoes his belt to fish out his cock. He presses the tip to my opening.

"Yes," I rasp, and he thrusts into me.

I scream, no longer caring who hears... or sees.

"I need you to come fast."

He pistons into me roughly—just how I like it. His hand reaches underneath my sweater, and he takes one of my nipples between his fingertips. He pinches and pulls on the aching peak, and my eyes roll into the back of my head.

"You're being such a good little slut for me. Letting all these passing cars see you getting fucked."

I whimper, not knowing how badly I wanted to be Elias's little slut until this moment.

He kisses me, his lips punishing against my own, and moans into my mouth when my walls clamp down around him.

"So good, Sage. You feel so fucking good. Will you come for me?"

I nod, my forehead flush with Elias's.

His mouth descends on my neck, and he sucks my skin—leaving his mark on me.

The move combined with his fast thrusts and his fingers pinching my nipples sends me over the edge.

He keeps pumping into me until he comes too.

After at least a minute of trying to catch our breath, he slowly removes himself and helps me put my underwear and leggings back on.

Then he twists me back around and secures the seatbelt before closing my door and walking around to the driver's side.

That's when I feel it.

His cum... leaking out of me... soaking my panties.

"What's wrong?" he asks, seeing my wide eyes and red cheeks.

"We fucked without a condom."

"We did. Should I be worried?"

"No. Should I?"

"No. I'm STD free. Just got tested a week ago. Want me to email you the results?"

I'm not sure why I'm making this a big deal. Him fucking me raw was hot as hell and felt so, so good.

The best sex we've had yet.

"Um, hello, babies? Birth control isn't 100% effective."

"I'd happily put a baby inside you." He winks, starts up the SUV, and merges into traffic.

I suck in a sharp breath. "You can't say things like that, Elias."

"Why not?"

"Because we barely know each other. We're not even in a relationship, and you're talking about babies?"

"Oh, we're in a relationship, Chérie. There will be no one else for me or for you. You. Are. Mine."

I scoff because Chase said those same words to me not long ago. Yet hearing them from Elias makes my heart thunder with excitement.

But babies?

As insane as it is to be talking about having a baby with a man I just met a few months ago and have spent a total of two nights with... or is it two and a half? Three? It doesn't matter because I don't hate the idea of having Elias's baby.

"Ugh! You're frustrating."

I cross my arms and turn my head to hide my smile. I can't with this man. He makes me reckless but at the same time, it's... freeing.

I can't tell him that. Not right now when he's so fucking proud of himself.

Let me humble him.

"I'm really the winner here you know."

"Oh?"

"Yeah. You tried to deny me an orgasm and when I threatened to do it myself, you caved and fucked me and gave me my orgasm anyway."

The smug smile drops, and I giggle. He shakes his head and grabs my hand, weaving his fingers with mine. The move makes my stomach flutter. It's such an affectionate act... sweet and loving in comparison to the big and scary man offering me this part of his life.

We don't speak for the rest of the drive, lost in a post-orgasm haze. Elias puts on an indie rock radio station to fill the silence.

Something else I wouldn't expect the violent mafia boss to enjoy. I guess stereotypes in movies and the mafia books I read had me believing he'd be blasting death metal or something.

We arrive in New York City within the hour, and Elias heads to Brooklyn to his penthouse. Two men are waiting outside the entrance when we pull up.

"I'll send someone to your apartment to get some of your things tomorrow."

"I can go."

"Not a chance. Chase will likely be there waiting for you. I'm sure he's already found out I've captured and killed some of his men. He's going to be pissed and want to take it out on you."

I shiver at the thought.

"No working—I need you to take some time off—and no going out in public unless you have my men with you. Understand?"

There's no use fighting Elias. I hold my hand to my forehead and give him a salute. "Yes, sir."

He grabs me by the throat and pulls me in for a kiss.

"Brat," he says against my lips.

Elias nods at someone over my shoulder and turns to get back in the SUV.

"Are you not coming up?"

"I have some leads I need to follow. I won't be around a lot this week, at least not until I find Chase. He's never going to lay another hand on you. I promise you that."

Chapter 16

Sage

"Do you want to tell me why you have two men following you around?"

I choke on my espresso martini, the brown liquid somehow making its way into my nose, burning as it drips out onto the table. I grab a napkin to clean up the mess I'm making.

Noah sits across from me, arms crossed, not amused.

"Someone's following me?"

"Cut the bullshit, bestie."

I roll my eyes. Nothing gets past Noah.

I was wondering when she'd figure everything out.

It's New Year's Eve. Nearly a week since Elias showed up at my parents' house, killed two of Chase's men, and captured about six others working with him. One week of being bored in the penthouse while Elias is out searching for Chase.

I've missed my bossy man.

He's been coming in late, cuddling up with me in my half-asleep state, then in the morning when I wake up, he's gone.

"They're... uh... Elias's men."

"I gathered. *Why* are Elias's men bodyguarding you?"

"Is bodyguarding even a real word?"

"Sage," Noah warns. She casually sips on her vodka tonic while I sit across from her, having a panic attack about telling her the truth.

Will she hate me?

Will she kill me?

"Sage?" Noah's voice has softened, and she reaches across the table to grab my hands. "You know you can tell me anything, right?"

I gulp down the rest of my espresso martini and signal the waiter for another.

"Okay, wow, ordering another drink. This is serious—"

"I've been lying to you."

She opens her mouth to respond, but I can't let her. I have to get it all out while I still have the courage to do so.

"Remember I told you about my ex, how he stole my identity and ran up my credit? Well, it was a lot worse than that. He never went to jail—"

"Wait, why did you tell me that he did?"

I shrug. "I didn't want you to judge me for not turning him in. I also didn't tell you that he cheated."

"Oh, hell no! Where do I find him?"

"Yeah, look, I don't care about the cheating. And I didn't turn him in because he scared me. He threatened me not to say anything to anyone or quote, 'I'd pay.' Well, you can judge me now, call me an idiot, because he moved on to bigger crimes. When he turned to drug dealing, I filed for a divorce. He just got worse from there. He's, like, some wannabe crime lord now. I changed my name so he couldn't find me. It didn't matter. He found me anyway. He showed up at my apartment the day after your father's Christmas party and hit me—"

"I'll fucking kill him."

"—then he threatened to kill my parents if I didn't help him." I know I'm speaking fast. I hope I'm making sense. I take a deep breath and continue. "He wants to take down the QBM and the Empire and start his own mob so he made me wear a wire to your father's dinner—don't worry it didn't work—then he wouldn't let me go visit my parents for Christmas without him, and his goons, escorting me. Elias showed up right as Chase was leaving, and Elias proceeded to kill the two goons babysitting me. For the past week, Elias has been trying to find Chase while I stay at his penthouse because I can't go back to my apartment... or back to work... or out in public without protection. Hence the two big guys back there."

I point over my shoulder.

The waiter returns with my second espresso martini, and I down nearly half of it.

"Holy shit, Sage."

"I know. And I'm sorry. I couldn't tell you. I really wanted to, but Chase said if I told you or Elias, he'd torture my parents."

"Where are your parents now?"

"Elias has them somewhere safe."

Noah shakes her head. "Elias is so fucking obsessed with you. I should be pissed, but it sounds like this is a good thing. He's taking care of it?"

"He is. Chase is behind a lot of the human trafficking that Elias has been busting lately."

"Unbelievable."

"I know. I'm sorry. I didn't want to bother you or Del with this. You two already have a lot to deal with."

"You will never be a bother. And don't worry about us. I'm just glad Elias is taking care of you. He hasn't mentioned any of this to Del or me, and I won't tell Del shit either. He and his brother need to work on their communication problems. If Elias wants to tell him about the woman he's obsessed with and protecting, that's on him. How the hell did he find you anyway?"

"Some real spy bullshit. Something about putting his phone next to yours and cloning it, which gave him access to the tracking app we use."

I refrain from telling Noah that I found this stalkerish behavior extremely endearing. Elias is full of red flags, but my delusional self only focuses on the green ones.

Is killing someone for me a red or green flag?

"Okay, don't ever tell Del about the phone cloning t hing... or the tracking app. He hates that I have a digital footprint."

Our food arrives, and we sit in silence while eating. It's been way too long since Noah and I have had a chance to go out to brunch at Boqueria, our favorite spot in SoHo. The Barcelona-style tapas are to die for, and I always imagine I'm in Spain at some cute little cafe on the waterfront.

Except I don't even have a passport because I've never been outside of the U.S. I've traveled across the country with Chase and his stupid band, but I never had enough money to go anywhere that required a customs check.

I wonder if Elias could take me somewhere in his private plane?

I frown at the thought. My poor parents are in hiding, Chase is still out there probably plotting my demise, and I'm thinking about escaping with the mafia boss who's obsessed with me.

"I actually have something to tell you too," Noah says the moment we're done eating. She takes a sip of her vodka tonic before setting it down and crossing her arms to lean on the table. "I'm not just some mafia princess."

My eyes light up, and Noah holds up her hand. I've heard people use the word to describe Noah before, and I've read it in plenty of mafia romance books, but knowing my best friend is an *actual* mafia princess just makes me giddy as hell.

"I'm not *really* a princess. It's just a term. Anyway, when I started investigating my mother's murder, I came across some vile humans... I couldn't let them live and harm more people, so I started killing them. I gained a reputation because I was good. Because no one expects the fat girl to be a contract killer. I was invisible for the most part. People lowered their guard around me. So, yeah, I'm a contract killer. They call me Colpa Sicario."

Wait.

Noah is a... contract killer. A... murderer?

Holy shit.

Is this real?

Am I having a nightmare or something?

I pinch myself until it hurts.

Okay. Real life, I guess. I mean, why not? My bestie is in the mafia, and she kills people.

"How... how many people have you killed?" I drink the rest of my martini and point at the empty glass when I get the waiter's attention. At this rate, I'm going to need a keg of this stuff.

"Not as many as Del—"

"Del?!?"

I know he's Elias's enforcer, a mafia hitman, but a contract killer too?

"Oh, yeah, he's kinda my rival. He's called the Marionette because of how he sets up the murder scene, including the bodies... like they're puppets. He's killed way more than me which is funny since people say I'm just as good as him." She shrugs. "I lost count, but I'd say dozens."

I must have made a face because she holds up her hands.

"They all deserved it, I swear."

A maniacal laugh bubbles out of me.

Probably because my best friend just told me she's a mother fucking contract killer—and apparently her mafia rival fiancé is too—yet I have no desire to run. I'm not even appalled.

I'm impressed because Noah has always been a badass bitch.

When my bestie laughs, I realize I said that last part out loud.

"It's true. You are a badass bitch. Have been since the day we met."

"So you're not mad at me for not telling you? You're not disgusted or scared of me?"

I shake my head. "I have no room to be mad, especially when I, too, was withholding important information from you. And maybe I've completely lost the plot, because no, I'm not scared. To be honest, I got that vibe from you."

"What vibe?"

"A murdery vibe. You always offered to kill Chase for me, and a part of me suspected you weren't joking. I almost took you up on that offer too. You just make me feel safe."

Noah's eyes fill with tears. Her shoulders, which have been tense all throughout brunch, relax as she reaches out for my hand again. "I was so scared to tell you because I didn't want to lose you. Thank you for being an amazing best friend."

"Well, I should tell you then that my real name isn't Sage Manilow."

Noah laughs and it's such a vibrant sound. A laugh that has only grown brighter the longer I've known her. I think that has something to do with Del.

"I assumed as much. I couldn't find shit on you when I did a background check."

"You did a background check on me?"

"Shortly after we met. Typically, learning someone has a fake identity is a red flag but, I don't know, there was something different about you. I didn't see you as a threat. Honestly, you seemed lost and broken like me."

I frown because she's right. I never knew how much I needed Noah in my life until we met. It's as if my soul had finally found its missing piece. Well, part of my soul.

Is Elias the final piece I've been searching for?

"So, what's your real name then?"

"Sage Morgan."

"It's nice to officially meet you, Sage Morgan." Noah checks her phone for the time. "Okay, it's noon. We have two hours before happy hour ends. Do you want to get day drunk? Del and I are going to celebrate New Year's on the couch later tonight, but I need more bestie time before sexy time."

"Absolutely. Elias and I are also supposed to hang out tonight, but he said he won't be home until closer to six."

"Home? Wow. That sounds serious."

"It's not, I promise."

It's a lie. It feels serious, which terrifies me, especially so soon after my divorce to Chase, but this is different. *Elias* is different.

I realize I still had a lot of healing to do from my time with Chase. Elias might have been exactly what I needed to move on.

My new drink arrives, and Noah orders another.

"Question," I say and take a sip. Noah must see the mischievous look on my face because she raises a brow. "What do you know about getting woken up with sex?"

Noah and I leave Boqueria sloshed, enough that my two bodyguards help me to the SUV. Noah threatened them with bodily harm if I didn't arrive back at Elias's penthouse in one piece, then she sent me off with the best bestie hug. Del showed up to escort her back to their place in Flatbush since Noah was just as drunk as me.

One of Elias's men, whose name is Aaron, hands me a bottle of water, and I suck it down before taking a nap in the backseat.

I wake just as we pull into the horseshoe driveway at Elias's building. He's out there waiting, arms crossed.

Uh oh.

I'm in trouble.

"Okay, who told on me?" I ask the two guards. Neither of them makes eye contact with me.

Narcs.

Elias opens the door.

"Hello, stranger," I say with a wink. "You're home early."

Elias leans in, and I close my eyes, licking my lips expectedly. His mouth tickles mine, but instead of giving me sweet smooches, he unlatches my seatbelt.

"Inside, troublemaker," he says and pulls away.

"Yes, sir." I giggle and give him a two-finger salute which I know he hates but do because it's fun to make him bristle.

Elias helps me out of the SUV, his hand clasping mine before leading me to the building's entrance. He's walking fast, but I have long legs, so I easily keep up with him.

"Am I in trouble, daddy?" I say in a childish voice when we step inside the elevator alone. "Are you going to punish me?"

I stick the tip of my finger between my teeth but my attempt to woo Elias fails. He's giving me the silent treatment. The elevator dings announcing our arrival on the penthouse level. The door opens, and Elias steps out. I rip my hand from his.

"Fine. Be mad at me. I'll just go home," I say as the doors begin to shut.

Before I can take my keycard out of my purse to get the elevator car moving, Elias's large hand stops the doors from closing.

He slowly steps inside, backing me up against the wall and caging me within his arms.

"You *are* home."

I scoff.

"And I'm not mad at you, Sage," he continues, his voice low and dangerous. "I'm *furious*."

"Why? Because I wanted to spend time with my best friend?"

"Because you got drunk. You let your guard down. What if Chase—"

"Your babysitters would have protected me, isn't that why they're following me around?"

He doesn't answer that question. He looks up at the ceiling, avoiding eye contact with me.

"I'm not sorry about getting drunk. I *needed* to get drunk. Can you blame me? Chase returning in my life. This world I'm now a part of—"

Fuck. My voice cracked.

Oh, God, not the tears.

I blame the booze. It always makes me weepy.

"It's *intense* and all too overwhelming. I've been losing my mind this week with you gone, and I've been bored, trying not to let my thoughts get the best of me."

I'm full on crying now, and Elias cups my cheek before wrapping me in his arms. We stand there in the elevator, holding each other for several minutes until he pulls away.

He dries the tears off my cheek—I melt every time he does that. It's such a gentle move from the big, dangerous mafia boss.

"I'm sorry. I was worried and overreacted."

I nod, but I can't say anything because I might start crying again.

"Let's get you inside," he says, his deep voice soft.

In the kitchen, he hands me a glass of water and stands there watching as I drink it all down. He refills it and leads me to his bedroom where he strips me of the sweater and leggings I wore to brunch. Then he puts me in one of his big t-shirts and sweatpants before tucking me in bed.

"I have to go take care of something. Sleep off all those espresso martinis—"

"Hey, how'd you know what I was drinking?"

"Justin sent me photos."

Justin's the other bodyguard.

Fucking narc!

"I'll be back later to make us dinner."

Dinner?

Oh, right. It's New Year's Eve. Elias wasn't even supposed to be home until six.

It's three in the afternoon.

Did he ditch his responsibilities for me?

I really fucked up.

I wanted tonight to be special. Instead, I made the day all about me by getting wasted. Now I can barely keep my eyes open as the man who's a green flag disguised as a red flag continues to save me.

Chapter 17

Elias

The drive to Queens takes longer than expected because of New Year's Eve traffic. Everyone is on the road, likely heading to their party destinations.

My driver pulls through the black iron gates of St. Orion's Cemetery in Fresh Meadows, past the brick arch that's covered in graffiti. Most of the headstones are barely readable and covered in dirt, bird shit, moss, or mildew. Lance has been working with the city to buy the land and take over maintenance. The place has been neglected for years because of the lack of funding.

My mother was one of the last people buried here. Her grave sits at the back in a corner; the last remaining plot of land before St. Orion's was declared at capacity. My brother keeps the grass around her grave cut and the gray marble tombstone clean, and there's always a fresh bouquet in the memorial vase next to her headstone because Lance comes here to visit more often than I do.

Because I'm a shit son.

I add my bouquet of white carnations, purple amaryllises, and pink peonies, complemented by a colorful butterfly decoration to the memorial vase. My mother loved butterflies. She used to spend hours at the Brooklyn Botanic Garden, sitting on a bench, letting the bugs land on her. When I was young, and before my father made me abandon my childhood to shadow him, I'd go with her. The butterflies never liked me. They were drawn to my mother, though. She believed a butterfly landing on you represented joy or change.

I place my hand on the curved top of the headstone.

"Hey, Ma," I say, barely able to push my voice past the ache in my throat. "Sorry I don't come around much."

I could list all the reasons why, but there's no excuse.

It took me years to build the courage to visit. I was too overcome with my grief and guilt about her death to allow myself to mourn her. Lance was forced to end her life, yet he manages to come here at least once a week, sometimes more.

I meant to come by on Christmas Eve this year, on the anniversary of her death. Yet again, I failed.

It's just... every time I'm here, when I see her name and the year of her death, I'm taken back to that night twenty years ago, holding her in my arms, blood covering her front side.

Seeing her corpse haunts my nightmares, and I couldn't let it bleed into my waking hours.

Meeting Sage has changed my perspective. Seeing her sacrifice herself to protect her parents from Chase made me realize I'm a fucking asshole. I wasted years not honoring my mother by refusing to visit her final resting place.

She deserves better than that.

"We're close, Ma. I can feel it. We're so fucking close to nailing your murder—all the mafia wives' murders—on Lenetti."

I crouch and trace the letters of her name.

Imogen Carter

A Loving Mother & Wife

"I met someone... her name is Sage. She's a firecracker. You would have loved her. She keeps me on my toes and doesn't take any of my bullshit. She reminds me of you in a way. She's brave, defiant. She hasn't let me, or this life, scare her away."

Yet.

The word sits on the tip of my tongue because it's only a matter of time before Sage sees too much and leaves me.

They always do.

She's different, though.

I let the thought give me hope because if Sage wants no part of this life, my life, then that means having no part of Noah's life too.

Would she abandon her best friend just to run away from me?

Maybe she's tired of running.

I now know a big part of her fear is Chase.

I wipe my palm down my face.

"You might think I'm crazy, Ma, but I might just love this woman. I mean, we haven't known each other very long. Well, that's mostly because she kept running from me, but now that I have her... I don't think I can let her go."

I stand and palm the headstone one last time.

"I should get back to her. I'd love to bring her to meet you next time. I know this was a short visit, but I promise I'm working on that. I just want you to know that I think about you all the time."

I turn to leave and wipe my damp eyes with the back of my hand.

When I get to the SUV parked on the small roadway that winds through the cemetery, I turn back to the corner where her grave sits.

A chill washes over me and the hairs on the back of my neck rise.

I let my eyes scan the cemetery, but despite the feeling of being watched, I see no one.

Maybe it was Ma letting me know that she's always watching over me.

After leaving the cemetery, I check in with my uncle.

We still have a couple of Chase's men locked in the basement of Underground Park Slope. I've been torturing them for information, but they're useless. Either Chase told them the bare minimum, or he's been one step ahead. Every lead we follow has led to a dead end.

Lance knows I've been trying to destroy this asshole human trafficker, but I haven't told him that it's Sage's ex. Though after Sage and Noah's boozy brunch, I'm sure he'll find out soon. If Sage told Noah, surely she'll go blab it to my brother.

He's texted me a few times this past week, asking where I disappeared to. He's worried I'm going to back out of this plan to take down the Lords. I keep assuring him I'll be there, but I understand his lack of trust when it comes to me.

I don't fault him for that.

When I walk into the penthouse, the scent of cookies hits my nose. I follow it, drooling, all the way to the kitchen where I find Sage bent over at the oven. She's shaking her ass, mumbling unintelligible words.

Her phone sits on the counter with her music app pulled up.

Oh. She can't hear me. She has earbuds in.

I slowly walk up behind her, grab her by the hips, and grind my cock into her ass.

She yelps and jerks, then screams.

"Goddamn it, Elias Carter."

Oh, she pulled out the first *and* last name.

Sage closes the oven and takes out her ear buds with one hand while cradling the other to her chest.

Panic rolls through me. "What happened?"

"I burned my hand, asshole."

Okay, I deserve that.

After setting the ear buds on the counter, she turns the faucet on and sticks her fingers and palm under the water.

"Do you need ice?"

She shakes her head. "Ice could make it worse."

"I'm sorry. I was trying to be cute."

"No need to try, Elias. You're already cute."

"And sexy?"

She rolls her eyes, struggling to hold back her smile.

"Did you bake cookies?"

Her smile pushes through her anger, and her face lights up.

"I did. I started my period, and I desperately needed sweets. You didn't have anything, so I ordered delivery to make some." She holds up a finger, anticipating my complaint. "Don't worry. I used the credit card you left me. I'm broke, not stupid. And, yes, I sent one of your guards to get the groceries from the lobby."

She turns off the water and dries her hands with the towel hanging on the front of the stove.

Grabbing a cookie from the plate sitting on the counter, she holds it up to my mouth.

"Here, try."

I take a big bite out of the sweet treat. It's ooey, gooey, chocolatey, and...

Oh. Fuck.

"Sage," I mumble. "Are there nuts in this?"

"Yep! Walnuts. My fav."

I curse and spit the rest of my bite into the sink. Her eyes widen.

"Holy shit, Elias. Are you allergic to walnuts?"

"Walnuts, cashews, pecans... all tree nuts, but they're not as bad as peanuts."

The last two words sounded garbled as my tongue starts to swell. I take off my suit jacket and toss it to the floor before reaching for my EpiPen and inhaler. I keep them in a custom-made holster that sits under the shoulder holster for my guns. I check my Benadryl bottle, which I also keep in the holster, and curse realizing I'm out of pills and forgot to refill it.

"Benadryl. Bathroom."

She understands, despite my words being strained, and before leaving the kitchen, she tosses the whole plate of cookies into the trash.

While she's gone, I stab myself in the thigh with the medicine and use my inhaler. Sage returns after a couple minutes wearing medical gloves. Fuck, I didn't even think to tell her to wash her hands and put on gloves.

She hands me two pills, and I swallow them down without water.

"Should I call 911?"

I shake my head, already feeling the epinephrine working its way through my system. I unarm myself and loosen the collar of my dress shirt to help me breathe better, then I fish my phone from my pants pocket and shoot a text to my doctor. He lives in a condo a few streets away, so he'll be here within five minutes.

I also text my cleaner who lives in the building. They'll need to sanitize the kitchen and toss the contraband.

"What do you need, Elias? Let me help you."

Sage's concern nearly has me struggling to breathe for a different reason. I rarely have someone offer to take care of me.

"Oxygen tank," I wheeze. "Bathroom closet."

She's turning on her heel without a second thought and returns in record time. When I reach out to take the mask, she smacks my knuckles and puts the mask on me herself.

She's so careful and gentle, making sure the straps aren't too tight.

"You have a lot of medical supplies in your closet. You really don't want to go to a hospital, do you?"

I shake my head, unable to speak to tell her that hospitals complicate things. They leave paper trails—well, I suppose it's all digital now, which is even worse because Elias Carter, mafia Don, doesn't do digital. Even if most of New York City knows me as Johnny Goode, I'd rather not have my blood or fingerprints uploaded to a system that could be hacked or accessed by law enforcement officials who I don't have on my payroll.

I close my eyes, letting the air flow through my constricted throat. Sage stands at my shoulder, one hand rubbing up and down my pec while the other combs through my hair.

I might intentionally have allergic reactions if this is the result.

The Benadryl, oxygen, and epinephrine work fast, and my swollen tongue has gone down. When Doctor Wicker arrives, he gives me a corticosteroid shot before checking my vitals.

Sage watches intently as if memorizing everything he's doing to utilize at another date. Doctor Wicker then gives her instructions to monitor my symptoms for the rest of the night and hands over a card telling her to call him if I show any signs of the inflammation returning.

"I am so sorry," Sage says, the moment he leaves. Her eyes well up with tears, and I wave her over to the couch where I'm sitting. Doc let me take off the oxygen mask but said to keep it nearby just in case.

"There's nothing to be sorry about," I say, wrapping my arms around her waist when she sits on my lap.

She hugs my head to her chest, and I stifle the urge to motorboat the plush mounds.

Inappropriate, Elias. She's clearly traumatized.

"You could have died!"

"I've had plenty of allergic reactions, and I'm still here."

"Walnut and chocolate chip cookies are my favorite, and I just wanted to share something I love with you. I legit almost killed you."

"I should have asked before taking a bite."

Sage gasps. "Wait. We had Pad Thai that one time. Doesn't that have peanuts?"

"Thai Villa is a nut free restaurant. And even restaurants that aren't nut free are fine. Cross contamination doesn't give me that big of a reaction as eating a whole nut, but it'll still make me itchy, and my throat will swell slightly. I'd rather not risk it, though."

"Oh."

She sighs, and we sit there in silence for a few minutes. I listen as her frantic heartbeat slows now that the adrenaline of my allergic reaction has waned.

"Could you imagine if your enemies learned this? Death by nut!" Sage giggles.

She loosens her hold on me and leans in for a kiss but pauses, her eyes wide.

"I need to brush my teeth. I put a lot of walnuts in the cookies and ate two before you got here. I need to clean up the kitchen too."

"Don't worry. My cleaning staff already scrubbed it down while we were in here with the doctor."

Sage's mouth drops open.

"I didn't even notice. I should have taken care of it. This is my fault."

I swallow hard. She thought of all this for me? Brushing her teeth, cleaning the kitchen, wearing gloves...

"I'm surprised this is the first time you've had a reaction around me. I really like nuts. I buy the cans that have the cashew, walnut, and peanut mix to snack on at work." She gets off my lap and winks at me. "Good thing I like you more."

I sit on the couch, stunned, at... everything. Sage not hesitating to help ease my symptoms. Her being proactive to make sure I don't get sick again. Her insinuating that she would give up her favorite foods for me.

After I've shaken off my disbelief, I head into the kitchen and start setting out everything for dinner: dough, sauce, pepperoni, sausage, cheese, onions, bell peppers, olives, and mushrooms.

When Sage returns from brushing her teeth, her face lights up upon seeing the spread.

"Pizza?"

"*Homemade* pizza." I point over my shoulder at the brick oven next to the stove.

"I was wondering what that was when I snooped earlier. I didn't open it though."

"Find anything interesting?"

She shakes her head, biting her lip. "I didn't get far because I got hungry, so I came in here and made a sandwich, then I craved the cookies and... well, you know the rest."

Now that everything's ready for assembling, we need some tunes.

"Help me pick out some music." I say and take Sage's hand, leading her into the living room to my bookcase full of records.

"Lord, how can I? There must be a thousand records here!"

I shrug. "About 500."

Her eyes scan over the spines of the albums. She nearly jumps for joy when spotting one of interest. I have them organized in alphabetical order, so I know exactly which one she picked, but she doesn't let me see as she hides it behind her body. She pushes me out of the way to stick it on the platter.

"Go stand over in that open space," she says, pointing to the area near the windows.

When I don't move, she puts her hands on her hips.

"Be a good boy and do as Madam Manilow says."

"Madam Manilow?"

A grin spreads across her face. "That's my name on the Madam app."

Before I can open my mouth, and maybe she can see my face fill with rage and jealousy, she holds up a finger.

"Don't get your panties in a twist. It's solely virtual."

"For your information, I'm a boxers guy."

"Yeah, because tighty-whities wouldn't be able to hold that horse in your pants."

She points at the open space again.

"Go, *Boss Man*."

I hold up my hands in defeat and do as Sage demands, but make a mental note to look into that fucking app.

The moment *Great Balls of Fire* by Jerry Lee Lewis starts playing, she shimmies her way over to me and takes my hand in hers then places my other hand at her waist.

"I don't dance."

"Neither do I."

"Yes, you do. I watched you on the dance floor of Underground Park Slope."

"That's different. I was just moving my hips around. We're going to swing dance."

The song is past the intro, and I move when Sage moves. We're making shit up as we go. I twirl her around and she spins, and I tug her back toward my body. We gallop around the open space of my living room for the rest of the song and despite having no clue what I'm doing, I seem to be in sync with Sage.

By the end of the song, I'm smiling until my cheeks hurt. I'm also struggling to breathe.

"Oh, shit," Sage says and rushes over to the table for the oxygen tank. It's not a large one. I always keep small portable ones nearby whether it's here at home or in the car.

She hands me the tank, and I sit on the edge of the couch to slip on the mask.

"Probably not the best idea to be dancing around after trying to kill you," she says, rubbing my back while I breathe.

"You didn't try to kill me."

After a few minutes, the album Sage chose—which is a compilation of rock-n-roll hits from the fifties—changes songs to *Can't Help Falling in Love* by Elvis Presley.

I take off the oxygen mask and stand, holding out my hand. Sage shakes her head.

"Hand, woman!"

She scoffs but smiles and gives in.

"Slow dancing I can do," I say, giving Sage a wink. "Rain check on the dance party for another night when I haven't just had an allergic reaction?"

"I'll hold you to it," she says.

"I don't doubt it."

Sage sighs and lays her head on my chest while we turn in slow circles in the middle of my living room.

I don't think I've ever slow danced in the middle of my living room. Or any living room, for that matter. It's only something I've seen in cheesy rom-coms.

My life isn't romantic.

But for Sage, I'd hold up a boombox outside her bedroom window while it plays *In Your Eyes* by Peter Gabriel.

I'd pay a marching band to play in a stadium while I sang to her from the stands.

I'd buy a ukulele and play it on a plane while singing a song about growing old with her.

I knew since the night we met she was going to be different. Especially when she didn't hesitate to choose death for the man who groped her. When she didn't let my dark side scare her. When she showed me her compassion and empathy by kissing the tattoo on my wrist in tribute to my mother.

I might have jerked it away from her in that moment, but it's only because I was confused. I was *surprised*. I was also worried that if I told her what happened, she wouldn't understand and leave.

The song comes to end, and Sage is the first to pull away.

I already miss her warmth.

We return to the kitchen, and Sage helps me assemble the pizza. She gasps when *Unchained Melody* by The Righteous Brothers comes on and we proceed to recreate the pottery scene from *Ghost* with the pizza dough. Except a lot messier because the dough sticks to our fingers.

It is far from sexy.

My favorite part of playing house with Sage is finding out she can sing. She's belting out words, hitting the notes, and outshining the artist.

"You're a singer?" I ask when the song is over.

"I'm alright," she says with a shrug. "I do love me some karaoke, though."

"I've never been to karaoke."

"What?"

"I never went to prom or been camping. Never went bowling or played laser tag. Never went to a haunted house—Mom wasn't a fan of Halloween. The last time I played a board game, or a video game, I was just a kid."

Sage is next to me now, assembling her pizza since we decided to make two, each with our favorite toppings. I chose everything. Sage forwent the sausage, olives, and mushrooms.

She frowns. "Is it because your father wouldn't let you?"

"Yes." I pause, not sure if I want to talk about what I went through in my childhood, but it's only fair since Sage has shared so much with me already. "I blocked out a lot of my memories from my childhood because of him. Mostly the bad things. I remember the good parts, like playing board games with my mom and Lance when I was twelve. Mom also got me a Nintendo for my thirteenth birthday. I used to kick my brother's ass at *The Legend of Zelda*. But when I turned sixteen, my father threatened to destroy the game system. He said it was a distraction from my responsibilities to the QBM. I didn't want Lance to lose the games, he deserved to hold on to his childhood as long as possible, so I pretended I was no longer interested in playing with him. I did everything I could to distance myself from him because if I showed him any sort of love or care, my father would have focused on him instead of me. I know Lance was upset about that, but I did it to protect him."

Sage stops assembling her pizza and puts her palm on my forearm.

"Have you told him any of this?"

"I can't. He would be heartbroken. He would blame himself. He already thinks I hate him. He thinks I blame him for what those men forced him to do to our mother. I didn't blame him, but I *did* shut him out. I regret it, but at the time, I was only sixteen. I felt *guilty* that he had to be the one to do it. But I shut him out because I knew that my father would punish him if he found out. I told Lance not to say a word about that night. My father tried beating it out of him, and when Lance refused to speak, he was sent to a psychiatric hospital. It was better that way. I was Percy Carter's heir. He saw Lance as a mistake and the reason his wife was dead."

Since both of our pizzas are nearly assembled, I turn from the island and preheat the oven.

"What happened after Del got out?"

"He was released when he turned eighteen. I picked him up and was an even bigger asshole, basically telling him to take care of himself because I didn't have time to be a parent to him. Our father was diagnosed with cancer at that point, and he disappeared upstate to die in hospice. He refused to let us see him in his state. Not that we wanted to. I already had too much to take care of because of Percy. He forced responsibility over the QBM on me, and he left it such a fucking mess. Corrupt to the bone, his own soldiers not trusting him and going rogue."

"I'm so sorry, Elias," Sage says.

I take the pizza peel and slide it under her pizza then transfer it to the brick oven. She watches in awe as I repeat the move with my pie.

"It was a relief that he died. My father was pure evil. He eventually found out my brother was forced to slit our mother's throat because he beat me until I gave it up. I think he was more pissed about being targeted than our mom being killed. He tried to connect Lenetti to the murders up until the day he died, then he left Lance and me all his notes. Now we've taken over the investigation."

"What piece are you missing?"

"The actual order. It's complicated, but I don't want to start a mafia war until we have solid proof." I lean up against the kitchen island, arms crossed, while we wait for the pizza to cook. "And we still haven't figured out who blew up Noah and Lance's apartment building."

"I thought Noah said that was an accident? A gas leak?"

"Nope."

Sage scoffs and shakes her head. Oops. Didn't mean to spill the beans on Noah's secret.

I push away from the island to stand in front of Sage. Extending my arms on either side of her to trap her in, I lean down.

"Have I told you how beautiful you look today?"

She shies away from the compliment.

"Don't lie. I feel so gross right now. I'm bleeding, bloated, and cramping."

"Hmm." My lips graze over the side of her neck, and she gasps ever so lightly. "Did you know sex can help alleviate period cramps?"

"Can it now?"

"Yep."

"How do you know that?"

"I just know." I slip my hand down the front of her leggings, and she freezes. "Have you never fucked while on your period?"

"No," she answers, her word barely a whisper. "Chase thought it was gross, and I never considered it for any of my one-night stands."

I tease her opening, my fingertip grazing over the string of her tampon.

She whimpers.

"Tell me to stop, and I will."

She bites her lip, lust and hesitation lighting up her face in a fight for dominance.

"I don't want you to stop," she finally says.

Slowly, I pull down her leggings and help her step out of the material.

"If you feel uncomfortable at any time, let me know and I'll stop, okay?"

She nods.

"I need you to use your words, Sage."

"Okay. I understand."

"Good girl."

Chapter 18

Sage

Holy shit. I can't believe I'm doing this.

I'm going to let Elias fuck me while on my period.

In my experience, men get uncomfortable when I talk about my time of the month. They frantically find a way to change the subject, don't make eye contact with me, or try to be funny, but it only ends up being weird.

Elias washes his hands, then crouches on the floor before me. The urge to cover myself is strong.

"Put your hands on the counter, Sage. I see you itching to use them."

I plant them at my sides, clutching the marbled edge.

"Open your legs for me," Elias says, tapping my knee.

I do as he orders and immediately feel exposed.

Elias's palm skims up the inside of my thigh, and I hold my breath.

"Relax, Sage. It's just a little blood."

Right. The murdering mafia boss isn't afraid of blood.

His fingertips tickle my opening as he attempts to grab the tampon string. Once he has a hold on it, he tugs and pulls it free.

The first day of my period is always the heaviest so of course blood drips out of me with nothing to catch it.

I jerk the moment Elias's finger enters me, pumping in and out of me slowly at first.

My breath hitches.

Fuck.

That feels good.

He picks up speed, and his thumb finds my clit and starts massaging it. My eyes roll back in my head.

He brings me to the cusp of orgasm before he stops. I'm about to yell at him but next thing I know, he's lifting me off the floor.

"What the fuck?!"

He lays me down on the island countertop, sending veggies, pepperoni, and sausage to the floor.

He spreads me open to get better access to my clit, then descends on my pussy and resumes pumping. My hands find his hair and fist the strands, attempting to pull him closer to me.

"Yes, fuck, Elias."

I slide my hands under my shirt and grab my nipples to pinch and pull.

"I'm close," I moan.

Elias sucks on my clit, lashing his tongue over the swollen nerves and adds a second finger. He drives into me at the perfect speed, and my walls clamp around the digits.

Then he stops and removes his fingers.

I'm going to stab him.

I feel around the countertop for the knife I'd been using to cut veggies, but Elias knocks it out of my hand just as I grab it.

"Naughty girl," he says, amused at the way he's torturing me.

He looks so sinister smiling with a bloody chin, mouth, and nose. He fishes his cock out of his pants and uses *my blood* for lubrication.

My head falls back with a groan.

"Hang on to me," he says and tugs my ass off the edge enough to slide into me in one fast thrust.

I hold on the best that I can while he drives into me.

The sound of our bodies slapping together is loud enough to drown out the music of the record playing in the living room.

"Yes, Boss, please," I say because he's worked me up to the point where I'm already reaching climax.

"Lift your shirt. Let me see your glorious tits, Ma Chérie."

I do, and he descends on them, latching on like a hungry man before a four-course meal.

His teeth graze over one of my nipples and Elias moans, clearly feeling my pussy walls work around him.

"Choke me," I say, and he doesn't think twice.

His large hands wrap around my throat, and he squeezes.

"Tap my arm if it's too much," he says.

I barely hear him because I'm lost in ecstasy. I've never been fucked like this... He's feral, his hips jerking into me as my ass hangs off the kitchen island. His hands—that have caused many deaths—tight around my throat. He could easily squeeze harder and kill me. The thought excites me and sends me over the edge.

He releases my neck and pauses while my walls massage his cock, then he picks up his thrusts to chase his own release.

It doesn't take long.

One last pump, and he stills while he pours cum inside me.

He buries his face in my neck, breathing hard. To be fair, he did all the work, holding up all 250 pounds of me.

Not to mention he just had an allergic reaction. He should be taking it easy, not dancing and fucking.

"Fuck, Sage, that was good."

The timer on the pizza oven dings, and I burst out laughing.

"Perfect timing," I say.

Elias chuckles, then he carefully removes himself from me.

He gives me a peck on the cheek, careful of his mouth being covered in my period blood.

"Go get cleaned up, and I'll get our pizza plated." He helps me off the counter. "What do you want to drink?"

"Maybe a ginger ale. I don't need any more alcohol after getting drunk at brunch today."

"I got you something," I say when we're done eating and sitting on the couch listening to another record featuring songs from the sixties. I've learned it's Elias's favorite era of music. He likes music from the seventies, eighties, and nineties too. He blanched when I told him my favs were Lady Gaga, Taylor Swift, and Adele.

"What do you mean?" Elias asks, finishing up a text message and setting his phone down on the table next to the couch.

"A Christmas present. I know it's a little late, but you obviously didn't get to celebrate this year because of me so..."

"You didn't need to do this," he says as I hand him a box and a bag. "I don't celebrate Christmas. Plus, I didn't get you anything."

"Yes, you did. You saved me from Chase."

"That's not a gift, Sage. It was a necessity."

"Still... I just wanted to make sure you knew how much I appreciate you being a Level 100 Clinger and stalking me."

He rolls his eyes at the Level 100 Clinger remark.

"Look, I know you couldn't save your mom, and you've been living with your guilt and regret over that... but think of all the lives you've saved since. The women in those shipping containers...me..."

He clears his throat and looks away.

I place my palm over his knuckles. He's clinging onto the wrapped box hard enough that they're starting to turn white.

"I don't deserve this," he whispers.

"You do, and if you don't open these gifts right now, I'm going to kick your ass."

He barks out a laugh, and I relax a little because I was worried giving him a gift was the wrong move. He wasn't mad about it... just surprised and feeling unworthy.

He rips the Christmas tree themed wrapping paper to shreds, then extracts a knife from his ankle to cut the tape of the box.

Inside is another box.

"A WWE Lego set?"

I nod enthusiastically.

"Did you ever play with Legos as a kid?"

He shakes his head slowly, staring at the box in awe.

"Wait, I just realized I don't know how old you are."

He lets out a puff of breath. "Thirty-six."

"When's your birthday?" I ask.

"July twentieth. What about you? You're, what? Thirty-three?"

"In February. My birthday is February 2nd. Groundhog Day."

I take the Lego box off his lap and hand him the bag decorated with a bunch of dancing Santas.

"Next one."

He doesn't hesitate this time and pushes past the tissue paper until spotting the gift. He lifts his head, tears welling in his beautiful, dark blue eyes.

"Sage," he nearly sobs. He pulls the gift out of the bag. "A championship belt?"

"Yep! And look," I turn it over and point at the name on the back. "John Cena signed it."

"How?"

"I know a guy who knows a guy."

I don't tell him that the bouncer at Club 99 SoHo, who I was sleeping with up until meeting Elias, is a part-time wrestler and good friends with John Cena's former agent. I made a call a few days ago and the belt arrived by courier last night.

I wasn't sure who his favorite is, but I know there are some wrestlers who don't align with his political views, but Cena does and based on his reaction, it was a good choice. CM Punk would have worked too, but I don't know anyone connected to him.

"And..." I reach into the bottom of the gift bag. "Tickets to see a live taping of WWE Raw. They film in California so we'd have to take a plane, obviously after all this mess with Chase is taken care of, but maybe we can go to Disneyland when we're out there. I've never been. I mean, I traveled all around the country with Chase, but we never had time to do tourist stuff. I haven't even been out of the country, so I have a lot of catching up to do. I'm sure you've been everywhere. You own a freakin' island for fuck's sake—"

"Sage," Elias says, interrupting my nervous rambling.

"Sorry, I know that's a lot of future promises, and we still don't know each other well enough for me to be making plans with you, so you can tell me if you don't want to go. The tickets are open-ended, and you can take anyone you want—"

"Sage!" he barks. "You're the only one and, yes, we will go to Disney World. If you want, I'll buy out the entire park for one day, just for you and me."

"It's Disneyland. Disney World is in Florida. I've never been there either."

He sighs and grabs me by the chin.

"After we get rid of Chase, I promise you that I will fly you anywhere you want to go. Disneyland, Disney World, London, Paris, Italy?"

I nod.

"Scotland, Tokyo, Costa Rica?"

I nod again.

"Turks and Caicos, Hawaii, Antarctica?"

"Oh, maybe not Antarctica. Too cold. Though, I wouldn't mind hanging out with some penguins."

Elias kisses me and it's the kind of kiss that would give rom-com kisses a run for their money. *Can't Take My Eyes Off You* by Frankie Valli plays on the record player and all that's missing is cheers from bystanders and my leg lifting up in delight.

When Elias releases me from the soul-searching kiss, he rests his forehead on mine.

"Thank you, Sage. This is the best thing that's happened to me in a very long time."

This time, I kiss him, because my heart breaks at his words. I can't imagine what it was like for him being forced to grow up too fast. To be abused by the person who was supposed to keep him safe and love him at all costs. And to find the one parent who actually showed him that love and safety dead in a pool of her own blood.

We spend the rest of the night watching movies, including *Ghost*, inspired by our pizza dough moment earlier. We turn the channel to the ball drop at Times Square just in time to count down to midnight. Then we kiss and fall asleep together on the couch.

Best. New Year's Eve. Ever.

Chapter 19

Sage

Staten Island?

Why was Noah on Staten Island?

It's been a little over a week since New Year's. Elias and I spent two whole days together before he had to leave to take care of mafia business.

Nearly a whole week of him being gone most of the day, only to return at night when I'm tucked in bed. I've been bored as fuck.

I texted Noah this morning to see if she wanted to hang out today, but now it's nearly nine at night, and she still hasn't answered me back—which isn't like her. I pull up the tracking app to pinpoint her whereabouts. It shows me everywhere she's been today, and she was out on Staten Island for about half an hour.

Now her location is no longer showing up, and her phone is going straight to voicemail. Del and Elias aren't picking up either.

I have a bad feeling.

I've attempted to grill Elias's security men but either they know nothing, or they've been instructed not to say anything. I'm two seconds from fighting these fuckers and leaving to track down my bestie and my—wait, how do I label this relationship... mafia boyfriend?—when the penthouse doors open.

I'm coming in hot as I approach the front.

"Where the hell have you..."

My words trail off and my steps slow when I take in his appearance. He looks like he's been hit by a truck.

"What happened?"

I reach up to take his head in my hands, and he closes his eyes before wrapping his fingers around my wrists. He says nothing as he lifts my hands away to kiss my palms, one after the other.

"Elias?"

"Let's sit down."

"What. Happened?" I repeat. Pressure builds behind my eyes, and my throat pinches with the threat of tears.

"Noah..."

I rip my wrists out of Elias's grip and step back, shaking my head.

"No. NO!"

"Sage." Elias moves toward me, but I step back again. Hurt fills his eyes, but he's quick to shake it off.

Staten Island.

Oh, God.

Was today the day they went through with their plan to take down the Lords?

"Tell me. Is she…"

I can't even say the words as tears begin falling.

"She was hurt. She's in a coma."

I cover my mouth with my palm and turn away. I hate how much I cry around this man.

Except he's never been turned off by the emotional mess that I am. Not like Chase was. Instead, Elias comes up behind me and wraps his arms around me.

I turn and bury my head in his soft chest.

"There was a shootout at the Lords Mansion, and Noah was taken by surprise by one of the members. He stabbed her. The doctor said she'll make a full recovery, but they had to put her in a coma to help her injuries heal faster."

"Did I do this?"

"What? Why would you think that?"

"I told Chase—"

"No. Sage, listen to me. There's no way Chase would have known the details of our plan or the day we were going to confront Finn."

I let out a relieved sob, and Elias squeezes me a little bit tighter. I don't even care that I can barely breathe. I would let him suffocate me right now to silence the worry taking over my thoughts.

We stand there for a few minutes while this big, scary mobster soothes me. A part of me feels like I don't deserve his gentle touches. The way he rubs his large hand up and down my spine. How he kisses the top of my head. How I feel *safe* in the hands of a man who uses them to end lives.

Out of all the women who walked through the doors of his club in Park Slope, he chose me. I mean, sure it was all about fucking at first, and yeah, he's a little stalkerish.

But he's *my* obsessive stalkerish mafia boss.

I pull out of his embrace... and immediately notice fresh blood on my arm.

"What the hell? Elias, are you hurt? Is this your blood?"

I start patting him down. He's wearing all black, which makes it difficult to locate the wound.

"Sage, I'm fine."

I ignore him and graze my fingertips up and down his chest and stomach then to his arms. He hisses when they skim over his right shoulder. I pull my hand away and find blood on the fingertips. Without saying a word, I take him by the wrist and drag him to the bathroom.

"Why didn't you go to someone to get this taken care of?" I ask, sitting him down on the toilet seat.

"One of my medics got the bullets out. I wouldn't let him stitch me up."

"Why the fuck not?"

"Because I needed them to treat my soldiers who had far worse injuries than me."

He says it so casually like his life isn't as important.

I know that's a trauma response of always being in charge and having no one to take care of him, especially growing up. It hurts my heart that he's never had the gentle touch of someone who cares about him.

At least, not since his mother died.

I don't know his relationship history, but I'm going to guess that he hasn't let anyone get close to him.

I have to wonder why I'm different.

The bandage that was slapped over the bullet hole in Elias's shoulder is doing nothing to stop the blood. It's soaked through the dark shirt he's wearing.

"Elias, you need stitches."

"I know."

"Can't you call that doctor who came over to help with your allergies that one time?"

"He's a doctor who makes home visits to Johnny Goode, business owner, not Elias Carter, mafia boss."

"Then what was your plan?"

"Stitch myself up. The wounds aren't that bad. Mostly superficial."

Shaking my head, I turn to the closet in his bathroom. A first aid kit sits on the middle shelf. It's not your typical first aid kit. It's bigger with a lot more supplies.

Because he gets injured all the time.

The thought both angers and saddens me. I remember seeing the scars on his other arm and shoulder and on the right side of his stomach. I counted five little circles total.

And that doesn't include scars from stab wounds and the ones he's yet to tell me about.

"I don't know how to do it," I say, my breath barely a whisper.

Surprisingly, the blood hasn't grossed me out yet. I think my concern over Elias is masking that.

"I can show you."

He sets supplies out on the counter including a suture kit with a packaged curved needle, the sutures, and scissors, some antiseptic and saline solution, soap, gauze, and bandages.

Picking up the needle first, he takes it out of the packaging and strings the thread through the eye. "It's just like sewing. Do you know how to sew?"

"Not anymore. I did as a kid, though. I sewed patches on my Girl Scouts sash."

"Perfect. It's like riding a bike."

"I fell off my bike all the time."

"I just mean stitching up a wound is as simple as sewing on your patches."

"I'm pretty sure it's not and actually my patches fell off because I sucked at sewing."

"Sage," he sighs. "If you don't want to do it, it's fine."

"Just... Tell me what to do."

He searches my eyes for a few seconds before pointing at the needle in my hand.

"Douse that with antiseptic first, then take the gauze and pour saline solution on it to clean the bullet hole."

"Not alcohol?"

"A misconception. Alcohol can cause tissue damage."

I swallow hard and nod. I won't let my nerves show. He needs me to be strong. Besides, I should get used to him coming home injured—

Did I really have that thought?

I'm talking as if we're married, and I've moved in.

Haven't I, though? I haven't stayed at my apartment since before Christmas.

"I can do it, Sage," he says, his voice soft and understanding.

He holds out his hand for the needle, but I shake my head. "I'm fine."

He cups my cheek. "It's really not that bad."

I playfully try to bite his fingers, getting a hearty chuckle from him, which lightens the heaviness resting on my shoulders.

"Blood is leaking out of you, and your arm is soaked."

"Some of that blood is not mine."

I hold back my gag and close my eyes, inhaling slowly before letting out a long stream of breath.

Then I get to work.

After washing my hands, I disinfect the needle and his arm as Elias instructed. Willing my hands to steady, I focus on the bullet hole. I sink the sharp tip into his skin. If it hurts, he doesn't let it show. In fact, he's on his phone, texting with one hand while I literally stitch him up.

I hate to admit that he was right about the 'riding a bike' remark. I even found sewing human skin together easier than sewing Girl Scout patches onto a sash. Or maybe I'm more motivated because if I fuck this up, I could nick a vein, and Elias could bleed out and die. Or it could get infected, and he could die.

Okay, maybe I'm being dramatic. There aren't any major blood vessels in shoulders. I don't think. Whatever, I'll Google it later.

By the time I'm done, I'm sweating, and my heart is beating a mile a minute. I use the scissors to cut the stitch and tie a little knot. I don't even know if I was supposed to tie a knot but how else would the stitch not come undone?

Elias looks down at my work.

"Impressive."

I roll my eyes and wash my hands in the sink. "Now what?"

"Use soap and water to clean the wound again, then cover it with the bandage."

Since the hard part is over, I'm ready for him to start talking.

"Tell me what happened."

Surprisingly, he doesn't hesitate and spills, telling me about showing up at the Lords Mansion on Staten Island and the plan to take down the crime organization. He went through every minute, including Noah killing Finn O'Connor and the shootout that injured him and Del, and Noah getting stabbed.

Fuck.

My best friend is in a coma.

I need to go see her.

"So what happens next?"

"Well, the Lords will be dissolved. I have my men out there now questioning any members who survived. We'll offer immunity to those who provide insider information that will help absorb their organization. They'll be vetted, watched. We can't trust them, but the more they cooperate, the better chance they'll live."

I scrunch my nose at the thought of him and his men ending a human life. I may not agree with it, but I'm not entirely put off by it.

"And what about Noah's father? Is he the one who ordered your mother's death twenty years ago? I know you suspected it, but you needed evidence."

"We're still working on that part. Once Noah has recovered, she's going to snoop in his Manhattan office."

I pause putting on the bandage and frown.

"What happens if her father did it? What happens to the Empire?"

"That's something Noah and I will have to discuss. I'm under the impression she doesn't want to follow in her father's footsteps. If that's the case, I will gladly take over both organizations. I've already cleaned up the QBM. I could do the same for the Empire."

I smile and return my focus to his arm, gently putting the bandage over the cleaned wound.

"You're a good man. You know that right?"

"I literally kill people."

"People who deserve it like Chase and whoever he's working with to kidnap humans to sell for sex."

He grinds his teeth, his nostrils flaring. "I'm going to really enjoy torturing those fuckers."

"Okay. All done," I say, turning to clean up the mess on the counter.

"You're a natural. Want to do that again?"

"No. Not really." I snort while scooping up the empty medical packages to throw in the trash.

He stands and hobbles over to the counter where I placed the first aid kit.

Wait... he's hobbling? Was he doing that earlier? Now that I think about it, he did say *bullets,* not bullet when talking about his injuries.

"Elias, what the hell is wrong with your leg?"

"Nothing."

I narrow my eyes at his back. "Did you know when you lie to me, your voice goes up a pitch?"

"It does not."

"It does not," I say, mocking him.

He slumps his shoulders and leans up against the bathroom counter. "I may have another bullet hole in my thigh. Allegedly."

I cross my arms and raise a brow. He holds up his hands in surrender.

"Get the fuck on the counter," I demand, and after giving me a mischievous smirk, he complies, like the good big boy he is.

He might pretend to hate when I boss him around, but I see the way his eyes light up anytime I bark an order at him.

He's been in control for far too long. He doesn't trust anyone with it.

Maybe I can be the one he falls to his knees for.

Maybe I can convince him to let me be in charge.

Maybe I can take away all the horrible things that have happened to him, even if it's just for one night, and replace those memories with ones of love, care, and pleasure.

Love.

It's crazy to think I could give my heart out so easily to another man. Especially since it's still being repaired after Chase abused it. But for Elias, I would be willing to risk the chance of another heartbreak.

Chapter 20

Elias

Word of Finn O'Connor's death, and the fall of the Lords, traveled fast. It's all the news has been reporting on this week. I let my FBI contact take the win for busting the mafia operation, knowing that I'll need a favor from the agency in the future.

I haven't been home much since the shootout, spending the past four days cleaning up the Lords territory and taking down his corrupt business ventures. I suspected Finn was the one working with Chase. He'd been known to exploit sex workers, and being involved in human and sex trafficking, but he always managed to weasel his way out of getting busted for it. I'd hoped one of his soldiers would have provided the evidence needed, but Finn either kept all of them in the dark—even the higher up soldiers—or Finn isn't involved at all, and someone is using his name to move up in the sex trafficking circuit.

I'd been at the Lords Mansion all day with my men, raiding Finn's office, when my tech guy called me. He remotely accessed Finn's computer and was scouring the files when he found something interesting: security video showing two men dousing Noah's apartment with gasoline before setting it on fire, causing an explosion. Lance said it was taken from his feed. He's a paranoid bastard who installs hidden cameras around the entrances and hallways of all his safe houses.

I suppose it makes sense since he kills people for a living. He likely has as many enemies as I do.

Speaking of enemies, why the fuck would O'Connor have video of Noah and Lance's building being set on fire? If he was responsible, he wouldn't keep incriminating evidence on his computer. It feels like a setup. Especially after Lance and I also found a manilla folder with pictures of him and Noah entering Cillian's apartment building the night he was killed. Someone was following them and snapped photos of the two.

We believe whoever took the photos didn't know Lance and Noah's true identities until the night of the Christmas party. Then they saw an opportunity and sent them to Finn. As if they wanted him to retaliate against the Empire and the QBM, especially after their engagement connected our organizations.

I just left Lenetti's place in the Lower East Side after Lance and I went over these discoveries with Noah. I was happy to hear she woke up from her coma. I called Sage to let her know, but she didn't answer. Noah said she'd already talked to her and the two women scheduled a bestie day later this week.

Sage was hesitant to visit Noah's bedside while she was in a coma. I think she's terrified of Lenetti. Especially after everything Noah has told her about him. He's too unpredictable. Too hotheaded. She needs me to protect her.

And I will.

She's the first person to give me hope that I could live a somewhat normal life.

I've always wondered what that would be like.

Would Sage let me marry her? Would she let me put a baby inside her? She's let me fuck her raw a few times now. I suppose now's not the right time to have a baby. I want to do parenthood the right way. I'd give my child all the love I never received from my father. I'd take them to the park, to get ice cream, to a baseball game, the zoo.

The zoo.

Another thing I've never experienced. When my second-grade class had a field trip to the Bronx Zoo, I was home with a bruised eye and busted lip. I missed too many days at school by my father's hands, and when they threatened to call Child Protective Services on my parents, Percy dug up dirt on the principal and threatened to expose him. The school backed off, but I was pulled out of classes the next year.

Lance and I were homeschooled by Mom until we reached high school, and Percy realized I could be recruiting my peers for the QBM.

Normalcy.

It's not something I'll get anytime soon, but Sage is the closest thing I have to experiencing it.

The sun has set when I arrive at the penthouse. All the lights are turned off, and it's eerily quiet inside.

My heart kicks into gear, thinking the worst.

"Sage!"

My feet move faster than my brain can think as I run through the kitchen. The living room is dark and silent, so I head to the bedrooms, opening doors and checking for Sage while calling her name.

My phone is in my hand, ready to call Jax to have soldiers deployed to search for her but when I return to the living room, the lamp on the table next to my armchair turns on.

"Hello, Elias."

Sage stares back at me, arms crossed and eyes narrowed.

"What the fuck?! You scared the shit out of me. I thought someone had taken you. I thought Chase..."

"Sit down. We need to talk."

Oh.

Fuck.

This isn't good.

My stomach sours and my mouth dries as I slowly sink to the couch adjacent to her.

Fear isn't something I'm accustomed to but the way Sage glares daggers at me, I am literally concerned for my life.

"Did you break into my phone?"

Shit.

"Don't lie. I know the answer."

I swallow hard. "I... I did."

"You deleted the Madam app?"

"Fuck yes I did."

She closes her eyes, uncrosses her arms, and fists her hands in her lap.

"You had no right—"

"I know."

"Then why?"

"Because that app is dangerous. Men could find out your true identity. They could become obsessed with you—"

"Obsessed like you?"

I scoff. "It's not the same."

"Why? Because you've had your cock inside me?"

"Sage," I sigh and run my palm over my face. "I had my tech guy do some digging, and the creator of the app is using it to harbor predators."

"What?" She shakes her head. "No... I... I don't believe you."

"You know I'd never lie to you. I have the proof. I'll show you. And the men... your clients..."

She gets out of the chair and stands before me.

"What about them?"

I reach for her, but she slaps my hand. Shit. I'm fucking this all up. Sweat gathers on my forehead because I'm scared as hell that this is going to be her breaking point. She's going to hate me for what I've done.

"Three of the ten who regularly hired you had incriminating material on their computers. So I..."

I look up at her, and she takes a step back.

Fuck!

I silently plead with her not to run, but I can't hold back this information from her.

"What did you do?"

Swallowing, I say, "I had them killed."

"Noah?"

"No."

Lance is the one who helped me, at least with the one man who was local. I sent him his information, but I didn't tell him I needed the man dead because of Sage. I knew he'd tell Noah, and Noah would tell Sage. I was hoping she wouldn't find out.

I should have known better. She's too fucking smart.

As for the other two men who lived too far for my brother to kill, Lance arranged for their deaths through an encrypted, untraceable site he uses on the dark web to accept hit jobs.

Sage stares at me for the longest time. At least a minute before she nods and turns her back to me, walking to the center of the living room.

"Sage—"

"You invaded my privacy."

"I know."

"You could have talked to me about this, and I would have deactivated my account and removed the app from my phone."

I stand and walk to her. She tilts her head up, nose high in defiance.

This woman has never, and will never, be intimidated by me. I think that's one reason why I can't stay away from her.

She doesn't treat me like a monster.

I just told her I had three men killed, and she's still here. Albeit she looks like she wants to kick my ass, but she's here.

"I'm sorry."

When I try to take hold of her, desperate to bring her into my arms, she once again steps away from me.

"No."

"No?"

"Sorry is not good enough. I want more."

"More?"

"I want you on your knees."

The words are like a bolt of lightning going straight to my cock. It jumps, just as shocked as I am.

"You want me to give you control?" I ask, realizing what she's implying.

"Yes."

"And what will you do if I don't give it to you?"

My heart pounds in my chest. The last time I didn't have control, I was being abused by my father. When he died, I was set free, and I vowed never to let anyone tell me what to do in both my professional and personal lives.

It's why I tend to have relationships with submissive women. Is that why those relationships always felt empty? They never challenged me like Sage does?

"What would you do, Sage?" I repeat.

She plants her hands on her hips. "Are you going to risk finding out?"

She's bluffing, but I can see how badly she needs this.

I think I need it more.

Slowly, I sink to my knees.

"I'm sorry I betrayed your trust and privacy by breaking into your password protected phone."

"Take your shirt off and keep talking. Eyes stay on the ground," she says and walks away.

"You were right," I say, removing my shirt and throwing it to the side. "I should have told you how I felt. I'm not good with communication, especially when it comes to my feelings. I hold things in because of fear. Because it's what

I had to do as a teenager. I know that's not an excuse, but it's the truth, and I vow to make it better. I'll be better for you."

Sage's feet come into view. She's wearing a pair of lovely red pumps; her toenails painted to match.

"Give me a safe word."

"I don't—"

"You do. Give me one, Elias."

I huff but oblige. "Barry."

"Barry?"

"Yeah, like Barry Manilow."

I can't see her reaction, but I just know she rolled her eyes.

"Fine. Barry it is," she says, and above my head she thwacks something against her hand.

I manage a peek.

Does she have a… riding crop?

My cock twitches, eager and ready for punishment.

"Anything else you'd like to say?"

I nod and inhale a deep breath. I'm in a vulnerable state and it's intense. It's also slightly cathartic. "The real reason I deleted the app was jealousy. You're mine, and I'm the only man you should be controlling."

The crop whips across my chest, and I gasp, not expecting the sting.

But fuck it felt good.

Sage clutches my chin. "Good boy."

She leans in and presses a soft kiss to my lips.

I finally get a good look at her.

Jesus Christ, she's wearing nothing but her pumps and a black bustier with a matching G-string and tights.

I'd been too distracted when she turned on the light after I had frantically searched for her because I certainly would have noticed the outfit. She must have been wearing a robe, covering up this delectable body of hers.

The crop strikes my thighs, and she makes sure to avoid hitting my healing bullet wound. Not that it matters. I'll gladly welcome the pain.

"No touching," she says, and I realize I had lifted my hands.

I desperately want to touch her.

Sage walks around me, her fingertips skimming across my back and sending a shiver down my spine. My cock aches, pressing against my zipper and begging for release.

When she makes it back around to my front, she viciously takes hold of my hair and jerks my head back to lock eyes with me.

"I want you to stand and finish undressing, then go into the bedroom and wait for me on your knees, palms flat on your thighs. Can you do that, Mister Carter?"

I clench my jaw at the formality. I'm Elias or Boss. Not Mister Carter.

But I say nothing because Sage is the one in control here. "Yes, Madam Manilow."

She smirks at me remembering the name she goes by on that stupid Dom app and lets go of my hair.

"You're doing such a good job, Elias," she purrs.

I'm not going to lie... the praise and validation chips away at my trauma ever so slightly. It's as if she's healing the parts of my past where I was left to fend for myself, physically and mentally. Piece by piece, patching up the holes from losing my mother and my brother when he was sent away.

Maybe one day Sage will make me whole again.

I've been waiting in the bedroom for an hour.

I know Sage is still in the penthouse. She's blasting music in the living room and singing at the top of her lungs.

She's fucking with me.

God, why does that turn me on even more?

I don't even care that my entire body aches. My feet have gone numb. My lower back screams with pain. I'm no longer young and limber. This thirty-six-year-old body of mine has been through shit. It's damaged and used.

But I'll endure the pain for her, for however long she wants to leave me here—my punishment.

When the music finally shuts off thirty minutes later, and I'm struggling to stay upright, a burst of adrenaline erupts within me. Sage enters the bedroom, and I manage to get a glimpse of her. She's carrying a can of whipped cream, the riding crop, and something else that I couldn't make out in time before averting my eyes to the ground.

"Someone's excited," she teases, likely seeing my cock harden. *Because I hope she's going to use that whipped cream on me.* "Get up. Sit at the end of the bed."

Everything inside me wants to fight her for control, but I've made it this far, I can't go back.

I'm not only doing this for her, but I'm also doing it for me. This is my chance to let go of the horrible things that have happened to me. To let someone else carry those burdens.

After setting the riding crop and whipped cream down on my dresser, she stands before me and holds up a blindfold.

"I'm going to put this on you now, okay?"

"Yes, Madam Manilow," I say, stifling a moan.

"You've been so patient, Elias," she says while putting the blindfold on me. Her warm breath on my lips makes me shiver. "And patient men get rewarded."

The bed beside me dips, and I feel Sage at my back. She reaches for my arms, and I let her bring them behind where she binds them.

"I for sure thought you would give up," she says, crawling back off the bed. "You're a reactive man. You don't take orders well, and I know that's because of how you grew up."

I hold my breath, realizing the lesson she gave me.

It wasn't punishment. It was a test.

"You don't let people get close to you, and you hold in your feelings. I understand that. I do. But you've grown so much since we've met. You've shared your life with me, and I'm honored."

The woosh of the whipped cream sounds, followed by a cold sensation on my chest... right over one of my scars.

"But you have to accept that you can't always be in control. That you don't always have to be the hero. Sometimes you can let other people take care of you. That's exactly what I'm going to do tonight," Sage says.

Her tongue laps up the dollop of whipped cream and I shudder, tugging at my bound hands. Precum leaks from my cock, and I can't help the moan that slips past my lips.

"Oh, Boss," Sage purrs. "Be loud for me. Don't hold back. Let me hear how well I fuck you tonight."

Sage's mouth closes over the tip of my dick, and I whimper for her. She wraps her hands around the shaft and massages while her tongue lashes over me. She takes me deeper, her hands moving to cup my balls. She grips them roughly while sucking me down to the back of her throat.

"Fuck, Sage," I moan.

She immediately slips my cock from her mouth and stands.

"Now, Elias, you know that's not what you're supposed to call me," she scolds.

Seconds later, the riding crop crashes down on my thighs—again, she's careful to avoid my injury.

I've never been into BDSM, even if what Sage is doing is just a sample of it. Being spanked *or whipped* never appealed to me because I endured too many beatings as a child.

But this is different. Sage is giving me pleasure with my pain.

She's taking away the horrible memories of being cut and bruised and replacing them with her mouth, her hands, her beautiful cunt.

Sage shakes the can of whipped cream and places dollops of the cool sweet topping on my neck, my pec, my stomach, and *my cock*.

Slowly, she flattens her tongue and laps up each spot.

When she gets to the one on my cock, I'm ready to burst.

"Please," I whimper.

"Please, what, Elias?"

"Please, I need to come."

"You'll come when I allow it," she says and takes my length down her throat.

I fist my hands, still bound behind my back, and bite my lip. Doing everything I can to stop myself from blowing my load down Sage's throat. She sucks me, slowly, barely putting pressure around my shaft.

She brings me to the brink of orgasm then releases me, replacing her mouth with her hands.

She fists my cock while her lips graze over mine. She's barely squeezing it because she knows how close I am.

"Tell me again. Tell me you fucked up, and you're sorry."

"I'm an asshole. I fucked up. I'll never do it again. I'm sorry, Madam Manilow."

She releases my cock, and I nearly growl in frustration.

"Get on the bed, back to the headboard."

It takes some time since I can't see or use my hands, but once I'm in place, Sage mounts my lap. She grabs my achingly hard cock and presses the tip to her soaked opening.

"Remember, no coming until I say so." It's the only warning I get before she sinks down to the hilt.

My moan is loud enough to echo throughout the room.

"Mhm," Sage hums. "So good, Elias."

She lifts up and sinks back down, using my shoulders as leverage.

Not being able to see her, touch her, squeeze her plump ass, is torture in itself. It's the punishment I deserve.

But it's exactly what I needed. I know it's what Sage needed, too, because her sweet pussy is already squeezing my cock as she approaches her release.

She's got a good rhythm going, riding me while clawing her nails into my shoulders.

"Fuck," she groans. "I'm going to come."

Sage takes my head in her hands and crashes her lips on mine. I open my mouth for her, allowing her tongue to tangle with mine.

And when I bite down, gripping her bottom lip between my teeth, she explodes with an orgasm.

Her walls spasm around me, bringing me to my release. I spill inside her.

She sits in my lap, my cock still inside her, while catching her breath. After a few minutes, she gets up, hissing when I slide out of her.

She takes the blindfold off and unties the binds of my hands.

"Apology accepted?" I ask, reaching between her legs to push the cum leaking out of her back in.

She smirks.

"I forgave you the moment you sank to your knees."

Chapter 21

Sage

It's been about a week since Elias gave me control in the bedroom. He seems lighter.

I'm not sure how often he'll let me tie him up and edge him, but I hope he knows it's always an option. That if he ever needs an escape, I can take over for him.

It's Thursday evening and tonight I'm taking Elias out on a date.

He walks through the door an hour before we're supposed to leave.

"Finally!" I say and walk over to him, arms crossed.

"Sorry, I had a lead on Chase, but it turned out to be nothing."

He boops my nose, and I playfully try to bite his fingers.

"Come on, let's get you ready." I take hold of his hand and turn to lead him to our bedroom closet.

"So what are these date plans you have for me?"

"It's a surprise," I tease.

"I need to know where we're going so I have enough men—"

"Taken care of."

"What?"

"I already talked to Jax. He'll make sure we have enough security where we're going."

Elias opens his mouth, then promptly shuts it.

I didn't think it was possible, but I've left Elias speechless.

"You're too good for me, woman."

I giggle. "I know. Now get dressed. Not a suit. Something casual. Bar wear."

"No suit?"

"No. Suit."

Elias rarely goes out in public in casual clothes. The only time I've seen him dressed down is when we're lounging in the living room. Which always leads to sex because I go feral seeing him in sweats and a t-shirt.

I go to the bathroom where I left my clothes and get dressed.

When I walk out, Elias is wearing a black, short-sleeve button down with a dark gray skull design throughout and a pair of black jeans.

It matches the black skull and rose design on my red cocktail dress with a full skirt.

"See," I say, smirking. "I knew you were going to choose a mobby outfit."

"Mobby? Is that even a real word?"

"It is now." I wave my hand up and down his body. "Mobby. You just need the hat."

"A fedora?"

I smile and nod and grab the collar of his shirt to pull him closer.

"I'm more of a trilby guy."

I place a soft kiss on his cheek, leaving a lipstick print behind. I'm not going to tell him because I want him to wear the mark all night.

"Ready?"

"I'm scared."

I snort. "No you're not. Nothing scares you."

"Karaoke?"

Maybe I was wrong about Elias because he *does* look terrified. A 300-some pound bear-of-a-man intimidated by... singing?

It's nearing ten at night, and we had a lovely dinner at an Italian restaurant in Little Italy. Elias has been a nervous wreck, glancing over his shoulder nonstop because we're in 'Empire territory.' It doesn't even matter that three of his men are on guard.

If I'm honest, it's probably more than three men. Some are likely hidden.

Now we're at my favorite bar in Midtown East where karaoke just got underway. The host starts off singing a fast-paced number where he puts on a show, dancing and walking around the bar to get people pumped.

Elias and I find a seat near the back where it's semi-private and somewhat quiet.

"Sage!" a familiar voice calls out.

My bartender friend, Allan, shoves his way through the crowd and nearly tackles me with a hug. I've known Allan for years, ever since I first moved to New York City, and we worked together at a hole in the wall bar in the East Village. But I haven't seen him since moving back. He's gotten even more handsome. Tall and slender with a head full of blond curls and piercing blue eyes.

I can't see Elias's reaction to the hug, but I flick my hand at him anyway, knowing he's already plotting all the ways to kill my friend.

To be fair, I'm also ready to sucker punch every person eyeing my man. He looks fine as fuck tonight. The mobby outfit makes him even more intimidating, if that's possible. He's also a massive guy so maybe people are wondering if he's a football player or someone else famous.

His thick black hair is styled short at the sides with a few long pieces hanging over his forehead. I always want to push it back.

"Oh. Wow," Allan says when he pulls away and spots Elias. "You've brought a scary one."

"This is..."

Should I introduce him as Elias? Or Johnny, his alias?

"Um..."

"Carter," Elias grumbles.

Okay, so we're going with last name.

Elias shoots death glares Allan's way, and I roll my eyes.

"Don't mind him." I wave my hand to distract Allan's heated eyes away from my man.

Okay.

Wowww. I've never been the jealous type. This overwhelming possessiveness is new.

And I don't exactly hate it.

"Do you two want anything to drink? I'm behind the bar tonight, but I'll send your server out with them."

"Can I get the usual? And Carter will have a whiskey on the rocks. Top shelf."

Allan smirks. "Fancy."

With a wink, he spins away, and I reach out my hand. Elias immediately takes it.

"We're just friends."

"I didn't say anything."

"Mhm."

He squeezes my hand gently. "What's your usual?"

I smile because there are a lot of things we still don't know about each other. Except, I know he loves whiskey. I always taste it on his kisses. I love the taste. *His* taste.

Do I have a taste?

"Depends. When I go out to bars or clubs, I get vodka soda with cranberry. For brunch I do mimosas or espresso martinis. If I'm chilling at home, wine. Tell me your favorite color—and black doesn't count."

He pouts. "Why the fuck not?"

"Because I said so."

He snarls at me, appearing adorable and grumpy instead of angry and intimidating, which is what he was probably going for.

"I love the color red," I answer first since Elias is being difficult. "It's seductive. To me, it represents power and love."

And I look fantastic in a short red dress.

"Now you."

"Since you won't let me pick black, I choose teal."

My mouth forms an 'o', surprised by that response.

"It's the color of your eyes."

Eyes that I roll. "You're such a cheeseball."

He shrugs, not at all concerned by giving a cheesy response.

"Favorite food?" I ask.

"Hot dogs"

I scrunch up my nose.

"Specifically, Nathan's Famous Hot Dogs because my mom used to take Lance and me out to Coney Island every summer." He looks down at his hands while revisiting this memory. "We'd start the day eating a hot dog covered in chili and cheese, then we'd get on every single ride until we were both sick to our stomachs."

He smiles sadly before looking up at me.

"What about you?"

"There's this dish my mom makes. Tater tot casserole. It has chicken—or you can make it with beef—sour cream, cheese, and a can of cream of mushroom soup. It became tradition to have it when we were celebrating something. It could be anything: an A on a test, a pay raise, passing my driving test. I could make it for you sometime."

The corner of his mouth turns up in a half smile. "I'd love that."

We spend about five minutes going through a few other favorites, including books, movies, TV shows, and music. We even talk about pet peeves.

Mine: loud chewers.

Elias: people being late.

"Tell me about your family. Your childhood," Elias says, moving on to the deeper stuff.

I shrug. "There's not much to tell. My life's boring... well, it was before I met *you*."

"I can be boring." He gives me that adorable half smile that makes me swoon.

I scoff. "Maybe when you're sleeping."

Except not even when he's sleeping. He mumbles and tosses and turns. If I wake up first, sometimes I'll just watch him. It's when he's his most vulnerable.

I notice someone waving at me from over Elias's shoulder. I wave back at the karaoke DJ, and he points at the television. I nod, letting him know to put in one of my usual songs to sing. It'll probably take half an hour to get to me so I guess I can share my boring life with the least boring person I know.

Especially since he's waiting so patiently like a good boy.

"I was born and raised in Connecticut in the same home where you found me on Christmas Day."

I frown, realizing my parents may never be able to go back to that home. Even if Elias finds Chase, I'd be worried about Mom and Dad being connected to Elias now. I wonder if he can put them in some sort of witness protection.

"I grew up fat, and I was bullied in elementary school for it, then puberty hit me, and my breasts got bigger which, despite still being fat, made me popular with the boys at school. It fed into my ego and gave me more confidence in myself and my body. I was happy for the most part and did well in school. I did everything a high school kid was supposed to do. Decent grades, extracurricular activities. I applied to dozens of colleges and got accepted to some of them, but I realized I didn't want to go to school anymore, so after graduation, I moved here to Manhattan.

"I made good money waitressing, so I saved as much as I could while I tried different things to see what I enjoyed and what direction to take my life. By the time I met Chase, I was itching for an adventure. To travel. I hadn't been anywhere except Atlantic City, a yearly trip my parents would take to kick off summer. We didn't have a whole lot of money. My mom was a teacher, and my dad had a safety officer position at this furniture making company before they both retired."

I pause when the bar roars with excitement as a singer starts belting out the latest Taylor Swift song. Elias winces, which makes me smile.

This is torture for him.

When the bar's enthusiasm becomes bearable, I continue.

"Chase was normal when we first met. He'd constantly compliment me, tell me how much he loved my body. Now that I think about it, he was definitely love bombing me. Then he'd slowly spew off micro-aggressions about my weight, tearing down all that work I did to build up my self-confidence. He used the fact that I'd never had a long-term relationship and convinced me that it was because of my wild nature, and no one could keep up with me like he could. Then it was my appearance... *no one wants to bring a girl who looks like you home to their parents.* I think I was excited about the idea of Chase—this beautiful rocker bad boy who gave me attention—that I believed his words. It got to a point that I didn't realize he was controlling me until it was too late, and I was too scared to leave him.

"When he started dealing drugs, that was my sign to get out of the abusive marriage. I wanted nothing to do with him so I changed my name and moved back to the city where I figured it would be too big for him to find me, but I didn't account for my parents. Even though he never let me visit them, they were easy to track down."

Elias brings our joined hands up to his mouth and kisses my knuckles.

"I won't let anything happen to them. To you."

The server drops off our drinks and Elias orders another round. I take a big gulp of my booze and close my eyes.

Because I'm about to go deep.

"I know you'll protect me, but Elias, what does my future with you look like? Will I always be in danger? Will I always need protection? Will I always be looking over my shoulder? Will my parents always need to be hiding?"

"Sage—"

"I have to work. I have to do something. I can't just be the mob boss's trophy girlfriend. I will lose my freaking mind. But I'm about to turn thirty-three, and I have no idea what I want to do with my life."

He sighs, and I expect him to appear hurt or worried by my words.

He's not.

If anything, he's determined.

"I promise you this will all be over soon. I will find Chase, and we're so close to connecting Lenetti to the mob wives' murders and taking down the Empire. I'm going to turn this city around, and I *need* you to be by my side, but you'll never be a trophy. You're not someone I can win. You're someone I earn. You're someone who will make me stronger. And you do not hesitate to take me down a few notches. So, I will never expect you to 'just be the mob boss's trophy.' I want you to be my partner, but not as my girlfriend. As my *wife.*"

"What?" The word barely comes out a whisper, and he must not have heard it. Or maybe he's ignoring the shock on my face because he keeps talking.

"What do you enjoy doing?"

Fuck.

How the hell can I function after he just laid into me with that speech? And to say he wants me as his wife? I know he's said shit like that before, but I honestly thought he was joking or just saying it to push my buttons.

It's fine.

This is fine.

Answer his question, Sage.

"I um… I think I'm pretty good at planning parties. I've worked at a few bars where they let me handle events or they'd let me book bands."

He nods and when he opens his mouth to say something, the karaoke DJ calls my name.

I numbly stand.

"I'm… I'm going to sing now."

Elias stands and follows me to the front where I get the mic, but he keeps his distance. Lady Gaga's *Bad Romance* starts playing, and I've sang the song enough to mindlessly sing the lyrics while I let my thoughts run wild.

Marriage?

Elias's *wife*?

It's… too soon.

Right?

I mean, we met months ago, sure, but we've only really been spending a lot of time together recently.

But on the other hand, if we got married, he'd protect me. Would I be, like, some powerful mafia queen or something?

Reine.

His queen.

He'd known from the moment we met, hasn't he?

That should terrify me, instead, it's endearing because the scary, dangerous mafia boss was enchanted by the mess of a divorcee that I am.

The crowd's amped up, and they scream out the chorus with me, pulling me from my thoughts. I can't help locking eyes with Elias at the part of the song about wanting his love and revenge.

Because it's true.

I want him.

All of him.

The drama.

The ugly.

The horror.

The psycho.

The bad.

The song ends to cheers, and I slowly make my way through the crowd back to where Elias and I were sitting. He beat me there and waits, holding his drink and that stupid knowing smirk on his face.

"So…" He stares at me over the top of the glass of whiskey. "Do you want *my* bad romance?"

God. I can't take him seriously sometimes.

He wiggles his brows at me and takes a drink before setting the glass down.

I burst out laughing and cup his face in my hands to kiss him. The kiss deepens and suddenly we're in the corner making out, not even caring about everyone around us.

But there was a reason I brought him to karaoke tonight.

He's going to sing too.

He lets out a grunt and pouts when I break off the kiss. I pat his chest.

"You're next."

That frightened look from when we entered the bar returns.

"No. That's okay. I'm fine. I don't need to... um... sing."

"Are you flustered?"

I can't help the amusement in my voice.

"I don't get flustered."

"You're flustered now. Why?"

"Because I can't sing."

"No one at karaoke can sing."

"You can."

I wave off his words and nod my head toward the man singing *Don't Stop Believin'* right now.

"This guy is horrible, but he's cute and a bit charming. Just use your good looks and everyone will love you."

Chapter 22

Elias

I lied.

I'm a decent singer.

My mother taught me to sing along with piano lessons. Every Friday night—at least up until I was forced to shadow my father—Mom would rearrange the living room and setup a makeshift stage. Lance would play the piano, since he was better than me, and I would sing. Mom would sit on the couch, beaming at her two handsome sons, crying at our performances.

Now I realize she always cried because she knew it would all come to an end someday.

I haven't sung since I was a teenager. Unless you count solo performances in the shower.

But I'm not as good as Sage.

She leads me to the front and introduces me to the karaoke DJ, a long-haired man dressed in a colorful outfit and red boots that remind me of the ones worn in that Broadway show *Kinky Boots*. He hands me a piece of paper, and I write down my song, making sure to hide it from Sage.

"No peeking," I tell her.

She holds up her hands in innocence.

I assumed the DJ was going to put me at the back of the list, and we'd leave before I was called up to sing, but he enters my song next.

Now.

The song is playing now.

New York State of Mind by Billy Joel.

God.

Why am I doing this?

Sage sits on a stool with her back to the bar. Her hands are clasped, and her eyes are lit up with anticipation.

That motivates me.

I belt out the lyrics and immediately, the crowd reacts with hoots and hollers.

Sage drops her hands to her lap; her mouth hanging open.

She's all I focus on as I croon. The song isn't even romantic, but the way Sage bites her lip and fidgets on the stool tells me she's ready to climb me right here in the middle of the bar.

When the song ends, I don't waste time and grab her hand to pull her toward the door. I ignore the accolades from everyone as I pass by, only pausing to pay our server before squeezing through the crowd to get outside.

We barely make it a few steps out the door before there's a loud pop followed by a scream. I stop in my tracks and reach for Sage, clutching her arm to bring her to the ground.

My men surround us, guns drawn.

"Are you okay? Did you get hit?"

"N-no."

Sage's voice is small and trembling.

"Someone's shooting at us. I need you to stay behind me, okay?"

"Okay."

Sage clings to my back, and I order one of my soldiers to protect our rear as we make our way to the SUV. People who were walking down the sidewalk are now running for cover as two more gunshots ring out.

I curse and reach for my gun when a bullet whizzes next to my ear.

"Where are they shooting from?" I ask Jax.

"Fifth floor window across the street. I already have men going over there."

"Have you called for backup?"

"On the way."

I need to get Sage out of here, but I also need to find who is shooting at us so I can brutally murder them.

I open the SUV's door and help Sage inside.

"Lock the doors. Stay down. I'll be right back."

I don't give her time to argue and close the door.

Chapter 23

Sage

My heart pounds against my chest, my nerves like a hot wire ready to combust.

What the fuck.

What the fuck.

What the fuck.

There's a literal shootout happening in the middle of the street in Midtown East. Muffled sirens pierce through the nearly soundproof windows, and I cover my ears.

Wait, Elias told me to get down.

But before I dive to the floorboard, the hairs on the back of my neck rise, alerting me that I'm no longer alone. When I turn to see who it is, praying to whatever God will listen that it's one of Elias's soldiers, a balmy hand covers my mouth.

And the cool tip of a knife presses against my neck.

"Hello, Sunshine."

I gasp and hold my breath at the sound of Chase's voice.

How the hell did he get in here? Elias and his men were everywhere, even before bullets started flying.

"You've been a busy little slut."

I attempt to respond, but his grip over my mouth is too strong, and he digs the knife's tip deeper. A burning sensation spreads from the cut, and I feel the slow trickle of blood down my neck.

"Tell your boyfriend to back off," he says, his hot breath making me shiver.

Tears streak down my cheeks, and I might just pass out with how fast my heart is beating.

"What... what are you going to do?" I manage to say clear enough when his hold eases up.

"I have your parents. I'll kill them the next time Carter busts one of my shipments."

He's lying. My parents are safe. I just spoke to them on FaceTime an hour before coming out tonight.

"Next, I'll kill that best friend of yours. Noah, or is it Noemi?"

Okay, he's clearly desperate.

Noah would kick his ass, and even if he somehow got a jump on her, he'd have to get past Del.

But I don't say anything because one wrong word will have the knife sinking deeper into my neck.

"Tell. Him. To. Back. Off."

The shootout has stopped, but the strobe of red and blue lights coming through the windows lets me know cops are on the scene.

Chase lets go and climbs past me to exit the vehicle.

I spin around, searching for Elias, but he's too far away speaking with police to notice Chase escaping. I spot Aaron and Justin, my two bodyguards, but they're on the other side of the SUV leaving the side Chase slipped out unprotected.

I try to yell for Elias, to anyone, but nothing comes out when I open my mouth.

Fuck. Chase is getting away, and as soon as Elias finds out what happened, he's going to be *pissed*. I hope he won't kill any of his men for this.

I scan the crowd, wondering if I can at least see which way Chase ran off, but he's somehow managed to blend in with the dozen or so people now gathering with their cell phones recording the aftermath of the shootout.

I lean my head back on the headrest and inhale deeply. The scent of blood burns my nose, and I skim my finger-tips over the cut that Chase caused.

Huh...

That's not that much blood.

Then where...

My eyes land on the SUV's driver, slumped over the wheel.

And, finally, I scream.

That gets Elias's attention.

He runs back to the car and opens the door, the same one Chase exited. I'm a crying, bubbling mess at this point, and I'm explaining what happened quickly and furiously, my words likely making no sense.

I point a lot... at my neck, at the dead driver.

Elias steps away and frantically searches the crowd for Chase, then barks orders at his men. A few of them run off while others stay behind to speak with officers.

Wait. Is that the mayor?

Elias knows the mayor of New York City?

Of course, he does.

I've calmed down drastically by the time Elias returns to the car. He holds out his hand, helping me get out since my legs are like Jell-O because of the adrenaline, and leads me to another SUV waiting around the corner.

"Let's get you home."

He opens the door for me, and I crawl in. Once he's inside, and shuts the door, he gives the driver a nod and the car takes off.

Watching him in his mafia persona is insanely hot. The way he can issue a command without saying a word? The way he jumped into the line of fire instead of running away from it. The way he makes sure I'm still safe while taking down the bad guys.

My distress about the shooting, about Chase, falls away and lust takes over. My body lights up.

I turn my head watching this powerful man beside me. He's typing away on his phone, probably still dealing with the aftermath of what just happened.

He can finish that later.

I need him now.

I grab his phone and toss it to the floor.

"Sage? What the fuck?"

I ignore him and crawl into his lap, swallowing his curses with a devouring kiss. My hands are buried in his hair, tugging at the strands while I grind my hips. His cock hardens beneath me.

"Fuck me right now," I groan, pulling away from the kiss. I fumble with his pants, desperate to have him inside me.

"Sage, I can't..."

"Please. I need this."

"You're in shock—"

"I'm not. I'm fucking alive. Elias, please."

Once I have his cock out, I fist the thick length up and down. Elias groans, his head falling back on the headrest. Behind me, I hear the car's privacy divider activate.

"He didn't scare me," I say.

I reach underneath my dress and pull my panties aside, allowing me to sink down to the hilt.

"Fuck," I moan at the same time Elias does.

Using his shoulders for leverage, I ride him. My movements are slow, calculated, torturous.

"Chase had a knife to my throat, but instead of cowering like I'd normally do, I held my head high."

"I'm so proud of you," Elias says and leans in to lick the blood off my neck.

I whimper and clench around him as I find a rhythm and pick up speed. Elias covers my mouth with his, capturing my moans and cries with rough kisses.

Just how I like it.

This might be the hottest sex we've had yet.

It feels important.

Because I can finally see myself in his world.

"You're perfect, Sage. Your pussy is perfect. My cock was made for you."

Elias holds my hips in place and bucks up into me. My head falls back with a scream.

Neither of us care that the driver and QBM soldier in the passenger seat can hear us fucking back here. The divider provides visual privacy. It appears to be soundproofed for casual conversations, but not screaming, hot sex.

Elias pounds up into me, bringing me to the edge of release. His mouth finds my breast, and he bites down over the fabric-covered nipple. My orgasm erupts.

He thrusts a few more times before following with his own release.

We sit there, his cock inside me to the hilt while we catch our breath.

"I'm sorry about your driver," I whisper. "Did anyone else... get hurt?"

He skims his palm up and down my spine. "No one else. At least nothing life-threatening."

"This is my fault. If Chase—"

"Chase is the only one to blame here. He's using you to get to me. Don't ever apologize for that man again, okay?"

I nod then, while still on his lap, his cock inside me, I tell him everything Chase said to me. We even FaceTimed my parents just to be sure. They were inside the beachside home, cooking dinner.

The call was less than a minute because I couldn't stop blushing, worried that my parents would somehow find out I was being used as a cock warmer.

As the driver continues towards Brooklyn, Elias explains that his men are canvassing the area around the bar, along with the NYPD. The mayor showed up so he could help spin the shootout to the media. I asked if he was worried about all the people who recorded the aftermath on their cell phones. There were too many devices to confiscate and wipe the evidence, so he said they basically had to explain that club owner Johnny Goode was targeted, believed to be a disgruntled patron who was denied access to one of his clubs.

Elias said it was a weak explanation, but it was going to have to do for now.

"Do you feel better?" he asks. "Did the car sex help?"

I snort and bury my head in the crook of his neck.

"It did."

I kiss along his throat and jaw before placing a gentle kiss on his lips. Since he's *still* inside me, I feel him getting hard again.

"You know, that was the first time I've fucked in a moving car," I say.

"But you've fucked in a parked car?"

"Yeah. Prom. Junior year." I roll my eyes. "I can see you revving up to be jealous, but don't. It was the dude's first time and my second. It was horrible."

He smiles at that.

"Good. You will never have terrible sex ever again."

"Is that a promise?"

He lifts my hips, and I gasp when his cock slides out of me, but only to the tip.

Then he jerks up, re-entering me again in one slick move.

I groan and wrap my arms around his neck, allowing him to pump into me easily.

"So," he says between thrusts. "What else haven't you done? Tell me all your fantasies, and I'll be happy to fulfill them."

"I want to..." I moan, temporarily losing my words. "I uh... fuck, Elias, that's good."

His arms are wrapped around my waist as he drives into me from below.

"Tell me or I won't let you come," he teases.

"I want you... to wake me up... with sex."

He pauses inside me, and I wiggle my hips because I was real fucking close to coming again.

"I've never done that before either," he says.

"Really? So you'll do it?"

"When? Tomorrow morning?"

I shake my head. "I don't want to know. I want it to be unexpected."

He curses, then resumes fucking me until I'm shaking with another mind-blowing orgasm.

When I crawl off Elias's lap to sit next to him, I curl up to his side.

"Why didn't you tell me you could sing?"

"Because I don't like to. It reminds me of my mother."

"Oh."

"But now I can sing and think of you."

I smile, and he kisses my forehead. I close my eyes, and the next thing I remember is Elias waking me when we get back to the penthouse. I'm half asleep as he leads me inside.

The excitement from the shooting and the adrenaline crash after has me falling asleep the moment he puts me in bed.

I dream about a life where Elias and I have a home in the suburbs with a backyard and a fire pit. Where our kids run around the yard and Noah and Del hang out while Elias grills.

It may not happen anytime soon, but maybe one day that could be us.

No more guns.

No more mafia.

No more brushes with death.

Chapter 24

Elias

It's been about two weeks since the shootout outside the karaoke bar and a month since the Lords were dismantled. Noah is fully recovered now, and her and Lance have been back to snooping for solid evidence at her father's businesses.

Things have been quiet. Despite Chase's threat for me to back off, there haven't been any human trafficking shipments. He's spooked. He knows I'm watching his every move. He's likely gone into hiding, knowing I'll murder him the moment he shows his face—especially after putting his hands on Sage.

My concern about Chase halting shipments is for the people he's kidnapped. They're likely being abused, malnourished, or worse while Chase and his partner or partners scramble to reorganize an auction or secure sales directly.

Sage has been my saving grace this past month.

She's there when I need an escape from my life.

Sage is *my life now.*

She officially ended her lease at her apartment and is now fully living with me. I had the rest of her belongings from her studio moved into my penthouse. She has her own room—something she didn't ask for, but I set up in case she wanted a space that felt like her own. Somewhere she could go when she needed to be alone.

She's yet to spend a night in there.

I haven't stopped thinking about our karaoke night, the post-shootout orgasms, and her request to be woken up with sex. However, I've been too busy for it to happen. When I get home, she's still awake and when I wake up the next morning, she's already in the kitchen cooking breakfast.

It'll happen. I will do anything Sage wants. I will give her everything she's ever dreamed of. Every fantasy she wants fulfilled. I just need to find her fucking ex and whoever he's working with. I need Noah and Lance to get that evidence on Lenetti so we can finally take the Empire down.

All these obstacles are getting in the way of my life with my queen and once they're gone, I can focus on her.

I've been at my office at Underground Park Slope all day because I'm still a legitimate business owner who has to do his job sometimes, but now I'm on my way back to the penthouse. I'm eager to see Sage.

My thoughts must have summoned her because she's calling me.

"Hey, everything—"

"I need you to come home."

"What is it?"

"I think... I think Noah is in trouble. Please, hurry. I'm worried."

"I'm almost there."

I bark at the driver to speed up, and five minutes later, we're pulling into the horseshoe driveway where Sage is waiting. I open the door and get out before the car is barely parked.

"Tell me what happened."

She pushes past me and climbs into the SUV.

"Sage?"

I stand at the open door, peering inside as Sage frantically taps at her phone.

"I texted Noah earlier to hang out since you were going to be gone most of today. She didn't answer, and I didn't think anything of it because she's usually with Del, but I had a bad feeling."

She turns the phone's screen toward me.

"Typically, if she's on a hit job, she'll warn me that she'll be out of commission, but she didn't today so I tracked her location, and it's showing she's in Queens."

I zoom in on the blue dot on the map and suck in a sharp breath.

"I know where she's at. Sage..." She raises a brow as if daring me to say the next words, but I have to. "I need you to stay here."

"Not happening."

"Please. I don't know what we're about to walk into, and I won't risk you getting hurt."

"I'm. Going."

I curse when she moves to the far door, locks it, and crosses her arms.

Brat.

But I can't say no to her.

As if she'd let me.

Before I get in, I give orders to my men and tell the driver where to go. I make calls to my uncle and deploy soldiers to my childhood home in Fresh Meadows. I call Lance next, and he doesn't answer. Texts also go ignored.

I have a feeling he and Noah are together.

"Do you know what's going on?" Sage asks about ten minutes into the drive.

"Nothing good," I grumble.

Twenty minutes later, the driver pulls onto the street where I used to ride my bike. We pass familiar homes, many left abandoned. I instruct the driver to park a block away where a few of my soldiers are staked out, watching the property.

I barely recognize the home where I grew up. It's been condemned for years, and the last time I was even here was in my early twenties. It holds too many horrible memories. The only reason I haven't bulldozed it to the ground is because it's one of the few places I have left of my mother.

Her handwriting remains on door frames when she used to measure mine and Lance's heights throughout the years. She also loved to paint and draw and decorated my room with snakes and wildlife, because I loved nature shit when I was a kid. Still do. It's why I have it tattooed all over my body. Lance's room was decorated in robots and alien drawings because he loved science fiction books and movies.

But the negative memories outweigh the positive ones.

"Stay here a sec," I say to Sage and get out, my gun drawn. I spot my uncle and approach him. "Report."

"About six men outside, captured or dead. Six more inside." He pauses, and I sense he's leaving something out.

"Say it."

"It's Percy... One of the QBM soldiers spotted him in the basement with Noah and Lance. Noah is tied up. Lance was unconscious but appears to be alive."

My eyes move past my uncle to the rundown three-story home with peeling yellow green paint and dark forest green sidings falling off the walls. Vines snake their way up the sides and the windows are either cracked, broken, or missing.

A ghost of a home with the ghost of the man who abused me inside.

Except, he's still alive?

"Impossible. How?"

An ache forms in the back of my throat, pressure building behind my eyes. The fucker's been alive this whole time. I'd always been suspicious of his diagnosis the moment he refused to let us see him on his deathbed.

He faked it all.

But why?

"Elias," my uncle urges, recognizing I was seconds away from having a mental fucking breakdown.

He's seen me at my worst. He's the one who arrived with my father that night twenty years ago and pulled me from my mother's body. He's the one who sent my ass to rehab when I tried to drown my new responsibility of taking over the QBM with drugs and booze to the point that I almost died.

My phone rings, and I scramble to answer, hoping it's my brother saying they somehow escaped and they're fine. Disappointment sinks in when 'unknown number' flashes across the screen. I only give this number out to a select, trusted few so I answer.

"Carter," a deep voice bellows from the other end.

Lenetti?

How the fuck did he get this number?

"Got a strange call from someone claiming to have Noah. They sent me an address in Fresh Meadows."

My heart skips a beat, and I swallow to wet my dry throat.

"The fuck did you say?"

"Fresh. Meadows. Got wax in your ears, boy?"

I ignore his condescending words. "What the fuck does that have to do with me?"

"Are you dense? That's QBM territory. Did you really think you could set me up by sending me to your child-hood home?"

"I'd never let the Empire in QBM territory. Fuck off with that."

He mumbles something I can't understand. "Look, Carter, just find Noah and make sure she's okay. I'm in the Bronx right now, and traffic is a nightmare."

"I'm close. I'll check it out," I say and hang up.

Lenetti doesn't need to know that I'm already here or that his daughter is, in fact, not okay. Gio would lose his shit. He'd risk starting a turf war by sending in every last Empire soldier. I'm surprised he even called me for help.

He's a monster, but one thing's for sure: He loves his daughter.

I return to Sage who's sitting on the edge of the back seat, door open.

"Things are about to get bloody. I need to stay focused, and I can't do that if you're out here and needing protec-tion."

Her bottom lip shakes, tears falling down her face, but she nods.

I turn to leave, but she catches me. Taking my face in her hands, she brushes her soft lips over mine.

"I want your bad romance."

I smile against her mouth, then devour her plump lips with a breathtaking kiss.

"Tell me," I say, breathless. "I want to hear you say it."

She peppers me with kisses on my lips, my cheeks, my nose, my chin, my jaw.

"I want to marry you. I want to be your wife."

"I love you, Sage."

With one more kiss, I walk off.

I don't allow her to respond because if I hear those three little words from her, I'll be tempted to get behind the wheel and drive off with my woman, leaving this world behind.

I can't do that to my brother again. I can't leave him when he needs me most.

Chapter 25

Sage

I love you, Sage.

The words repeat in my head as I watch Elias storm off.

He didn't wait for me to say it back.

I could have yelled it, made sure he knew I felt the same, but he's right. He needs to focus. If I were to distract him, and he gets hurt, or worse, killed, I'd never forgive myself.

I anxiously watch as Elias and his men enter the home. After no more than a minute, there's an explosion and gunfire erupts.

"Elias!"

Oh, hell no. My man is not going to die.

I'm going in. If I'm serious about being part of Elias's life, then I need to face my fears. I need to face the dangers of this world and learn how to fight back.

Plus, I'm worried as hell about my bestie and my *fiancé*.

My heart drums in my chest as I get out of the SUV. I don't get far when one of Elias's men stops me.

Jax.

The man I hit with a vase all those weeks ago.

So we meet again.

"Ma'am. You can't go in there."

"Don't make me fight you, big guy."

He smirks and crosses his arms, blocking my way.

"I already took you out once, I'll do it again."

"I'd like to see you—"

Before he can finish the sentence, I knee him in the nuts. He crumples to the ground, holding his jewels.

"Sorry," I hiss and run off toward the home.

Even though the gunfire has died down, I use caution as I approach. I divert my eyes from all the dead bodies and focus on finding Elias and Noah.

Broken glass crunches underneath my shoes when I walk through the open front door, and I'm glad I threw on my sneakers before leaving the penthouse.

In the living room, I spot someone. They're holding a gun, uneasy on their feet as they attempt to sneak up on Elias.

Not today, asshole.

I spot a gun on the blood-stained hardwood floor and grab it. My hands shake as I point it at the massive man stalking Elias. He lifts his hand, prepared to shoot, but I pull the trigger first.

He humphs when it hits him in the upper back.

"Sage?" Elias asks, turning toward me.

He reaches me in three large strides and brings me into his arms as more people pile into the home. I close my eyes and cover my ears as three shots are fired.

Exactly three.

Upon opening my eyes, I spot three men dead on the ground, including the guy I shot in the back... who now has a bullet hole in his head.

I didn't kill him.

Elias pulls away and smooths hair off my face.

"What are you doing in here?"

"The explosion. I thought... I'm sorry."

Fuck. I'm crying again.

"Don't be sorry. You saved my life. I didn't hear that man approaching. Have you ever used a gun before?"

I shake my head.

"You're fucking perfect."

"Elias!" a man yells and waves us over. He points down into the basement.

Elias releases me and calls Del's name from the top of the stairs.

He's on the move, descending the steps, careful to avoid the ones that are gone. I'm prepared to follow him down there, but he stops and glances over his shoulder.

"Stay here, Reine."

"Sage is here?" I hear Noah say, her voice panicked.

Noah! She's alive. I consider ignoring Elias's order, then take in the appearance of the stairs again. Okay, maybe not. They're not in good shape, and Elias, Noah, and Del still need to use them to get out. So I wait at the top, watching as Elias approaches his brother and holds out his hand.

"Give me the gun." There's a pause. I can't see Del because Elias is now blocking my view of him and the rest of the basement. "I need to do it."

"Pathetic," a man says. "Have I taught you nothing, Elias? This is not how the QBM Don should lead. I hand my legacy over, and you share it with the enemy?"

Wait... is that their father? I thought he died.

I jump at the sound of a gunshot followed by a muffled thump. Elias moves out of the way revealing a big man—who looks like an older version of himself—on the ground with a bullet hole to the head.

Holy shit.

Elias just shot his father.

Chapter 26

Elias

I stand over my father and watch as the life in his eyes slowly fades.

Closure.

It settles on my shoulders.

"Elias," Lance whispers, and I hold up my hand.

"He doesn't deserve our grief. Not after everything he's done," I say, still not looking away from the man who ruined my life.

"I don't give a fuck about him. I wanted to make sure you're okay. I know that wasn't easy."

Finally, I turn toward my brother. He stares back at me with concern and sympathy. Emotions I haven't earned.

"He made my life miserable as a kid. Killing him was easy because I needed to do it for my own closure. I'm sorry I wasn't there for you that night twenty years ago."

"I thought you always hated me for killing Mom. I thought you wished I had died instead."

The tears I've been holding back pool in my eyes, threatening to fall.

"I never... Lance-a-lot... I hated *myself*." I rub my hand over my face. "I hated that you were the one forced to do it. I was the big brother. I should have been there to protect you. It should have been me, not you."

Lance walks to me, and I expect him to be mad that I pulled out his childhood nickname. Instead, he places his hand on my shoulder.

"It shouldn't have been either of us."

A lonely tear falls, and it tickles as it creeps down my cheek.

Crying is such a strange sensation. I rarely do it, but the relief of letting myself *feel* after all these years is welcoming.

"I'm sorry I let you believe... I'm sorry. I love you. I always have. I've been punishing myself for that night, and I dragged you into my suffering."

Lance brings me into a hug, and I freeze, but only for a moment before I melt into his embrace.

My baby brother.

This might be the first time we've hugged since we were kids.

I know it won't be the last time.

Noah sniffles behind us, and Lance pulls away.

"That's so sweet," she sobs.

"What?" Sage screams from the top of the stairs. "Someone fill me in."

Lance and I help Noah walk over debris as we make our way out of this hellhole.

Tomorrow, I'm calling in the order to have the place demolished. Mom wouldn't have wanted us to hold on to this part of our past.

"Are all of Percy's guys dead?" Noah asks. "How many people knew he was still alive?"

Before I can answer, my brother adds, "And why the fuck did you blow us up? You could have killed us."

I scowl at Lance, the ungrateful brat. I literally just saved his life, yet he still has something to complain about.

I answer Noah first. "We caught a couple of them for questioning. Hopefully, we'll have answers soon."

I turn to my brother.

"And we didn't blow you up. This place was rigged with explosives. One went off during the gunfight when we first arrived."

"I can't believe you brought Sage here." Noah clucks her tongue at me. "She could have died."

I puff out my chest. "Are you kidding me? You think I had a choice?"

"I can hear you guys talking about me," Sage scoffs, glaring at us as we make our way up the unstable stairs. "I wasn't letting him leave without me. Literally locked myself inside his car. Besides, I was the one who knew where you were. He had to bring me."

I would have found out after Lenetti's call, but I won't tell Sage that. Especially since I would have arrived too late. Sage is really the one who saved them.

"How *did* you know where to find us?" my brother asks, narrowing his eyes at my woman.

He better stop looking at her that way or I'll fight him.

"Noah and I installed apps on our phones to track each other at all times."

"Right. I forgot we did that," Noah smirks, and something tells me she didn't forget. She just likes pushing Lance's buttons.

"Seriously, Noe?"

Yep. He's pissed.

He hates leaving digital footprints. I mean, I do too, but my aliases still have normal lives with streaming subscriptions and legit credit cards.

"I texted you about hanging out," Sage continues. "But you didn't answer right away, which is normal if you're with Del because you two fuck all the time."

I roll my eyes at Lance's cocky smile.

"I had a bad feeling, so I checked your location. You were heading into Queens, which I thought was weird. You never go that deep into Queens. I called, and you didn't answer. I panicked and called Boss, um, Elias."

My cock twitches at the nickname, which I haven't heard her say in a while.

Did she say it on purpose to get me all hot and bothered? Jesus. Inappropriate time to get hard.

I narrow my eyes at her, then clear my throat, needing to distract my horny thoughts.

"Once Sage gave me the location, I knew exactly where you were heading. This was our childhood home."

I glance around the kitchen where we just emerged from the basement. Mold and mildew cover the walls, and the cabinets are nearly rotted away.

I remember waking up to the smell of Mom cooking us pancakes and bacon. I remember late nights when Percy was busy with QBM business and Mom would let us help her make pasta from scratch.

She was the perfect mom who did everything she could to protect us from the devil himself.

Percy.

"A part of me never believed Percy died," I say. "Him getting sick and refusing to let us see him on his deathbed always rubbed me the wrong way. Then there was one night a year ago when I swore I saw him. I thought I was losing my mind, seeing ghosts."

I booked a session with my therapist the next day to talk about it, and she convinced me it was my trauma, which could be triggered by anything... a smell... an object that reminded me of my childhood.

"So, when I found out this is where Noah was being taken, I sent in a few soldiers ahead to scope out the place. One of them spotted Percy through the basement window."

"Fuck," Lance whispers. "At least you were mentally prepared. They drugged me, and I woke up thinking I had died and gone to hell and Percy was the devil."

Sage brings her best friend in for a hug, and I glance around the home while they speak to each other.

"Are we sure none of these people are traitors?" Lance asks.

I shrug. "I think they would have made their move by now."

Sage and Noah are done with their reunion and my *fiancée* locks eyes with me.

Fiancée.

I have a fiancée.

"Thank you for saving them," she says and tucks her blonde hair behind her ear.

I want to bring her into a hug and announce to the world that I'm going to marry this woman, but I know she'll want to tell Noah first. Now's not the time.

Is that why she's being so shy right now? Because now's not the time to celebrate?

We might have ended a lot of lives today, but ours is about to begin.

I clear my throat again because my emotions are all over the place. I've been on the edge of breaking out into tears ever since killing Percy and letting the relief of closure wash over me.

"Cops are on their way. You two should go," I say to Lance and Noah.

As much as I want to know what the fuck went down before I showed up, including everything Percy said to them, Noah and Lance are contract killers who do *not* need to be on the police's radar.

I have cops and the mayor on my payroll. They'll help me cover up this mess.

I can follow up with Lance later. He needs to be with Noah right now.

"I'll stay with you," Sage offers, and I widen my eyes.

I expected her to want to go with her best friend.

I'm honored that she chose me instead.

Noah and Lance slowly make their way toward the front door, and I walk with them.

"Your father called me after he couldn't get a hold of either of you," I say to Noah. "He told me about the strange call and text, which I assume came from Percy."

"Yeah, he was trying to lure Gio here. I bet that's what the explosives were for," Lance concludes. "He was going to level this place with him inside."

"He was in the Bronx, and it was going to take him too long to get here so I told him I was closer, and I'd check it out." I nod my chin at Noah. "You should call him back. He's worried."

I shouldn't care about Lenetti and his relationship with his daughter. He's the monster responsible for our mother's death, but Noah should still know he never stopped loving her.

Noah turns to Lance. "Let's head back to the townhouse. I'll tell Gio to meet us there. It's time I finally confront him about all this."

Lance points his thumb over his shoulder. "There's a guy downstairs. Lenetti's head of security went rogue. He was working with Percy. Save him for us, okay?"

I nod, then snicker at Noah's delight. She's clearly excited to torture the fucker.

Matt, I believe is his name.

I wonder if I can get some information from him first. If he was working with Percy, he might have been working with the Lords too. Or maybe he knows something about Chase. Lance wants me to save him so they can kill him, but that doesn't mean I can't have fun first.

"Elias." I turn at Sage's voice. "Are you okay?"

She reaches up to palm my cheek. Her brows furrowed.

"You just killed your father. I know you hated the man, and you already thought he was dead, but he was still your father."

I turn my head to kiss her palm.

"He wasn't my father, though. Not in the way that matters." Her beautiful blue-green eyes glaze over with tears. "I was only born so his legacy could live on. He didn't love me, and I never loved him. I'm relieved he's dead. I'm sad, but not because he's gone. I'm sad because I didn't kill him sooner. I could have saved my mother, and Lance would have never been forced to kill her."

"You don't know that," Sage says, attempting to reassure me. Her palms are resting on my chest, and I'm sure she can feel my heart thrashing beneath.

I know she's right, but I still wish I could go back in time and fix this.

"I almost killed Percy when I was fourteen. He came home wasted smelling like booze and cheap perfume. He passed out in a chair in the living room. I went to the kitchen and got a knife. I held it to his throat. But I was a fucking coward. I didn't kill him, and he went on to become power hungry enough to taunt the Empire and Lenetti. He made too many enemies which put a target on my family's back. I could have stopped it all if I had just plunged that knife into his throat."

Tears stream down Sage's face, and I wipe them away.

"You were just a kid. That wasn't your responsibility. Please don't let this burden you."

Fuck.

I don't deserve her.

I bring her into a hug, and we stand there for a few minutes, ignoring the people around us as they clean up: removing bodies, confiscating weapons, deactivating and removing the explosives. Police officers are pulling up to the home now, likely with the mayor in tow.

"I'm mad at you by the way," Sage says when she pulls away.

I let out a tear-filled laugh.

"You are?"

She crosses her arms and raises a brow at me.

"You just drop the 'L' word and leave? Without letting me say it back?"

I reach out for her and despite her claims of being mad, she lets me cup her face in my hands. I rub my thumb back and forth along her jaw.

"Well? *Are* you going to say it?"

She shrugs, failing to hold back her smile.

I lean in and brush my lips over hers.

"Tell me when you're ready."

"I'm ready. I just want to torture you a little."

"Speaking of torture…" I glance over my shoulder and see two of my soldiers bringing an unconscious man up from the basement. Lenetti's head of security. "I have some business to take care of. I probably won't be back until tomorrow morning."

I devour my future *wife* with a kiss that leaves her panting when I pull away. I call over Jax, who cringes as he gets close.

"Jax is going to take you back to the penthouse. Try not to hit him over the head with another vase."

"Sorry about your balls," Sage says with a wince.

What?

She must see the shock on my face. "I kinda kicked him in the nuts when he wasn't going to let me go inside."

"It wasn't kinda," Jax mumbles. "You *did* kick me in the nuts."

I lean in.

"I'm proud of you," I say and place one last gentle kiss on her lips. "But maybe stop injuring my head of security."

"I did it because nothing or no one was stopping me from getting to you," she whispers, her breath sweet and tempting on my tongue. "Because I love you."

Chapter 27

Elias

Alot can happen in a day... or two.

Like the downfall of the Empire.

And the death of Giovanni Lenetti.

Noah confronted him at his Lower East Side townhouse, and the moment he confessed, she put a bullet through his head.

Fitting that I had done the same thing to my own father just hours before.

After years of chasing evidence to pin the deaths of the mafia wives and children on Lenetti, we finally got our reason why.

It was all a power move. It was about weakening the other mobs, to have them fear him so the Empire could rise to the top.

Noah's mother overheard this plan, and she was terrified. She tried to escape and take Noah away from Lenetti, but when he found out she was trying to leave, he panicked and hired some men to scare her. But the men weren't professionals. He hired them off the black market and they went off orders and killed Noah's mother instead.

They're the same men who forced Lance to slit our mother's throat. They're the same men who set fire to the Lords Mansion and killed Finn O'Connor's wife and daughter. And they're the same men Lance later tracked down, captured, tortured, and killed.

Then there's my father.

His lies.

His betrayal.

Lance told me everything.

How Percy received a large manilla envelope shortly after our mother's death with information on the men Lenetti hired. When Percy faked his death, he left us that envelope—but without anything connecting Lenetti to it—so we could only seek our vengeance on those men, but *he* wanted to be the one to kill Lenetti.

Percy claimed it was revenge for killing Imogen, but he didn't love our mother. He didn't mourn her. He mourned his toy. He mourned the control he had over her.

He was pissed because Lenetti took something that belonged to him. So he planned to target Lenetti through Noemi, the little girl who saw her mother killed. Lenetti let everyone believe she died that night too, but Percy had spies embedded in the Empire. He knew she was alive.

Percy's plan was to kill Noah, then lure Lenetti to our former home in Fresh Meadows and set off the explosives. With Lenetti dead and no heir to leave his Empire, the QBM could rise to the top, especially after the Lords were dismantled.

I may have wanted the Empire and the Lords gone, but I was going to do it the right way. I wasn't going to end innocent lives over greed. I was going to clean up the corruption.

Percy wouldn't have allowed it. He would have tried to dethrone me.

Matt was the one who sent Percy the envelope all those years ago with the proof that Lenetti was behind the kill orders. It turned out that he was spying on the Empire and feeding information to Percy. We just haven't figured out why yet.

It's now been two days since Lenetti and Percy were killed, and we need more answers. Lance and I have been beating the shit out of Matt, the double-timing fucker, but he's held out a lot longer than expected. Typically, I bring targets to my torture room in the basement of Underground Park Slope, but Lance had a different idea.

We brought him to the near abandoned St. Orion's Cemetery.

"Talk," Lance orders.

I pick up my brass knuckles from the top of the empty casket inside a decrepit mausoleum. After slipping it on, I cock my arm back.

"Fuck, okay!" Matt growls.

He's likely already lost sight in one of his eyes. We've cut off a few of his toes as well. We bring him to the brink of passing out then stop, giving him reprieve, only to start up again.

He's had enough.

"Start from the beginning," I say.

After a few seconds of silence, Matt talks. "I didn't want to be an Empire soldier, but I had no choice."

He's struggling to breathe, and his words are slow. Lance might have broken a rib. It's fine. We have time.

"My father got sick, and Gio would only let him out if I took his place. Lenetti threatened to harm my family if I refused. So I accepted. As a rookie, I was ignored for the most part. It allowed me to hide in plain sight. Which meant I heard a lot of things I shouldn't have.

"A few months after the Christmas Eve murders, I overheard Lenetti bragging about it. I was still furious about being forced to join at eighteen, so I thought I could use this information to my advantage. I snooped for physical proof. Lucky for me, I knew how to pick locks and sure enough, Lenetti was dumb enough to keep files on the men he hired in his safe. I made copies, then anonymously sent them to Percy Carter and Finn O'Connor, and waited for war to break out. Except, it never did.

"Years passed, and my dad got sicker. He had emphysema after being a lifelong smoker. He spent his days gambling, trying to win enough money to pay off hospital bills or buy booze and drugs for the pain. When he spent all our rent money, he went to Lenetti for a loan. But he couldn't pay Gio back. Lenetti ordered my mother and sister killed as payment. I begged Lenetti to let me pay the debt, but he refused. Instead, he beat me for interfering."

Matt wheezes and inhales as deeply as his body will allow before having a coughing fit and hawking a bloody loogie on the ground.

"Their deaths were the last straw. I wanted revenge, but Elias had just taken over the QBM, and I knew he wouldn't get involved. And the Lords were useless. I was ready to give up. I was going to end my life, so I went to a bar to get wasted first. That's when I met Percy. He was still alive. He'd been following me because he recognized me as an Empire soldier. He knew what Gio had done to my family and used that to his advantage.

"I became Percy's spy. He already suspected Noemi was still alive, and I confirmed it, but Lenetti hid her well. We never could find her location. Then last year at the end of August, Gio comes to me saying Noemi is moving back, but her name's Noah now. He tasked me with finding her a place to live after she refused to move into his townhouse with him. I was also keeping tabs on Lance for Percy so I knew I needed Noah to move into his building so I could watch them both.

"Percy found out Lance had become obsessed with Noah—the enemy's daughter—so he had me hire men to kill you two in an 'accidental' building explosion."

"You sent Finn O'Connor those pictures of me and Noah outside Cillian's apartment the night Noah killed him, didn't you?" Lance asks.

Matt coughs up more blood.

"Yeah. After you two survived the explosion, Percy was hoping Finn would take you two out himself."

"Wasn't Percy's plan to use Noah as bait to lure her father out to the Fresh Meadows home to kill him?" I ask. "How would that have worked if Noah died in the explosion or if Finn took her out?"

Matt shrugs. "Fuck if I know. The man claimed to know what he was doing, but I think he'd lost his fucking mind. He got desperate there at the end."

"I've heard enough." Lance sighs and turns to me. "I'm going to bring Noah back here. She needs to hear all this herself. Maybe she can get more out of him too."

He clamps my shoulder.

"You good?"

I nod. "I have questions for him, but I'll keep him alive."

Once Lance is gone, I face Matt.

"What do you know about a man named Moonlight?"

Matt was more than happy to give up information on Chase.

I didn't even have to torture him, and I almost felt bad for the fucker for what Lenetti did to him, but he felt absolutely no remorse for partnering with my father and putting Lance and Noah through hell.

Matt said Percy was working with a man named Moonlight.

God, I still can't stand that name.

Percy apparently saw the potential in Chase and put him in charge of human trafficking. It's how my father had been making money since faking his death all those years ago. He slowly built a customer base in the states along the Gulf of Mexico, but he needed to move his operations to the East Coast.

Chase already had connections with the Lords who funded trafficking operations and supplied buyers. Turns out, Chase was double timing Finn O'Connor and my father. He'd been building a repertoire with powerful people and planned to cut out Finn—which we did for him—and then my father—which I also did for him.

Matt said he couldn't stand Moonlight. He said Chase was cocky and reckless. Especially since he couldn't keep his mouth shut about wanting to take down the Empire and the QBM to form his own crime syndicate. My father either didn't care that Chase was aiming for the QBM, or he didn't believe Chase would succeed with his plan, and let the man continue to run the shipments.

It's because he was making a shit ton of money. He wasn't going to kill his cash cow.

Luckily for me, Chase didn't know Percy was dead so when I used my father's phone to set up a meeting with the fucker, he didn't hesitate to accept.

I pull into the South Brooklyn Marine Terminal in the SUV my father had been using and drive to a secluded area with shattered streetlights and an abandoned warehouse full of broken windows.

Where sketchy deals, assaults, and murders happen.

I spot Chase standing near the water's edge, smoking a cigarette. He's got two men with him.

"That's unexpected," Jax says from the passenger seat. "Thought we captured all his men."

"Me too."

Clearly, I've underestimated this fucker.

I bring the car to a stop far enough that when I get out, he won't know it's me. For once, being a near spitting image of my father is to my advantage.

"Percy, Percy, Percy," Chase says the moment he spots me walking toward him. "Or should I say, Elias Carter."

I stop in my tracks and reach for my gun.

"I wouldn't."

The two men standing behind him move to the side.

They have Sage.

I nearly collapse to my knees—my heart stopping for a second before it revs up in fear.

My Reine.

My fiancée.

Captured by this asshole.

How?

"Let her go, Moonlight. This won't end well for you."

Sage's hands are tied behind her back, and she's struggling to break free from the men's grip on her arms. She's screaming at them, but there's a gag in her mouth, so her words are unclear.

"Now, Elias," Chase goads. "Did you really think you could trick me into thinking you were Percy?

"Worth a shot." I shrug, attempting to keep my cool and not think about the fact that the woman I love has a gun to her temple.

I lock eyes with Sage and instead of fear staring back at me... I see rage.

My beautiful queen.

I subtly shake my head, trying to tell her not to do anything crazy. She nods, understanding.

"Percy told me his plan. He said there was a chance shit would hit the fan. He left everything to me. He told me what to do if he was killed."

I take a step forward, and Sage squeals as the man next to her digs the gun in harder.

"He said all I had to do was take the one thing you loved, and you'd hand over the QBM. And since Lenetti is also dead, I think I'll take the Empire off your hands as well. Unless." He glances back at Sage. "I'll let you have Staten Island... but Sage will have to die."

"That's not going to happen."

"Yeah?"

Chase nods to the men, and they bring Sage to him. He pulls her flush to his side and grinds his gun into her head.

"What's the plan here?" I say, taking another step closer. My eyes drop to movement at Chase's hip. Sage's hands are attempting to grab the knife he has hooked on his belt. *Didn't I just silently tell her not to do something crazy? Brat.* Thankfully, the two men beside her haven't noticed because they have their eyes trained on either me or Jax, who's out of the car behind me.

Chase has no idea that I have a dozen more men planted around here.

One hand signal from me and these three are dead.

I just need to get Sage away from them first.

She might be able to help with that if she manages to get a hold of that knife, but I still worry she'll get caught in the crossfire.

"I hand you the QBM, you give me Sage, and then what? We all live happily ever after?"

Chase laughs, leaning back and barking at the sky for dramatics.

"Of course not. You hand over the QBM, and I give you Sage, then you die together."

He fires a shot at me, and I duck down just in time. I crawl to a nearby shed for cover while his two goons bombard us with bullets. Jax returns fire while running toward the other side of the small lot to take cover behind a light pole.

"Jax, hold fire!"

Sage isn't safe yet.

"Not fucking smart, Elias," Chase growls.

I peek around the edge of the shed and notice Sage holding her arm with blood dripping down to her wrist. I curse because that bullet definitely came from Jax's gun.

"Any last words, sunshine?" Chase says, tearing the gag out of Sage's mouth.

"Yeah, eat shit," she growls and the next thing I see is Chase's eyes widening. Because she stabbed him. "Now, Elias!"

Sage drops to the ground, pulling Chase with her. I walk around the corner of the shed, a gun in each hand, and rain bullets down on the two men who are distracted by their boss on the ground injured.

I litter man number one's body with bullets: to his head, chest, stomach.

Jax takes care of man number two, allowing me to run over to Sage.

"Are you okay?" I ask, helping her stand.

My eyes quickly scan her body, searching for any other injuries.

"I'm fine. Can you untie me?"

Jax points his gun at Chase, who writhes on the ground in pain, making sure the asshole doesn't try to escape.

Once the binds are off, Sage turns to me and nearly jumps into my arms.

"Thank you for saving me again."

"This was all you, Reine. You were so brave."

"Actually, I was scared as fuck. I peed my pants a little."

I bark out a laugh. How can this woman go through something so traumatic yet still bring humor to the moment?

She's amazing.

I inspect her arm and realize the wound isn't as bad as I first thought. Just a graze. She'll still need it stitched up.

"Bitch. Fucking bitch."

Sage's nostrils flare. She stomps over to her ex and kicks him in the stomach. Right where she stabbed him.

He coughs and pulls his hands into tight fists.

I close my distance to Sage and grab her by the nape to claim her mouth. It's not a quick kiss either. It's a kiss of ownership. Sage. Is. Mine. I make sure Chase watches every lap of my tongue and pull of her lips.

"I'm so fucking proud of you," I say upon coming up for air. "I'm going to take Chase to Underground Park Slope. Jax will ride back to the penthouse with you. I'll have a doctor meet you there to stitch you up, okay?"

Her eyes trail to Chase.

"Don't worry. I'll keep him alive so you can play with him."

A cruel smile spreads across that beautiful face of hers.

Does the idea of torturing him excite her?

She really is meant for this world.

Meant for me.

Sage nods, kisses me one more time, then turns towards a waiting SUV. Jax helps her inside, then he sends another soldier in his place to assist me with this fucker.

A cleanup crew has already been called to take care of the men we killed.

"Here's what's going to happen, Chase. You're going to hand over the list of buyers, and maybe I'll let you die just a little bit quicker."

I take a pair of gloves out of my coat pocket and slip them on.

"I uh... I don't know what you're talking about."

"Sure you do. The shipments? The containers with women and children inside?"

"That was all Percy." Chase trips over his words as I stalk toward him. He's still crumpled on the ground, holding his side where Sage stabbed him.

"See, I know you're lying because my father's spy, Matthew, told us you're in charge of shipments."

I came prepared for this meeting and brought some of my favorite tools to use on idiot criminals. Like my crowbar. I nod to my soldier, Rogan, and he hands it to me.

Perfect to break kneecaps with.

"I'm not, I swear," Chase pleads, his eyes wide.

I swing the crowbar and crash it down on his right knee. Chase lets out a pierced wail.

"Here's the thing, *Moonlight*. I'm going to get that information from you one way or another. Because you're special."

Chase holds his injured knee, sobbing. "Wh-wh-why?"

"Because you threatened the woman I love. You *harmed* her."

He sucks in a deep breath and swallows, his face scrunching up.

"Sh-sh-she's yours. I don't want that fat fucking slut."

Another swing of the crowbar, and it whacks Chase in his other knee.

I tsk. "Now, Moonlight... that's my *wife* you're talking about."

He doesn't need to know we're not married yet, but I plan to remedy that soon.

Chase attempts to cradle both of his knees to his chest, but he hisses as it causes the stab wound on his side to open further. I kick him in the back just because I fucking can.

"You just couldn't keep your mouth shut about the woman I love, could you?"

I crouch down and secure Chase's hands behind his back with the zip ties I pulled from my pants pocket—like I said, I come prepared. I haul him up onto his feet, but he struggles to stay upright because of the blood loss and his bruised kneecaps—they might be broken.

I didn't hold back.

I start walking and Chase trips. I don't stop and drag him to the car. Rogan helps me shove him into the back-seat.

Once I'm behind the wheel, and Rogan in the back with Chase to make sure he doesn't die on me, I drive off.

"Where are you taking me?"

I should have put tape over his mouth.

"I'm innocent!"

Sighing, I open the middle console and take out my small handheld cattle prod—who knew that was a thing? I was delighted when I discovered it while drunk shopping online a few months ago—I hand the device to Rogan.

"You fucking dick! I will kill you. I'll kill Sage too. You two deserve each other."

I nod and Rogan digs the prod into Chase's back, sending high voltage throughout his body.

The fucker tries talking a few more times and proceeds to get shocked until he passes out, remaining unconscious, but alive, for the rest of the ride to Underground Park Slope.

I let Rogan take him to the torture room so Chase can sweat it out for a few days before I kill him.

Right now, I need to get home to my soon-to-be wife. After everything she did tonight, I have no doubt that she's going to want to help me end Chase's life.

Chapter 28

Elias

I's been nearly a week since I took Chase to the basement of Underground Park Slope.

He tried dying on me, but he wasn't getting out of this so easily.

I sent my medical team in to give him enough blood and food to keep him alive long enough for me to torture him.

While Sage recovered emotionally and physically—not that she'd admit to needing rest, but Noah helped me convince her of it—I stayed busy killing or capturing more of Chase's men. We missed about ten in the original sweep.

I also spoke with Aaron and Justin, the two soldiers assigned to protect Sage. They explained how Chase was able to grab her. It happened when they were headed to Brooklyn. Sage wanted to hang out with

Noah and console her best friend, who had just ended her father's life earlier that week. While at a stoplight, they were ambushed.

The driver was shot in the head and killed. Justin, in the passenger seat, was shot in the chest and is now recovering in the surgical unit I have set up at Underground Park Slope for situations like this—to avoid hospital visits. Aaron was in the backseat with Sage and was able to get in a few shots at Chase's men before he was shot in the leg and left to bleed out while Sage was abducted.

Aaron said she fought back the entire time, using her nails to claw at the two oversized goons who carried her to their SUV. She screamed and kicked and attempted to use her weight to escape, but they were still stronger than her.

Chase's men were smart enough to confiscate the phones belonging to my soldiers, so they weren't able to immediately contact me. Not that they could have since they were either dead or unconscious and bleeding out.

I'm really going to have a hard time securing a driver as this is the second one to die in the past few weeks.

The sun is close to rising when I return to the penthouse. Sage is asleep, and I should be exhausted, but my *fiancée* went to bed naked.

My cock hardens as my eyes scan over her full ass, barely covered by the thin silk sheet.

I spot the cut on her arm where she was grazed with a bullet.

The stitches are nearly dissolved by this point, the wound healing to leave a badass scar.

I walk over to my dresser and begin taking off my clothes. I need a shower to wash off the grime from tonight.

Then I'm going to fuck my fiancée awake.

After showering, I find some lube inside my dresser drawer where I keep condoms and other sex toys. I slather my cock and crawl onto the bed. Slowly, I take the sheets off her, making sure not to wake her. With lube still coating my fingers, I line them up to her opening and inch them inside.

She hums and stirs but doesn't wake up.

I make sure she's nice and wet before I readjust myself between her legs and press the head of my cock to her pussy.

And I thrust inside her with one quick jerk of my hips.

She wakes up with a scream, and I cover her mouth with my palm.

"Good morning, Reine."

I slowly slide out, then thrust back into her. Her confusion and panic over being woken up this way quickly fades to muffled moans against my palm.

I pound into her; the slapping sound of our bodies is music to my ears. She's making all kinds of wonderful noises, but I need her to be louder, so I remove my hand. Grabbing her long, blonde hair, I wrap it around my wrist and tug her head back. My other hand crashes down on her plump ass cheek, and I relish the recoil. The pain causes her walls to flutter around me, so I do it again and again.

She reaches her orgasm quickly, and I pause to let her pussy spasm. Once she's done, I flip her over and slide into her again.

"You never sleep naked," I muse while casually fucking her.

She claws at my ass, trying to get me to go faster.

"It was hot in here."

"No, it wasn't. Tell me the truth."

"You said you'd wake me up with sex."

"I've been busy."

"I know," she moans when I withdraw to the tip of my cock before slamming into her to the hilt... and I stop.

"You're still injured."

"Barely," she groans.

"Naughty girl."

I lean over to take her nipple into my mouth, letting my tongue lash over the hardened peak.

"I've got a surprise for you," I say and resume pumping my hips, picking up speed.

She whimpers because I'm not being gentle.

"I'll show you tomorrow, but I need you to be a good girl and give me another orgasm."

My own orgasm is getting close, and I close my eyes, savoring how wonderful my fiancée's sweet pussy fits around me.

Sage buries her fingers into my hair and pulls me down for a kiss.

"I love you," she says against my lips. "My *husband.*"

Husband.

That did it.

I spill into Sage, no longer able to hold back, and she moans with me, coming for a second time.

She's too good for me.

I rest my forehead between Sage's breasts to catch my breath. She hums and combs her fingers through my hair.

"That was amazing."

"You liked waking up to my cock inside you?"

She groans. "Yes. I'm going to need you to do that every week."

"Every week?"

"Yeah, at least once a week."

I lift my head and give Sage a quick kiss on the lips before removing my cock and collapsing onto the bed next her.

I bury my nose into her neck and inhale her sweet strawberry and vanilla scent.

"Do you want to get married?"

"We are getting married. You proposed, silly."

"No, I mean tomorrow. At the courthouse."

"Really? Why?"

"I don't want to wait a day longer."

Chapter 29

Sage

I always thought I was weird growing up not having a dream wedding in mind. My friends had scrapbooks with photos of beautiful women in extravagant gowns. They had floral arrangements, the cake, and the color of the bridesmaid dresses decided.

They always wanted to play wedding with Barbie dolls or Cabbage Patch Kids.

I'd play along, but I never had the same excitement as them.

My wedding to Chase was bare minimum. It was held at a park in New Jersey. I had the white dress I bought at Walmart. It was beautiful, don't get me wrong, but it wasn't fancy. And the ring Chase got me cost a hundred dollars.

It was all I needed at the time.

I think it's because a part of me knew my marriage to Chase wouldn't last. That it wasn't true love, no matter how much I tried to convince myself it was.

Now, here I am in a car with the man who really *is* the love of my life, my *husband,* and saying our vows in front of a judge with some stranger as our witness was more special than any of those dream weddings my friends could have planned.

Elias surprised me with a twelve carat, pear-shaped, Harry Winston ring that cost nearly $700,000.

I almost passed out.

"If you want a ceremony—"

"I don't," I say, beaming at the ring.

"What about a party instead? A celebration?"

I gasp. "Can I plan it?"

"I think that's a great idea. In fact, how do you feel about being in charge of charitable events for the Alliance."

"The Alliance?"

"Noah doesn't want to take over the Empire so it's in the process of being dissolved. I'm forming the Five Borough Alliance. FBA. Or just the Alliance. No more corrupt mafias. No more lowlife politicians and abusive assholes in power. I'm cleaning up this city and, in a few months, I'm hosting a fundraiser where I'll strengthen my connections and make new ones. I want you there so I can introduce you as my wife. Then we'll celebrate. I was hoping you'd want to organize it. And there will be plenty more parties needing organized, which is why I want you to be the event planner for the Alliance."

I bite my lip, suddenly shy that this man believes in me despite not knowing if I can do such an important job.

"Are you sure?"

"I've never been more sure of anything," he says, taking my hand to kiss my knuckles.

"I would be honored to be the event planner for the Alliance."

He flips my hand over and kisses the palm. He loves doing that.

I also love when he does that.

It's such a sweet and loving thing to do. It reminds me that he's not only a scary killer mafia boss but a cuddly teddy bear.

"So where are we going now?"

"Back to the penthouse to change and then we're going to the place where it all began."

Chase is being kept in the basement of Underground Park Slope.

The closer we get to the neighborhood, the faster my heart beats. My stomach twists and sours. It's not that I'm scared about what's about to happen... I'm anxious.

Excited.

Elias is going to kill Chase, and I'm going to watch him do it.

"You okay? You're shaking your leg and picking at your nails."

I nod and examine the pastel polish I picked out for our courthouse wedding ceremony. My nerves have me wanting to rip the acrylics off one by one.

The SUV slows, and Elias puts it in park.

We're here.

He gets out first and greets a large man with a shaved head and tattoos all over his skull. After slapping the man on his shoulder, he hands him the keys to the SUV. I'm getting out when Elias reaches my side and holds out his hand. I take it, and we walk inside.

It's barely noon, so all the lights are on with only a handful of workers cleaning, stocking the bar, or doing admin work.

Are they real workers or mafia soldiers?

Elias leads me across the empty dance floor. A chill runs down my spine remembering the last time I was here.

The night it all began.

The night we met.

The night my life changed.

We stop at a black door, and Elias turns to me.

"Are you sure you want to go down there?"

I fidget on my feet and chew on my lower lip.

"Sage, listen to me." Elias takes my face in his hands. He rubs his thumb over my bottom lip, pulling it from my teeth. "The things I'm going to do—"

"I want to go. I need to see."

He closes his mouth and grits his teeth, his nostrils flaring.

"I'm not going to hold back, and you might see me... a different way after."

I catch his thumb when it passes over my lower lip again, and I take it into my mouth. My tongue lashes over the tip, and Elias lets out a puff of air.

"I know. I don't care. You're my *husband*. I... I want to help."

Elias drops his hands, and he's preparing to argue, but I hold up my finger.

"I need to help. Please."

I've come a long way from nearly puking after watching Noah's father stab a fork in Del's hand all those weeks ago, but that was different. I wasn't expecting it, and I was already nervous as fuck about wearing the wire.

Now I've seen dead bodies. I've sewed up bullet holes on my husband's body. I fucking shot a man.

And I stabbed Chase.

I'm not letting Elias go in there alone when Chase is the one who abused me. He threatened me. *My family.*

He should die by *my* hands.

I'm not sure Elias will allow me to be the one to take his life, I'll worry about that once we're down there.

He studies my face for a few seconds, then gives me a curt nod. After putting a code in the keypad next to the door, we descend the stairs.

I don't know what I was expecting. Maybe a cold, dark, and haunted basement like the ones in horror movies. But the staircase is solid, not some decrepit wooden steps.

The walls are clean and painted red with beautiful minimalist artwork hanging throughout.

The floors when we get to the bottom are a lovely, stained cement.

There's a black cotton couch and matching recliner, a coffee table, and large television hanging over a fireplace.

A few arcade games, including pinball, are tucked in a corner.

This place is cozy and nothing at all like I'd expect a torture chamber to be.

We walk through another door and into a red-walled hallway. There are four black doors on each side, all closed.

We pass them until arriving at a door in the very back of the hallway.

Elias pauses before turning to me. "Are you ready?"

I inhale deeply and let the breath slowly creep out.

I stretch my neck from side to side and crack my knuckles. "Let's do it."

Elias shakes his head with a chuckle and opens the door. Chase looks up from the chair he's slouched in. He's naked, his hands are tied behind his back, and his ankles are secured to the chair's legs.

His face is swollen and littered with cuts and bruises and instead of feeling sorry for the man I once convinced myself I loved, I pity him. I offered him all my support after his mother's death. I was there for him when he lost his job, and I started working a second job just so we could pay bills. When I discovered he was using, I offered to pay for his rehab.

He wouldn't let me help him.

Now there's no one to save him.

His eyes fill with hatred the moment he spots me. He tries to talk over the gag in his mouth, but the words are too muffled.

"Chase Henley," Elias says and closes the door behind us. "Or should I call you... Moonlight."

Elias walks over to the wall across from Chase and picks up a tool.

"Locking pliers," he says, answering my questioning stare. "Used to... extract things."

Chase squeals and thrashes in the chair.

"What would you like me to start with, Reine? The nails or the teeth?"

Chase whimpers this time, and his pleading eyes turn to me.

I tap my finger on my chin. "Hmm. I think the nails. Maybe after you're done plucking them, you can cut off his fingers."

Elias groans and grabs me by the back of the neck, crashing his lips against mine.

I open my mouth for him, and he thrusts his tongue in, massaging my own.

Chase's muffled roar encourages me, and I'm ready to ride Elias right here in front of my ex, but he releases me when my hands take aim for his cock.

"Not yet, Ma Chérie. Let's have some fun first."

My pleasure.

Chapter 30

Elias

Fuck, my beautiful Sage is tempting me.

I want to sink deeply inside her and force this piece of shit to watch.

It's going to happen, but I need him in pain first. I need him on the brink of death so he can witness hell on earth before facing the devil himself.

I give Sage one more quick peck on the lips before releasing her and walking back to the asshole. He grunts and jerks around, doing whatever he can to escape the binds, but he's not going anywhere.

I rip off the gag so I can hear his screams for what's about to happen. His hands are bound behind his back, but I need them in front. Instead of untying him, I swiftly lift them up and over his head, the sickening crack of his arms dislocating from his shoulders echoes throughout the room.

Sage's gasp is drowned out by Chase's guttural scream. Spit dribbles down his chin and tears streak down his cheek.

I glance at Sage, and she stares at him wide-eyed.

Not yet scared.

She appears more in awe than anything else.

That's good.

His arms hang limp in front of him. He might have lost feeling in his hands because of the dislocation.

I guess we're about to find out.

I pick up his bound hands and isolate his middle finger. His nails aren't too long, but it's just enough for my pliers to take hold.

"Chase, Chase, Chase," I goad. "This is only the beginning. Relax... enjoy your breaths while you can."

I jerk my hand up. Chase's high-pitch cry lets me know I did some damage.

Fingernails are notoriously difficult to remove. It's not a one and done process.

I've managed to dislodge his nail off the bed just enough to get a better hold with the pliers.

"You're going to give me some information, Moonlight."

"Fuck. You," he slurs, more spit pouring from his mouth.

"That's Sage's job," I say and rip his fingernail the rest of the way off.

Blood pools out and drips down to the ground.

I move on to the next finger.

"I need all the names and addresses of your men, including anyone who knew about Sage."

We thought we had caught everyone, and we managed to capture a few more this past week, but I've been underestimating this fucker. He proved he was deeper into his attempted crime syndicate takeover than we thought. I want to be sure we have everyone this time.

He still didn't have the numbers compared to me, but it was a nice effort.

When Chase doesn't say anything, I rip the nail off his pointer finger.

"I've got eight more to go and then we can move on to your toes. After that, I'll start removing your fingers. I've got all the time in the world. You can tell me now and maybe I'll spare some of your little piggies."

I stomp my boot down on his bare foot, hard enough to possibly break something.

"Oops."

Chase clenches his mouth, suppressing his scream with a groan.

Still, he doesn't say anything.

Guess he's going to make this difficult.

I finish one hand, and the fucker is holding strong.

This isn't working.

I turn and walk back to the table where I have my torture devices laid out and set the pliers down.

"What's wrong?" Sage asks. She's looking a bit queasy, but she's doing great keeping it together.

"I need a new... incentive."

Picking up the plastic bag, I give Sage a wink and return to Chase.

"No. NO!" He shakes his head frantically and jerks around in his chair again.

Idiot. That's only going to wear him out quicker.

"I need names," I say. "Give me names, and I'll let you breathe."

He clenches his jaw, grinding his teeth.

"Very well."

I slip the bag over his head in one slick move and pull it tight. The sound of Sage's gasp is once again silenced by the crinkle of the plastic and Chase's choking as he struggles for oxygen.

I wait until his fight starts to wane before removing the bag.

"Names?"

"Fuck you," Chase wheezes.

I put the bag back over his head. This time his fight dies quicker. His body is likely overworking to stay alive.

"Names," I say the moment the bag is off his head.

Chase huffs and puffs and greedily takes breaths while I allow it.

Yet... he still hasn't learned.

He says nothing.

This time, it takes less than a minute for him to reach the brink of passing out.

When I remove the bag, I don't say a word, only lifting a brow.

"Okay!" he rasps, his voice full of spite.

I call for Jax, causing Sage to jump at the sound of my deep voice in the quiet room.

When he walks in, I motion to Chase who begins rattling off ten names and addresses of the remaining men and women who were working with him. I instruct Jax to gather a team to find them and turn them over to the FBI. I could kill them, but we found a few of the people helping Chase had been blackmailed. Chase preyed on their vulnerability. They were forced to do bad things, and that doesn't automatically mean they should die. I'll let the FBI deal with it, that way they can owe me.

I also confiscated Chase's phones and laptops and handed them over to Phil. He'll make sure any mentions of Sage in texts or emails will be removed. He'll be able to scrub any record of Sage and Chase being married as well.

Phil will then scour Chase's correspondences. I need information on every lowlife scum he made transactions with. He was selling to some powerful assholes. People who have money and connections who are desperate and sick enough to buy humans to use for whatever fucked up fantasy they have.

If Chase is smart, his client list will be hidden, or in a secure location.

I'll know soon enough.

When Jax is gone, I turn to Sage.

"Tell me what you want to do to him."

Chase's head whips up, and he narrows his eyes at Sage. "Bitch," he spits and snarls.

"Don't you fucking talk to my *wife* like that."

"Wife?" Chase says uncertainly.

"I told you this when I captured you. Did you forget?" I ask. "Sage and I are married."

Sage holds up her left hand and flashes him her diamond.

Chase scrunches his face in disgust. "Whore!"

Did he learn nothing? I guess the lack of air made him dumber.

I cock my hand back to punch him, but Sage beats me to it. His head wrenches to the side, and blood spurts out of his mouth and nose. A huge gash is left behind from the engagement ring. Pride swells within me for her using the diamond like a weapon... but I also worry she'll damage it.

She doesn't look concerned—not that it matters. I could always buy her another one.

"That's for hitting me," Sage says, pivoting on her heel and walking over to my torture table. Her eyes travel over the knives, and I expect her to grab one, but instead she picks up the thin bladed scalpel.

My cock jerks at the sight of her holding the tool.

She whips back around, smiling like a deviant queen ready to let her true nature come out to play.

Fuck, she's beautiful.

When she's back standing in front of Chase, she puts the tip of the surgical knife to the corner of his mouth.

She secures her hand on his shoulder, in the dislocated spot, and Chase lets out a wail.

Fuck she's amazing.

A natural. No instructions. No hesitations.

She's a woman who knows what she wants.

"This is for controlling me."

She slices and the skin peels apart.

"This is for threatening me."

She moves the knife to the other side and slices again.

"This is for threatening my parents."

She slowly, expertly, sinks the thin blade into his eye.

Goddamn I want to put a baby inside her so fucking bad.

She leaves the scalpel embedded in his eye and turns to face me.

Shit, she's crying.

"Oh, babe." I open my arms.

She wipes her cheeks and falls into my embrace.

"I'm fine." She laughs through her tears. "That was really fucking cathartic is all."

"I know. I know," I say, petting her silky hair. "It's like a rage room… and I know you have so much more rage to show him."

I release her and clutch her chin, claiming her lips with a gentle kiss that leaves me wanting more.

But we've got work to do.

"Please," Chase mumbles when Sage rips the surgical knife from his eye.

Thick blood seeps out, mixing with the streaks from the cuts in the corners of his mouth.

"Now that we have names of the low-level idiots working with you, I need names of clients. Anyone who bought human beings from you, you piece of shit," I say as my beautiful, vindictive *wife* starts slicing little cuts all over Chase's chest. Not too deep, but enough for the wound to sting with pain and slowly leak blood.

When he doesn't answer, Sage walks over to my tool table and picks up a knife, then proceeds to stab him in the thigh.

"Tell him."

"Fucking cunt!"

Sage extracts the knife from his thigh only to stab him again on the other side.

I groan at how sexy she is right now… but at the same time, Chase is losing a lot of blood, so I need her to slow down, or he'll die before we get answers.

I grab Sage by the throat and graze my lips over hers. "You're doing such a good job, Ma Chérie. But you're going to kill him if you keep at it."

She shyly looks away and giggles. "Sorry. I got excited."

"I know," I say and kiss her.

Her vengeance tastes so good.

I release my stabby little queen and turn to Chase. He glares at me, and I relish it. He hates that I have the woman he lost. He hates that he was caught. He hates that I'm more powerful than him.

"Here's what's going to happen," I begin and take out the knife Sage left in his thigh. I press my palm down on the wound to stop it from bleeding. "You're going to give me names or tell me where to find the list. The longer you hold out, the longer I'll keep you alive. I'll bring you to the brink of death, then patch up all your wounds, let you heal, just so Sage can come over here and stab you all over again. You think this isn't that bad? That the plastic bag was child's play? Just wait until I bring out the water."

Sage says 'oooo' beside me. "What can you do with water?"

I don't look away as I forcefully clutch Chase's chin so he can look me in the eye.

"There's always waterboarding." I shrug. "Or... I could fill a pot and put it on a portable burner." I point to the ground. "I'll stick his feet in the water while it heats up.

Slowly, his feet will cook until the water is boiling, and the skin melts off."

Sage gags.

I glance at her over my shoulder and grimace. She has her hand over her mouth, but waves at me to keep going.

God she's perfect.

Despite the grotesque threat I just described, she hasn't let that scare her away.

"So... what will it be, Chase? Your client list or your feet boiled off your body?"

His skin is covered in a sheen of sweat, his chest rising and falling rapidly. He's lost a lot of blood, and I'm surprised he hasn't passed out yet.

"It's on a drive," he says between breaths. "At my bank. Safety deposit box."

When Chase gives me the name of the bank, I pull out my phone and text it to my men. Getting access to it won't be easy. Phil might have to dig up dirt on the branch manager. I could also go the legal route and call my FBI contact for a warrant. I'll worry about that later.

When I put my phone away, I turn to Sage.

"What do you want to do next? He's likely going to pass out soon because of blood loss."

Sage chews on her bottom lip while thinking and the moment a vindictive smile spreads across her gorgeous face, I know exactly what she's about to say.

"I want him to watch."

Chase slowly lifts his head. He narrows his one eye and snarls.

There's some fight left in him after all.

"The man Percy and I partnered with is going to find you, and he's going to kill you... and your families. He's powerful and—"

"And he's next," I say, turning my phone around to show Chase the text I just got from Phil.

He managed to hack into Chase's burner phone and get the man's name.

Some billionaire prick.

The top funder of this operation.

Chase's one functional eye widens.

I backhand him, his head whipping to the side in a loud thwack. He spits blood on the ground, aiming for me, but he's too far away for it to reach.

I shoot a text back to Phil to gather the evidence and send it around to news outlets and my contact at the FBI.

They can have him.

All we want is Chase.

He's my gift to my wife.

"Take control, Reine," I say, tucking my phone away. "Show this fucker who he gave up."

Her eyes widen. "Take... take control?"

I clutch Sage's chin.

"Order me around, Ma Chérie."

Chapter 31

Sage

My doubt slowly fades, replaced with determination and desire.

Elias is giving me control again.

He knows how desperately I need it right now, especially in front of the man who denied me control for years.

"Undress me. Slowly," I say.

Elias leans in to give me a kiss, but I stop him, catching his face in a clawed grip.

"I didn't say you could kiss me."

I release him, and he smirks, like a brat. He glances over his shoulder, then holds up a finger.

"One second."

Elias turns and walks to a sink behind Chase to wash his hands.

Right. He got Chase's blood on them.

After drying his hands, Elias grabs what looks to be a helmet and puts it on Chase whose head lolls as he struggles to stay conscious.

Elias latches the helmet to chains hanging from the ceiling. I'm guessing it's to prevent him from moving his head around. Elias then picks up a roll of tape off the torture table and tears off two pieces. Chase squeals and jerks around in his chair as Elias puts the tape on his eyelids to make sure they stay open.

"That's sick," I whisper. Not so much in disgust but in awe because Elias has literally thought of everything. I mean, who has a specially made helmet that prevents head movement?

I guess mafia bosses who need it for torture.

Elias pauses once he's done, seeming to gauge my reaction. The corner of his mouth turns up.

"This turns you on, doesn't it?"

I bite my lip and nod.

Elias returns to me and wraps his large hand around my throat.

"You're perfect," he says against my lips, brushing them against mine.

Teasing me.

"May I undress you now?" he asks.

"You may."

Elias moves his hands to the bottom hem of my sweater. He slowly lifts it, as I commanded, and when the material reaches my breasts, Elias leans in to press his lips in between them.

"Listen, brat, you better stop disobeying me," I say, my voice infused with lust.

He chuckles, his hot breath on my skin makes me shiver. With one final kiss to my sternum, he removes the sweater the rest of the way.

Next, he gets on his knees to work on my leggings. His fingertips hook the band, and he begins inching them down.

Okay. I know I told him to undress me slowly, but I didn't know what I was talking about.

This is torture.

He's peeled the leggings down to thigh-level, allowing him to give me more kisses—one on each thigh. My hands fall to his luscious black hair. I comb my fingers through the loose curls and fist to lift his head away from my body.

"Changed my mind. Go faster and once you're done, I want you to put your mouth on my cunt."

"Yes, ma'am," he says and smiles. God it's such a beautiful smile, lighting up his entire face. He's got a small dimple on his left cheek—barely visible unless you're close enough—and crow's feet around his vibrant blue eyes.

I yelp when he shoves the leggings the rest of the way down.

"Step out... please, Madam Manilow," he says, and I hold on to his shoulders.

He tosses the bottoms toward Chase, and they land at his feet.

Fuck. I forgot he was there.

I smirk, and my ex squirms in the chair, distracting me from what Elias is doing. Because I didn't notice my underwear was gone until I'm being lifted off the ground and placed ass naked on a table. Elias gets on his knees again, allowing his face to be pussy-level, and he wraps his arms around my thighs.

He says nothing as he dives in, licking up my slit to my clit and sucks.

My head falls back with a moan, and my hands return to Elias's hair. I tug on the strands, attempting to bring him closer.

"Yes, Elias, that feels good," I say as he lashes his tongue over the sensitive bundle of nerves.

He lets go of one thigh and seconds later, two of his fingers are teasing my entrance.

"I need them inside me," I whine.

He slides them in and pumps casually while his mouth works my clit. He hums, feeling my walls clench his two girthy fingers, and the vibration sends a shot of lust throughout my body.

"I need to come. Make me come, Boss."

The nickname is like a catalyst, and he pumps his fingers faster. His mouth sucks my clit rougher. When he lets go of my other thigh to reach his arm up and pinch my nipple, my release washes over me.

Elias stands when I'm done shaking, and he walks over to Chase, forcing him to watch while he sucks my pleasure off his fingers. I stifle my moan at how fucking hot and sick that is, and I think I need to question my morality after today.

But right now?

I need more.

"Take off your clothes and fist your cock," I say.

I lean back on the table and watch Elias remove his shirt. I've explored the mesmerizing ink across his expansive chest and thick arms more times than I can count, and I can never get enough. The same theme along his chest and arms continues down his thighs and legs: roses and greenery, guns, knives, and snakes.

When his underwear is off, his dick springs up, pointing directly at me. Elias steps between my legs.

"Not yet," I tsk. "I want to watch you touch yourself."

Elias closes his eyes, the lids fluttering at my words. He takes hold of his cock and slowly strokes the shaft.

"Faster."

"I can't. I'll come, and I'm not coming unless it's inside you."

I slap him.

His head whips to the side, and his hand pauses mid-stroke. I cover my mouth with my palm, failing to hold in my giggles.

"Sage," he warns.

"That's for being a brat," I say. "Brats don't get to come until I say so."

Chase grunts, but I ignore him, relishing the fact that he can't look away. That he gets to see what it's like to please a woman.

"Touch. Yourself," I order, and Elias resumes fisting his cock.

He grits his teeth, I assume to stop himself from coming. I lock eyes with him as I pinch and pull my nipples.

"So good, Boss," I whisper.

He growls and before I can give him his next order, he's grabbing my legs and shoving his cock inside me.

"Not fair!" I scream, which turns into a moan when Elias drives into me like a madman. "Fuck, yes, Boss."

He kisses me. It's raw and consuming, and his teeth catch on my lips. I taste blood, but I don't care because I've never had a man lust over me the way that Elias does.

It's slightly toxic... definitely full of red flags... but it doesn't matter because they're my red flags now.

Because he's my husband.

Mine.

"Please," I whimper against Elias's mouth.

"Tell me what you need," he nearly growls.

"Make me come. Please. I need to come."

His hand finds my neck again, and I can't stop the moan when his grip tightens. He pistons into me harder, the loud slaps echoing around the cold, dim room. My vision blurs from his strong hold around my neck. It's skirting that wonderful line between pain and pleasure.

When my eyes begin to droop from the lack of oxygen, Elias lets go and the relief of getting air while getting fucked so brutally has my body erupting with a second orgasm.

Elias pumps a few more times before he spills his cum inside me.

He rests his forehead on mine, breathing heavily. I rub my hands up and down his back—something he rarely lets me do. He usually grabs me by the wrist and gently shoves my hands away.

Not this time.

My fingertips pass over several scars—too many scars. I've seen them before, but I never asked about them, and he hasn't told me about them either. Most of them are hidden underneath tattoos.

"Elias," I whisper, my voice laced with tears.

He pulls back and cradles my head in his hands. "Some are from getting shot or stabbed. Some are from my father."

"I'm so sorry."

"Don't be. They made me stronger. They made me the man I am today."

He kisses me, then slowly removes his cock and turns me, legs spread wide for Chase to watch as cum slowly seeps from me.

Elias uses his finger to shove it back inside.

"That's how you fuck someone," Elias says to Chase while pulling up his pants. He zips and buttons them, then walks back to the chair Chase sits in limply. Only his head is still being held up, his eyes taped open. "This amazing and beautiful woman deserves to be worshipped. To get all the orgasms. That was only two. I've given her plenty more."

"Glad you enjoy my leftovers," Chase says. His voice is weak, but full of arrogance.

Elias's arm cocks back and before I can stop him, he punches Chase square in the jaw.

"Elias, wait," I say as he tears off the helmet and rips the tape off my ex's eyelids. "I want to do it."

I'm slipping my clothes back on as he storms over to the torture tool table, next to the one he fucked me on, and grabs a knife. He shakes his head. "No, Sage, I can't let you do that."

"Let me?"

"You know what I mean. Killing someone..."

"I almost killed that man who was going to shoot you."

"But you didn't. One of my men put a bullet in his head. Taking a human life changes you. And this is different. That man was a stranger. You didn't have a history with him."

"Elias... I'm fine. I promise. I *want* to do this. Please. I need to."

I reach for the knife he's clutching in a deathly grip.

Instead of handing it over right away, he searches my eyes waiting to find my fear, any hesitation from me.

I've never been more certain of something in my life.

"Okay," he says, softly.

"Bitch," Chase gurgles, spitting out blood and a couple teeth from the impact of Elias's punch.

"Seriously?" I say and slowly sink the knife into his thigh. Chase clenches his jaw and groans. "Haven't you learned that talking gets you in more trouble? More pain?"

I take the blade out of his leg and blood pools to the surface.

Elias is off to the side watching me, but I keep my focus on Chase.

I never imagined I'd get to carry out all the fantasies I've had about ending this man's life.

"I did everything for you," I say, my voice quiet. I hold the knife to his chest. My hands shake ever so slightly. "I was *good* to you."

The muscles in Chase's jaw ripple. He's desperate to say something, but he's smart this time and stays quiet.

"You made me believe I was worthless. You mentally and verbally abused me. I left and yet, you couldn't let me be at peace. You came back into my life and used my *parents* as leverage to force me to help you."

I vaguely register Elias's steps before he's at my back. He snakes his arms around me and covers my hands with his on the knife. I hadn't realized how badly they were shaking. Or that I was crying.

Sobbing.

"Fuck you." It's all I have left to say before I sink the knife into Chase's heart.

He sucks in a sharp breath, his eyes widening before they slowly close as the life drains out of him.

I let go of the knife as if the handle burned me and turn to bury my face in Elias's chest. He cocoons me in his long, strong arms.

"I'm so proud of you," he says softly and kisses the top of my head.

We stand there for a few minutes before he releases me.

"Come on, my wife." He holds out his hand. "Let's get you cleaned up."

He leads me down a hallway to a room that has a bed and a bathroom, and we quietly shower together.

No sex, just a few kisses, and a terrifying and dangerous man taking care of the woman he keeps saving.

Who he chose to spend the rest of his life with.

Chapter 32

Elias

It's been a few months since Sage killed her ex. She's handling it better than I expected. I should have known because Sage has always surprised me with her strength and determination.

Tonight is the fundraiser and the unofficial introduction of The Five Boroughs Alliance.

The news of Gio Lenetti's death spread fast across New York City. Some knew about his life of crime, but he was mostly known as a prominent businessman. He owned some of the best restaurants and nightclubs in Manhattan and the Bronx.

His death was reported as natural causes, a favor I cashed in for my new soon-to-be sister-in-law.

Lenetti left all his money to Noah, but she gave it away to charity organizations and sold his businesses for pennies either to staff or to those Gio wronged over the years.

The Lords and the Empire are gone.

The QBM is dead along with Percy's pathetic legacy. We kept his fake death a secret, only letting a few we trusted know what really went down in Fresh Meadows. I didn't want him to have any more undeserved attention.

I'm sitting in the living room when Sage walks out, ready for tonight's event.

Fuck me. She looks amazing.

My eyes scan her body from the black stiletto heels, up her tanned legs and the side split of her red dress. The fabric clings to her body, draping down to the ground. The top is a corset with sheer sleeves that hang off her shoulders and pushes up her plush breasts fantastically.

"My wife," I nearly growl, standing.

She smiles as she walks to the kitchen while putting on her gold hoop earrings. Her blonde hair is styled in a half updo with wavy strands falling down her back.

"My husband," she echoes.

I reach the kitchen island and grab my wallet sitting on the counter, placing it in my back pocket. After putting on the holster holding my EpiPen, inhaler, and Benadryl, I pick up my guns and knives. Sage watches me place them in holsters all over my body: shoulders, waist, shins.

My Reine's eyes fill with desire as I roll my sleeves down, covering the ink along my forearms. I grab my suit jacket draped over a chair and slip it on.

"You better stop looking at me like that, Ma Chérie, before I throw you on this counter and feast on your sweet pussy."

She smiles and rolls her eyes. "You're insatiable."

"I'm not the one who was eye-fucking my forearms."

She shrugs. "I couldn't help it. They're sexy."

I lean in to give her a kiss, but she turns her head and taps on her cheek.

Right.

Can't mess up the lipstick.

It matches her dress, and I'm already counting the hours until I ruin the beautiful color with kisses and face fucking.

"Shall we?" I say and hold out my arm for her.

The drive to the Wyndock Hotel in Midtown Manhattan takes about forty-five minutes because of traffic. The moment Noah and Lance told me Lenetti was dead, I knew I wanted to hold my party announcing the Alliance there. It was always a favorite party location for Gio.

Now it's all mine.

We never found out who invited me to Lenetti's Christmas party all those months ago. We assumed it was Matt since he was playing both sides. My father knew I'd jump at the opportunity to attend to make connections and possibly steal some of Lenetti's contacts. Inviting me was smart, but also risky.

It ended up being one of the best nights of my life because I was reunited with Sage. I have no doubt we would have found each other again through Noah, but it wouldn't have been the same.

A team of my men lead us through the doors and into the lobby where people stop and watch us like we're two celebrities walking the red carpet.

They're likely all staring at Sage because it took all my willpower not to ravage her in the SUV on the way here.

It helped that we picked up her parents on the way.

They've been back for a month, and they're already talking about selling their house and moving to my island permanently.

I'm all for it, but Sage is throwing a fit.

She doesn't want to be far away from her parents, but I think I've convinced her that we could visit them often.

Blue water, white sand, fun in the sun.

She knows I'll always have guards there watching over them. They'll always be safe no matter who my enemies are.

When we enter the grand ballroom, heads turn our way, and I can already see excited faces wanting to approach and start conversations.

Thankfully, we're saved by Lance and Noah.

The two turned their fake engagement into a real one but before tying the knot, they want to travel.

The women squeal as they assess their outfits. Noah is wearing a sparkling black gown to match her black hair.

Lance is dressed in all black: suit, shirt, tie.

He smiles, watching Noah and Sage fangirl over each other.

"You look... happy," I say to him. "Is this what the suburbs do to you?"

Last month, Noah and Lance moved to Westchester County. They've got a normal looking home with a white picket fence, and even a cute little corgi named Kevin.

They've stepped back from New York City's crime underworld to travel, fuck, and kill.

It actually sounds amazing.

"This is what it means to find your soulmate," Lance says, barely taking his eyes off Noah. "You've got the same goofy look, brother."

He takes a sip of his whiskey, watching for my reaction over the top of his glass.

He's right. I've never been happier to have the woman who now owns my heart and soul by my side.

"I need to see the ring," Noah says, greedily grabbing Sage's hand.

"Wait, you two are engaged?" Lance asks.

Sage giggles. "We're *married.*"

"Seriously? Before us? Rainbow Bright, why didn't you tell me?"

Noah scoffs, possibly at the weird nickname or because Lance is clueless.

"I figured you knew. Don't you and your brother talk?"

I wince. I'm still working on that. Lance knows that I'm trying. He pretends to hate talking to me but anytime I miss a text or phone call, he chews me out.

I didn't tell him that we got married because that's something to reveal in person. Plus, I honestly thought Noah would tell him.

I roll my eyes. She's just as stubborn as Sage.

"No, he didn't," Lance whines. "We've both been a bit preoccupied with asshole traitors."

"And starting new crime syndicates," I add.

"Yeah... You two should work on that," Noah says, goading us both.

I'm not taking the bait.

"They really should," Sage says and elbows me in the side.

I narrow my eyes at her. She also knows I'm trying.

"Are your parents here? I want to meet them," Noah asks Sage, thankfully changing the subject.

"Yeah, they've already found people to chat with at the bar. They're both extroverted like me, and by the end of the night, they'll probably have a dozen new friends."

"Mr. Carter, Mrs. Carter," a man says approaching our group.

The mayor of New York City.

Lance and Noah use the interruption to slink away, and I narrow my eyes at my brother when he catches my glare. He waggles his brows at me.

He's totally planning to find a place to fuck Noah.

Except, she drags him unwillingly to the bar where they find Sage's parents... who proceed to give the two contract killers the most enthusiastic hugs I've ever witnessed.

My poor brother stiffens and blanches, as if the man and woman have the plague.

I chuckle and return my attention to the mayor and his wife.

Time to network.

Next month, Sage is launching her new event planning business, and I will be making sure everyone here knows she's the one who organized tonight's festivities.

"Mayor Quam, nice to officially meet you," Sage says, going heavy on the charm.

She's holding my hand, and I squeeze it not so gently.

The mayor is a handsome man. Tall, dark skinned, mesmerizing dark brown eyes—Sage's words, not mine that I totally didn't get jealous over—and a smile worth a million bucks.

He came to me for help when his father got mixed up with the Lords, and in exchange, we used his budding popularity in community activism and fast-rising political career to claim the city. He's believed in what I've been working hard for years to do: clean up crime and corruption across the five boroughs.

"Please, call me Enzi," he says to Sage, giving her a wink.

Sage brings my hand up to her lips and kisses the knuckles, as if anticipating my jealousy.

She knows me well.

"Congratulations on your new... business," Enzi says, giving me a nod. It's as if he knew not to shake my hand after that wink. Smart man. I might have broken it if he had. "The city thanks you for bringing down the Moonlight trafficking ring."

Still a stupid fucking name.

"It was the least I could do," I say, lost for words.

I hate networking, but it's a necessity. I always feel awkward, but tonight's a little bit easier with my wife by my side.

Sage is speaking with Enzi's wife, Nia. The two are laughing, and my woman is absolutely glowing. I can't help smiling, an ache forming behind my eyes and in the back of my throat at how normal this all feels.

I mean, sure, I still lead a crime syndicate, but it's one that aims to do good. One that has to be the bad guy sometimes to take down the bad guys. I'm hoping that someday, I can leave it all behind and live the rest of my years with the woman I fell in love with.

"Are you ready for your speech?" Enzi asks, pulling me from my thoughts.

I nod, and we enter small talk for the next few minutes, talking about our honeymoon, which we delayed while dealing with the aftermath of the trafficking ring bust. Next month I'm taking Sage to Aruba.

The mayor is eventually called away by a prominent businessman whose name I can't remember. I breathe a sigh of relief when Enzi and his wife excuse themselves and walk off.

Sage and I make our way to the stage at the back of the room. It takes us about thirty minutes because we're being stopped every few steps by people I know either through legal business connections or others who know who I truly am and want to be part of my trusted few.

Right before we get on stage, Sage turns to me.

"I want to tell you something. It's kinda important so you can't freak out."

"And you feel right now is the best time to tell me?"

"Yes."

She bites her lip, nearly jumping with anticipation.

"Go on then, brat."

She giggles and takes my hands in hers.

"Remember all those times we fucked without a condom?"

"Yeah..."

"Well... I kept forgetting to take my birth control, and you can't really blame me because things have been really fucking stressful, and the way you kept talking about marriage and babies and how you'd always put your cum back in me... well..."

My heart stops beating. The noise in the room fades, and all I hear and see is my wife.

"You're pregnant?"

That's what she's trying to tell me?

She beams and nods enthusiastically.

I scoop her up in my arms and spin her around.

She squeals and laughs, slapping my back. "Put me down, I'm going to puke!"

I gasp and immediately set her feet on the ground.

"Shit, I'm sorry."

I kneel and place my hands on her stomach. She covers my knuckles with her palms.

"How far along are you?"

"Ten weeks."

I do the math in my head then smirk.

"Are you telling me that when we fucked in front of your ex…"

She bites her bottom lip and nods.

"Isn't that some karma bullshit?" I say and laugh.

I stand, and Sage reaches up to lock her fingers around the back of my neck. Lifting on her tiptoes, she nuzzles my nose before kissing me. It's a consuming kiss that has me wanting to devour her.

Sage is better than me, and she's the first to pull away. Our guests are waiting.

The chatter in the room comes to an end once the music stops playing and people notice us on stage.

"Good evening," I begin, pausing to scan the room. "My name is Elias Carter, though, some of you might know me as Johnny Goode, businessman."

I glance at Sage, and she gives me a wink that somehow settles my nerves. I've always hated speaking in front of strangers.

"Tonight is more than a fundraiser. It's a party to celebrate my marriage. I'd like to introduce you to my beautiful wife, Sage."

Applause erupts from the room, and Sage waves like the beauty queen she is. She's a natural.

Once the noise in the room dies down, I continue.

"I also wanted to share a new venture of mine. One that will ensure the days of corrupt politicians and dangerous criminals are over."

There are a few nods across the crowd, some shocked faces, but mostly those who are eager for what I'm going to say next.

"The Lords are gone, the Empire has fallen, and the QBM is no more. The Five Boroughs are now united. Together, we will work to ensure humans are no longer sold for sex, and drug dealers aren't targeting children. I know it's impossible to rid the world of these lowlifes completely, but you are now part of the New York City syndicate that will make sure those responsible will not get away with it."

I pause, letting the words sink in.

The silence in the room as the crowd hangs on my every word sends chills throughout my body.

Sage squeezes my hand and urges me to finish.

I'm just a mafia king with his queen by his side.

A man who went from obsessing over this woman to having the honor of calling her mine.

And now she's here as I start this new chapter of my life.

"Welcome to the Alliance."

Epilogue: Sage

Two & a Half Years Later

It took a lot of sex and some threats of releasing a video of Elias singing karaoke, but I finally convinced him to move out of the city and to the suburbs.

Mafia Dons don't live in homes with white picket fences, he had argued.

Well, they do now.

I'm in the kitchen grabbing an iced tea and some chips to bring outside to the barbecue. I waddle my ass out the door and down the steps with the bowl of Doritos on my hip and the glass of tea in my hand.

"Sage!" Elias grumbles, reaching me the moment I step on grass. "You should be staying off your feet."

He grabs the bowl and holds out his arm for me to use as a crutch.

Despite my stubbornness about not wanting to accept his help, I sigh at the release of pressure it provides.

"I'm fine. I've been through this before. I know my limits."

"You almost died giving birth the first time," Del snorts as we reach the chairs placed around the fire pit in the backyard.

I scowl at my brother-in-law and motion the tips of my fingers across my neck.

"I didn't almost die," I say as Elias helps lower me into the Adirondack chair. "I passed out because of a uterine rupture that caused blood loss."

Noah slaps the back of her hand against Del's chest. He mouths 'what' at her, and she shakes her head.

"This pregnancy is being closely monitored too." I turn my scowl to my husband. "By the live-in doctor somebody just had to hire."

Elias holds up his hands. "I'm not taking chances."

I roll my eyes but smile because my Level 100 Clinger hasn't changed at all.

"I'm on Elias's side," Noah says, giving him a wink.

She does that to piss off Del, and he reacts accordingly by balling his hands into fists.

"The only person I trust with her life is Elias," she continues.

"Yeah, because he's fucking obsessed," Del grumbles.

Kevin, the corgi that Noah got for Del a few years ago, barks as it chases Imogen around the backyard. My little girl giggles, her little fingers trying to get a hold of the dog, but Kevin is too fast for her.

She trips over something in the yard, and I jolt, ready to get up to help, but I don't move as fast as I normally do with this baby boy in my belly, now four weeks away from entering the world.

Elias prepares to stand, too, but Immy gets back up and continues laughing while running around after the dog.

She's the spitting image of Elias. Dark wavy hair and blue eyes. Elias says her chipmunk cheeks and attitude are from me.

Little Gene better have blonde hair and greenish-blue eyes like me.

"I don't know how you do it," Noah says with a sigh.

She takes a drink of wine and relaxes in the chair. She's wearing shades and a bikini top with short shorts since it's summer and hot as hell.

Noah and Del live next door, but we have a pool, so they're always over here on sunny days. At least, when they're not traveling the world killing the corrupt and powerful.

"So you and Del are still not interested in having kids?" Elias asks.

"No, no, no," she says with a laugh. "I'm perfectly fine being Aunt Noe."

"And Uncle Dwel," Del adds.

Dwel is what Immy calls him since she can't say Del correctly yet.

"We have Kevin. We have our weapons. We have lots of uninterrupted travel and sex."

"Hey!" I protest. "We have that too!"

Never mind that Immy tried to barge into our room this morning while Elias was balls deep.

I've never been hornier in my life. My obstetrician said increased libido is normal for pregnancy.

We also travel plenty. Last year, Elias and I made it to LA for a WWE taping and a trip to Disneyland. And just a few months ago, we went to Disney World. Immy was in heaven the entire time, and I can't wait to bring her back when she's older.

My parents were also more than happy to watch Imogen for two weeks while Elias and I traveled to all the places he promised he'd take me.

I flip off my best friend, and she sticks out her tongue at me.

Elias kisses the top of my head as he stands to check on the burgers and hot dogs on the grill. Del joins him, beer in hand as they talk animatedly. It's probably about wrestling, or baseball, or something stupid like if they would win in a fight against a bear.

Elias is in full-on dad mode, and my heart squeezes at the sight. He's wearing an apron that says, 'Hi Hungry, I'm

Dad,' and he was so fucking proud of that purchase. He's also retired some of his all-black mob outfits in exchange for brighter shirts. I nearly choked on my juice the other morning when he walked out in a Hawaiian shirt and blue shorts.

He's still in charge of the Five Boroughs Alliance, but he's stepped back some to spend more time with his family. His uncle, Martin, and head of security, Jax, are taking charge, only looping in Elias when necessary.

He's more of a CEO now.

My event planning business was a near-overnight success, and I know it's all because of Elias and his connections. I've had to expand three times now, adding dozens of employees each time just to keep up with demand. Of course, now I'm on maternity leave, so I've left other people in charge for the next year—which is how long I plan to be out of commission.

As for Noah and Del, they run a successful business that appears legal on paper—a travel agency—but it's just a cover for their murder-for-hire company. They still take on jobs, mostly pro-bono ones, but they've also scaled back on that life.

We're getting a little bit of both worlds.

That normal life and the one that brought us all together.

Noah picks up her book and sighs as she flips it open.

I'm so glad to see her happy.

She deserves this peace and the man who helped her get to this point.

"Deadly Obsession?" I ask, noticing the title and the half-naked couple embracing on the cover.

Noah peeks over the top of the book and wags her eyebrows.

"It's so good. This woman walks into a nightclub owned by a mafia boss. She's in trouble, running from an abusive ex, so she asks this dangerous man for help. He becomes obsessed with her, killing everyone who's hurt her in her life. But then she becomes a target to his rival so they get married that way he can protect her."

"Sounds familiar," I snort.

"There's a ton of sex too. Like, chapter one he's fucking her."

"Sold. Can I read it after you?"

"What's mine is yours, sister."

I still get giddy when Noah calls me that. Neither of us had siblings, so I never imagined I'd have someone who I can call sister, even if it's only through marriage. Noah has always been my best friend. From the moment we met, I knew she'd be someone special in my life.

"Food's done," Elias announces. He's already preparing mine and Imogen's plates.

Noah helps me out of the chair, and we all head over to the picnic table.

We pile food on our plates. Noah and Del brought pasta salad and brownies that they baked together.

I call Imogen over, and Elias sets her on the bench next to me. She's perched on her knees as she picks up the hotdog to eat, smearing ketchup and mustard on her face.

"What's in this pasta salad?" Elias asks, taking a big bite. "It's really good."

"Nothing crazy," Noah says. "Some feta cheese, red wine vinegar, garlic, and Dijon mustard."

"And nuts," Elias wheezes.

"Yeah! Walnuts. I almost forgot," Noah beams.

"Oh, shit. I forgot to tell you, Rainbow Bright." Del winces. "My brother's allergic to nuts."

I sigh and scooch myself out of the picnic table.

Elias is already stabbing himself with his EpiPen that he keeps in a cute little holster around his shoulders. Not all the time, mostly when he's expecting to eat somewhere.

I'm not taking chances, he'd said.

"Noah, watch Immy," I say and point at Del. "You help me. Thankfully walnuts aren't as bad as peanuts."

Del follows me into the house to grab Elias's oxygen tank from the bathroom. By the time we return, Elias is breathing somewhat normally, likely after using his inhaler and taking some Benadryl.

"Did I tell you about the time I baked chocolate chip and walnut cookies for Elias and almost killed him?" I say to Noah.

She snorts. "Girl, this is so funny."

"Thanks a lot," Elias grumbles.

"No, I just mean you're this scary, dangerous mafia guy, but a little ole nut could literally take you out. Could you imagine if your enemies knew this?"

I gasp. "That's what I said! Death by nut."

Noah and I break out into a fit of giggles and Imogen joins in despite having no idea what we're talking about. She just knows something's funny.

Even Del is amused.

"You're all so fucking hilarious," Elias gripes.

"Dada, you said a bad word," Immy scolds.

"Sorry, belle fille." *Beautiful girl.* "Daddy will put a dollar in the jar later."

She twists herself on the picnic table bench to hug Elias's big belly.

The other day, she asked if he was also growing a baby in there, and I peed my pants laughing so hard.

Elias kisses the top of Imogen's head and gives me a wink. Pressure builds behind my eyes.

My perfect little life with my obsessive mafia man.

He gave me the bad romance.

Except it was never bad at all.

The End

Thank you

Thank you for reading Sage & Elias's story. Did you love it? Please consider leaving a review on Amazon, Goodreads, or any other outlet you use to talk about books! Feel free to tag me, as long as it's not a negative review!

Acknowledgements

I didn't know Elias was going to get a book when I started writing Deadly Deceit, but he spoke to me the more he appeared in Del & Noah's story. I also wanted him to be a big boy because that's the type of stories I write: romance for all sizes. I believe all body types deserve to be the main character. All body types deserve to be loved, worshipped, and fucked.

Not to mention Elias is a green flag running around as a red flag. A big ole teddy bear wrapped up in a mafia boss's body. And the tattoos? Hotttttt! He's exactly what Sage needed.

I want to thank my alpha & beta readers: Xan Garcia, Gina Hejtmanek, Kascha Stern, Mikaelynn Rose, Kim Holsapple, Suzi Vee, and Violet G.

Your critiques helped bring this story to life and fix all the things I missed.

To my editor, Jenny. Again, sorry about the commas. They are evil. You always go above & beyond. Thank you a million times!

To Kate Farlow with Y'all That Graphic. Thank you for working your magic with the ebook cover and making the discreet cover for the paperback as beautiful and cohesive as Deadly Deceit!

I should also thank my neighbor who gave me the vague idea to this world after hearing him cough through my apartment walls. It kinda got out of hand with the mafia aspect, because I'm pretty sure he's not in the mafia... unless... is he?

Also by Settle Myer

Deadly Deceit

A Rivals to Lovers Mafia Romance (New York City Syndicate Book 1)

Deadly Deceit is the first book in a standalone duet. It's a dark cozy romance meaning the romance is sweet... but the story includes dark themes. Find it on Amazon & KU

Guardians for the Vamp

A Manhattan Monsters Romance

FFM with a Vampire/Sphinx/Gargoyle

The monsters of Manhattan are tired of living in the shadows. The new vampire queen, Layla, is tasked to come up with an unveiling plan, but she finds herself distracted by her new broody gargoyle guard... and the bossy sphinx on the unveiling committee. Find it on Amazon & KU.

Gaga for the Gargoyle

A Fated Mates Monster Romance.

Gaga for the Gargoyle is about 999-year-old gargoyle king, Xander, who has 6 months to find his fated mate before permanently turning to stone. Enter a strange dating app that pairs him with Evangeline, a 40-year-old human. This book is part of the Fated Dates series, a shared world about plus-size MCs meeting their monster mates through a mysterious dating app. Find it on Amazon & KUIt's also on audiobook everywhere!

A Vow for the Vamp

A Manhattan Monsters Romance.

500-year-old vampire queen, Millie, is ready to face the sun, no longer able to live with the guilt of the monster she's become. When she goes out for one last feed, she meets a 29-year-old golden retriever man named Teddy... who just might be the reason she lives. It's on Amazon & KU

The Off Script Series

Beyond the Bright Lights is the first book in the Off Script series of spicy standalone contemporary romances. It features Lana & Mylan's story. Beyond the Fame is book two and features Rebecca & Jensen's story. Beyond the Spotlight is the third and final book and features Savannah & Reynold's story. Find them on Amazon & KU. Beyond the Bright Lights & Beyond the Fame are on wide on audiobook.

The Trinity Trilogy

If you love action & adventure, badass women with superpowers, diverse characters, found family, and fated mates—check out my sci-fi romance trilogy. Book 1 is a sweet romance with some cursing and violence, but books

2 & 3 have a sprinkle of spice in them. Trinity Found, Trinity Returns, Trinity Rises. Find them on Amazon and Audible.

Social Media

Check out my website and sign up for my newsletter for updates on new books, discounts, and sneak peeks!

https://www.settlemyerauthor.com/

Join my readers group. Become a Settle Myer Star and be a part of the discussion with other fans. I also posts fun facts about my books, characters, and more!

Follow me on social media

 tiktok.com/@settlemyerauthor

instagram.com/settlemyerauthor

facebook.com/settlemyerauthor

twitter.com/settle_myer

About the author

Settle Myer lives in New York City with her cats Zombie, Michonne & Birdie. She's currently a TV news writer who hopes to one day leave a world of death, disaster, and politics to write about worlds with plenty of cinnamon roll men and badass women. She loves all things zombies, cats, karaoke, and tattoos... but not necessarily in that order.